"Now no more than a pebble on the beach of time" p 126.

Check the history - not always reliable.

THE TRAITORS OF BOSWORTH

Henry Morane had some tough assignments even before the battle of Bosworth Field. In *The Killing of Richard the Third*, the first of his narratives to be published, he described those he had carried out on King Richard's behalf, ending on that disastrous day in 1485. How he escaped with his life and won a measure of trust from the new king, Henry the Seventh, was told in *Tudor Agent*. But Morane's loyalty to the memory of King Richard remained undiminished, and his hatred for the two men who had betrayed him at Bosworth never faded.

In this, the third of Henry Morane's narratives, the King's business takes him from the turbulent London he knew so well, to York and to the Bristol of the early navigators as well as to Flanders, where a new pretender to the English throne was being trained by Margaret, Duchess of Burgundy and King Richard's sister, an implacable enemy of the Tudors. With the double threat of invasion and full-scale rebellion at home, only a man of Henry Morane's resource and ingenuity could have used events for his own ends, vengeance upon the traitors of Bosworth.

THE TRAITORS
OF BOSWORTH

Robert Farrington

1978
CHATTO & WINDUS
LONDON

Published by
Chatto & Windus Ltd.
40 William IV Street
London WC2N 4DF

*

Clarke, Irwin & Co. Ltd.
Toronto

British Library Cataloguing in Publication
Data
Farrington, Robert
    The traitors of Bosworth.
    I. Title
    823'.9'1F   PS3556.A774T/
    ISBN 0-7011-2278-1

© Robert Farrington 1978

Printed in Great Britain by
Redwood Burn Limited
Trowbridge & Esher

For
GWEN

'It is to the Tudors in general that Britain owes the development of national espionage. Henry VII . . . had first sought to protect his throne by developing a system of Secret Service and Christopher Urswick, Recorder of London, was his chief agent . . .'

Richard Deacon
A History of the British Secret Service

AUTHOR'S NOTE

The betrayal and killing of Richard the Third at Bosworth Field was the work of two men. The first, Henry Percy, earl of Northumberland, in command of the reserve, refused to come to Richard's aid when called upon, leaving him to be overwhelmed. The second took a more active part. Sir William Stanley, his three thousand men likewise mustered for the defence of the realm, was secretly pledged to the Tudor invader. Keeping his red-coated division out of the battle until he could see which way it was going, he charged in, breaking up King Richard's final, desperate attack, and hacking to pieces the last Englishman ever to sit the throne of his own country.

Yet these treacheries were unconnected. Each man was out for his own ends, and seized his opportunity as it arose. Two years later there was to be another battle — at Stoke Field — in which neither took part, and thus survived to be dealt with as is here related. While the facts are in the history books, it is also true that many attributed those facts to Divine Intervention, for was it not the Lord who said, 'Vengeance is mine, I will repay'? Yet perhaps even He was nudged by one Henry Morane, who had some account of his own to collect, and who was a firm believer in the old adage that 'God helps those who help themselves.'

This, then, continues Henry Morane's narrative of what took place following Stoke Field, the last battle of what later became known as the Wars of the Roses, and, as in the previous narratives, it may be helpful to note the other characters who play their part, but whose names have not been recorded in those history books:

JOSEPH ANDERSON — captain of archers, and a Lincolnshire man. Morane's companion on previous assignments.

MATILDA — once mistress of the cultured William Bourchier. Now serving-woman to Queen Elizabeth of York, and wife of Henry Morane.

ROGER LEOPOLD — an obliging astrologer.

JAMES HERRING — master silversmith, with his shop in the Strand.

MATTHEW COOMBE — James Herring's apprentice, and Matilda's nephew.

RANDOLF EU — military retainer to Sir William Stanley.

MEHMET — a Saracen with a horse-trading establishment near London Bridge.

ALI — his nephew.

MARTIN CAILLOU — former chaplain to the Earl of Surrey.

JOHN MAN — ex-soldier of Brabant.

ANDROMEDA — who kept an establishment of 'geese'.

CHAPTER 1

A S I rode slowly away from Stoke Field along the gnarled stones of the Fosse Way I heard cymbals and trumpets on the hill behind me. The battle was over, the rebel leaders had been killed, and the boy they had tried to set up as king was cowering inside the royal tent. But would this be the end of our troubles? In the two years since Dickon had been killed at Bosworth there had been little but trouble in the realm. And it seemed to me that this affair of Lambert Simnel could not be the last while there were still Yorkists left to dispute the issue, and the most implacable of them all, Dickon's sister, out of reach in Flanders.

They were singing now, up there on the hill. The Welsh liked their music, and none more so than this Tudor king. He himself had seized my arm in a gesture of gratitude for my capture of the boy Simnel, and had promised to see to the matter of the bond I had been forced to sign as a pledge of loyalty after Bosworth. Loyalty? Mine was to the realm and the authority over it. Yet this new authority did seem as if he might act as a king should, restoring order in the countryside and imposing the law. But as a man? I did not know. Dickon had been a man first, and then a king, and my loyalty to him had been absolute. He had demanded none that could be measured in gold like this Tudor.

I rode alone, although all round me on the thousand-year-old Roman road were shouts and swearing as tents were being set up, tents for those magnates who had arrived too late to fight. The Stanleys would be among them, as at Bosworth, where Sir William's men had hacked Dickon to pieces as I watched, appalled. A lump came into my throat at the memory, and then as suddenly went as I saw his banner, the all too familiar Hart's Head, drooping over his tent, and a red-coated sentry leaning on his pike outside. I stopped and swore aloud, and in that moment would have forced my way in and killed him then and there, taking the consequences. But loud voices were coming from inside. Lord Stanley was in there too, and a bitter quarrel was going on.

Saluting the sentry, who nodded his indifference, I rode on until I was behind the expanse of silk and gilded canvas, and then dropped quietly from the saddle.

'I tell you, brother, I will have no part in such a business!'

It was Lord Thomas Stanley. He was another of those who had tried to predict the outcome of events to his own advantage, veering from one side to another in the recent civil wars. Yet not long previously I had heard him voice his respect for Dickon and, as he had had no direct part in his murder, I did not feel the same resentment for him as I did towards his brother.

'But then, you,' another voice said, and it was harsh with the arrogance I knew so well, 'you have now the earldom of Derby, whereas I, brother Thomas, still lack that of Chester.'

'And you think treason will achieve it?'

'Treason? When treason is successful it is not called by that name. Besides, it will not be imputed to me. Thomas Howard of Surrey will hang for it, not I.'

Surrey? I listened more avidly. Thomas Howard still lay in the Tower. Taken captive after Bosworth, I had come to know him well, being his servant there for part of the time. Thomas Howard, though no longer the earl of Surrey, was not a man I wished to see hanged for treason, or for anything else.

There had been a pause. 'So you think that by sending a false message to London of King Henry's defeat here today . . . that it will cause Surrey to act treasonably?'

Sir William Stanley laughed. 'The lieutenant of the Tower is my man. When the news reaches him he will offer Surrey the keys of the fortress. And that worthy, if I know him, will not miss the opportunity of making his escape and raising forces against the Tudor. And if the forces that he raises seem to have enough strength, why then we shall join him and upset this present regime. If not, then our own men, unjaded by this recent battle, will move swiftly to take him prisoner to King Henry. Either way our rewards will be great.' He laughed. 'But I forget that you have already received your reward, my respected brother.'

'Aye, and if you wish to receive yours you will not meddle in this.'

'Then you will not join me?'

'I have already said that I will not.'

'Or oppose me?'

A long silence followed. At length his brother spoke. 'I will not oppose you, William, for the sake of the family. But take care . . .' he lowered his voice '. . . lest it be said I knew of this.'

'Then I will see to it myself. I have three thousand men camped out there, enough for the purpose . . .'

'And a sentry out there, too. If his ears have been big his tongue may be bigger.'

Sir William Stanley chuckled. It was not a pleasant noise. Then he spoke quietly. 'He will have no need to keep either now.'

It was time for me to go. Surrey had to be warned. I moved away quickly, the soft grass deadening any sounds I made.

Three days later, when the Lieutenant of the Tower told him that King Henry Tudor had been defeated and killed at Stoke and offered him his liberty, Surrey refused outright, saying that he had been imprisoned by the proper authority of the realm, to which his loyalty was pledged, and until King Henry, or a new authority, granted him his freedom he would remain where he was.

That was the end of the matter, or so I thought, for nothing was heard of it for two more years, and then King Henry Tudor decided to release the earl of Surrey from his confinement in the Tower.

11

CHAPTER 2

S E E N from any direction, the Tower of London stands as a grim, grey pile. But from the muddy end of Thames Street on a February afternoon, with the sky overhead the colour of rotting flesh, it seemed as if it were the very outpost of Hell. The wall along the moat was streaked with rain, and the stench from the moat itself was only exceeded by that of the Royal Menagerie. Damp lions and sodden bears growled white puffs of vapour through the wooden bars of their cages, but they would not have long to wait. Their food was on the way. A herd of oxen was being driven down past the scaffold posts on Tower Hill. I gave a long sigh. Two years had passed since Thomas Howard had refused the freedom offered him by the Lieutenant, yet he was still confined inside. But at least on this occasion my black-bearded escort was not taking me there as a prisoner. I told him this, and he laughed.

'You think not? Wait till you are inside, Henry Morane. The Lieutenant in there has a score to settle, if I remember.'

'Not with these warrants,' I said, waving them confidently.

The sentries of the Tower-at-the-Gate passed us across the moat causeway to those at the Middle Tower. I showed the warrant again, and they were impressed. So was the Lieutenant, until he saw who carried it.

He had come running, and was breathing hard. 'Morane, eh?' he said. 'I thought I had seen the last of you.' His eyes went to my escort. 'And you too . . . Anderson, the archer-captain.'

'Of the King's Own Company of Yeomen,' Joseph Anderson put in.

I held the paper under the Lieutenant's well-curled moustache. 'The signet seal is attested by Richard Foxe, secretary to his highness Henry the Seventh, King of England, Ireland and France, and . . .'

'Yes, yes, I can see that as well as you.' He ran his

eye down it. 'You carry another warrant as well?'

'For the earl of Surrey. And I will deliver it myself.'

'There is no earl of Surrey here. I have in my charge one Thomas Howard, formerly of that title. And any communication for him will first be delivered to me.'

I raised my eyebrows. 'Indeed, Sir Oswald? Then am I to return to Richard Foxe with that message?'

He glared at me and muttered something about presumptuous clerks, then stood aside and waved us toward the stair that led up to the battlement. I heard his boots on the stonework as he followed.

Thomas Howard, a saddle-faced veteran of forty-five years, most of which had been spent in war, was at the distant end of the walk by Saint Thomas's Tower, under which his servants huddled for shelter, barely distinguishable in the mist that crept up over the wall from the river.

'Buttocks of God!' he exclaimed. 'Henry Morane, my old servant.' Then he clapped Anderson on the shoulder. 'So you're bringing him back again, hey? What devilry has Morane been up to this time?'

'None at all, my lord,' I said with a bow. 'I bring you a warrant from King Henry Tudor.'

'A warrant, hey?' The grey eyes narrowed. 'So he has finally made up his mind to dispose of me?' He looked across at the White Tower, whose ramparts stood in the gloom. 'Although I have not yet heard the carpenters banging away at a scaffold.'

It was a noise well-known for its encouragement during the last hours of doomed prisoners. He took the paper, and when he saw the superscription he gave me a quick glance before breaking the seal.

I watched him as he read. Taken prisoner after fighting for King Richard at Bosworth, he had been in the Tower now for four years. However, after the more recent battle at Stoke Field he had been pardoned, given more comfortable quarters and his own servants, as well as two pounds every week for his board, and allowed the liberty of the Tower precincts. But he had still remained a prisoner.

For two pounds every week, and lodgings, I thought,

13

I too could have lived like an earl . . . but Surrey had folded the paper and was looking at me.

'You know its contents, Master Morane?'

'Aye, my lord. Your earldom is restored, and you are at liberty again . . .'

'What's this?' the Lieutenant demanded, taking the warrant. He read it carefully, first wiping the dew off his moustache.

'Free!' Anderson exclaimed. 'My lord of Surrey is free!'

Yet while Thomas Howard's liberty and his title were restored, his estates were not. He was only to be allowed the income from those of his wife. But his stewards, although they had new masters, had all this time been manipulating their accounts so that their former earl had not suffered too greatly, as witnessed by the supper he provided for us in his Tower apartment, a supper on dishes of silver, and wines in cups of pure glass veined with gold . . . The Lieutenant had sent beer from the Tower brewery, and even two swans from the Constable's store. As the Constable of the Tower was the earl of Oxford, and no friend of Surrey's, the Lieutenant might have some explaining to do when that officer made his next inspection, but no doubt he wished to ingratiate himself with his former prisoner.

When he had eaten, and the remains taken back to the kitchens for the servants and hungry dogs, Thomas Howard turned to me.

'What of the country, Master Morane? I receive little news here in the Tower. Has all been quiet since Stoke Field? Were the rebels all killed?'

'All of them, except the Irish lord, Kildare, who was pardoned.'

'And the lad they set up as usurper, Lambert Simnel,' Anderson said, 'is spit-boy in the royal kitchens now.'

'So all his dreams of glory now bubble in a cooking pot,' Surrey laughed. 'And the country has been at peace these two years?'

At peace? No rebels these two years; no imposters claiming the throne, no foreign enemies invading our shores. All that was true. Yet the courts of Europe were restless with ambition, and King Henry's business was to

14

ensure that his small country, weakened after thirty years of civil wars, was not swallowed up by a mightier power such as France, whose eyes were known to be turning northwards. He had no ships of his own, and few soldiers other than those provided by his barons and magnates, while across the Channel stood a royal army with the most powerful train of artillery in Europe, guns which had blown us out of France thirty five years before. But the immediate threat was to Brittany which, if it fell, would give France the whole of the opposite coastline except for Calais, which bastion he would find it hard to retain if it came to war. It was a state of affairs no English king could tolerate. Yet that same king had an obligation to France for her support of his venture to seize the crown at Bosworth, and no less a debt to Brittany for giving him asylum during his years of exile.

An ambassador had been sent to Paris and to Brittany to promote peace between them. That ambassador was Christopher Urswick, King Henry's confessor and Dean of York, to whom my services were retained.

All this I recounted to Thomas Howard of Surrey, whose first question was as to how I had such information. I told him that, as Urswick's agent, and from conversations heard at Court, it was possible to piece together the state of affairs.

'Then there is likely to be war with France, hey?'

'Not if King Henry can avoid it, sir. It is too expensive. But now Duke Francis of Brittany has died, leaving only his daughter Anne, of fourteen years, and Charles of France has announced his intention of marrying her and acquiring the dukedom in his own right. The Breton nobles have called upon King Henry for help.'

'He cannot avoid it, then,' Surrey decided.

'I do not know. He continues to talk of peace. Yet a great council has been called, and parliament summoned to impose new taxes. And in all counties musters of archers are being made.'

'Then it must be war.'

'If the country will pay the taxes, my lord.'

The logs in the chimney place had burned low, and a chill began to sweep the room. Surrey pushed his mug across the board and eyed me.

'Morane,' he said, 'why at this particular moment am I restored in title and given my liberty? Has any especial event occurred to cause it?'

'I do not know, sir. But if there is to be war the King will need men of experience. Also,' I smiled, 'he has learnt that your eldest son, young Thomas, has eyes for no one but the princess Anne, sister of the Queen. It would be better, then, if he were heir to the earldom of Surrey, would it not?'

That made him laugh. 'Thomas, eh? So the boy has ceased whoring then? Ah well, it comes to all of us. But tell me, Morane, how is it that you, a scrivener, have been charged to bring this warrant for my release? Have you risen high in the King's service since we last met?'

I shook my head. 'No, sir. Archbishop Morton and Richard Foxe see to it that I keep my station. I asked audience of the king and gained the privilege. I reminded him that I was your servant here, and of the false news of his defeat at Stoke that had been sent to London, when the Lieutenant out there . . .' I waved a hand at the arras over the entrance '. . . offered you the keys of the Tower and your freedom.'

Anderson laughed and went across to the pissing gutter by the wall. 'Aye, my lord,' he called back, 'and Morane sent me back hot-foot from there to warn you that the news was false.'

'And so,' I went on, 'I urged that, while you might think even a Royal Warrant had been tampered with, you would believe the man who brought it.'

'You spoke directly, Henry Morane.'

'Aye,' Anderson agreed. 'It will hang him yet.'

'It also served to remind the king of what occurred two years ago,' I pointed out.

Surrey tugged at his beard. 'And yet,' he mused, 'the Lieutenant still keeps his post here.'

'Why yes, my lord. He explained away his action as a test of loyalty.'

'He did, eh? Did he know who sent the report?'

'Of course. He is Sir William Stanley's man.'

'Him?' Surrey's face grew hard. 'Dickon's murderer. I shall not forget . . . yet what advantage was there in

16

spreading a report of King Henry's defeat and death?'

'He was sure you would escape and raise the standard of the Yorkish succession. Probably that of the young earl of Warwick.'

'Warwick? The boy still prisoned here in the Tower?'

'The same. He is after all Clarence's son. Dickon's nephew.'

'I know that. But . . .' he shook his head '. . . he would never do for a king. Fourteen years of age and still plays with dolls,' Surrey ended with disgust.

'He needs some of the Malmsey his father was drowned in,' Anderson suggested.

'You seem very sure, Morane. How do you know it?'

'It is better not spoken of, my lord, since Stanley remains Lord Chamberlain, although not earl of Chester which he considers his rightful reward after Bosworth.'

'And he hoped to obtain it that way?'

'He did. He would have gained favour by putting down your rising, and giving the king the excuse of chopping off Warwick's head, removing one more of the Yorkist line. And then of course you would have been hanged too.'

Surrey laughed. 'Well then, Morane, now that I am free I shall have to tread warily, hey? And from what I once heard I believe Sir William Stanley would appreciate your demise as well.'

Anderson turned back. 'Aye,' he agreed, 'and even more so if he knew that Morane had disparaged his report of the king's death.'

'Then speak not so loud, Captain Anderson.' Surrey pointed past him. 'Those walls have mice. And mice have ears.'

'Ears or not,' I laughed, 'they tasted well enough when you and I were starving in the dungeon here, my lord.'

But Joseph Anderson was not laughing. He drew his dagger and stepped quickly across to the arras. Brushing the fabric aside with the blade, he leapt through. I heard footsteps pattering away along the stonework outside.

'You were right, my lord,' he growled when he came back. 'There were two of them. Little mice that scuttled away in the darkness.'

17

I put my ale-mug down and got to my feet. 'Then those little mice of yours will soon be recounting to the Lieutenant how I disparaged Sir William Stanley's report.' I glared at him. 'And how long will it be before Sir William himself hears of it, do you think?'

CHAPTER 3

MATILDA turned on to her side and put her chin in her hand. Her deep blue eyes regarded me reproachfully. 'Two years have passed since you were a danger to Sir William Stanley. Yet now you must arouse his enmity again, just when the Queen is to move from here to West Minster and join the King, and Stanley may be there.'

'As Lord Chamberlain he dare not be otherwise,' I said, pulling the coverlet over me, for the servants' quarters at Sheen Manor were chill with damp. 'But if there is to be enmity it will at least keep King Henry's curiosity alive as to who sent the false report. Although there is little likelihood of it expiring if I know him.'

'Know him? Who does? Not even his wife. Possibly the Lady Margaret Beaufort, but even she as his own mother does not have his full confidence.' She sighed. 'But what advantage is there?'

'It is part of the reckoning, my sweet apple. Sir William murdered Dickon by treachery . . .'

'But not a crime King Henry will hold him accountable for.'

'And his endeavours to kill me, three times . . .'

'The first of which . . .' she touched the scars on my chest and back '. . . brought you to me.'

'Maybe.' I smiled at her. 'But he will pay for the others.'

'I cannot see how. Unless it is by the intervention of God.'

'Then God will intervene,' I said confidently.

'If so, I hope there will be no part for you.'

'There was one when Lord Francis Lovell so nearly killed you.'

At that she shut her eyes quickly, and tears came. I felt as if I had struck a child, and reached out to comfort her. 'There now,' I told her. 'That is two years past as well.'

'Aye, and you have not spoken a word of it since!'

'Should I have, my poppet? It was a matter between

him and me, now settled. I do not wish to hang for it,' I concluded grimly.

She put her head on my shoulder and cried. 'But could I ever have a child now, after what he did?'

'Why not? The surgeons say so.'

A smile came through her tears. 'Aye, and the astrologer. You know him? The old man with one eye who lives near Charing?'

I knew him. I had taken him by the throat and threatened to break all his fingers if he had said otherwise.

'It was strange,' she went on. 'I had come out from praying to the Holy Virgin for a child, when I saw him drop a silver coin. When I helped him pick it up he was so full of gratitude he said it would bring me good fortune, and gave it to me. But I would not take it, for he was such a poor old man . . .'

In fact he was young and lusty, but he affected the gait of the old for the purposes of his trade. Hair and beard well laced with chalk, he also had two eyes, keeping the left shut at all times when others might notice. Once an Abraham-man, he had found the profession of astrologer more lucrative, especially among women. Oh yes, I said to myself, I knew Master Roger Leopold very well.

'. . . so he said he would read my fortune . . . why, Henry Morane, what makes you smile?'

'Because what an astrologer can do I can do better,' I said, reaching out for her.

Somewhat later, she murmured, 'Did you know that there was a Queen of Naples who made a law forbidding husbands from having intercourse with their wives more than six times a day?'

'Would you have such a law?' I smiled down at her.

'I might,' she smiled back, 'if it were anyone but you.'

'Aye,' I agreed. 'It was Joanna of Naples. But that was a hundred years ago. Where did you hear of it?'

'You know it, then?' She was disappointed. 'I heard the Lady Margaret telling Queen Elizabeth the virtues of restraint.'

'Who else?' I laughed. 'I should have known. Does she still refuse Lord Stanley all communication of the flesh?'

'It was part of their marriage contract, as is well known.

The Lady Margaret is most devout. And . . .' she saw my smile '. . . and I will hear no jibes about her, Henry Morane!'

'No, no!' I protested. 'I have great affection for her too.'

'Then do not preach that she should offer oats to Saint Uncumber.'

'Saint . . .? Oho! Now you wait for me to ask who is this Saint Uncumber.'

At that Matilda began to laugh. Pushing me aside, she got off the bed. 'Why, sir,' she said turning round a little, and arousing the desire in me again, 'so Master Henry Morane, who knows all the saints, and most of everything besides, has never heard of Saint Uncumber? Well, well, well . . .'

'Come now,' I said, getting up after her. 'He is the saint of horses, if he must have oats.'

'But no!' Matilda exclaimed with glee. 'Saint Uncumber is the bearded Virgin, who, if given an offering of oats, rids women of unwanted husbands!' With that she ran into the closet for her clothes.

*   *   *

The scarlet-coated guard outside the Painted Chamber brought the butt of his halberd to the tiles with a bang and held the shaft across my path. 'No one may enter,' he said. 'The King confers with his council, as you should be aware.'

'I wait only for Master Christopher Urswick, lately returned from Brittany. He is reporting to the King.'

'Then wait over there by the window.'

The other guard chuckled through his black beard. 'The window is not far enough for Henry Morane. His ears can hear through the stone walls of a castle.'

'Like a mouse?' I asked him, and Joseph Anderson's grin faded.

The Lady Margaret Beaufort was seated at one side of the stained window. She looked up when she heard me and nodded, the trace of a smile on her face. Still no more than forty-six years of age — for she had borne her son, the present King Henry, at the early age of fourteen

21

— she nevertheless had the appearance of one much older. It was on account of the clothes she wore, for the wimple and coif were more suitable to an elderly prioress or a widow than the wife of Lord Stanley, the newly created earl of Derby. I knelt and kissed her knuckles, once again surprised at their softness.

'Ah, Master Morane. You seek audience with His Grace?'

'No, madam, by your leave. Master Christopher Urswick. He will require my report on affairs here while he has been away.'

'Ah, yes! When the council has finished its business then. Do you know what William Caxton says?' She held up the book that had been on her lap. It was one of the newer kind that Caxton was making at his printing factory close by where, instead of cutting the letters of a whole page on a single piece of wood, they were made individually of lead and assembled together in a frame and copied thus in print. The older method of carving a whole page meant throwing away the wooden board afterwards, but by Caxton's process the individual letters could be taken out and used again in whatever order was required to compose another page. He had been working this way for more than ten years, having acquired it in Europe, and for much of that time I had been promising myself to go and see how it was done. But, like many intentions, I had never raised sufficient energy to carry it out. And now, it seemed, neither was I to hear what Caxton was saying, for the doors of the Painted Chamber opened and Lord Stanley came out.

Pushing past me as if I had been one of the Palace hounds, he went up to his wife and bowed stiffly. He very nearly ignored her outstretched hand, then thought better of it, and brushed his moustache swiftly across its back.

'Madam,' he said, 'I heard that you were gracing West Minster with your presence. It seems that your constant attendance upon the Queen instead of your husband is causing some comment here at Court, and little of it is to my advantage. I regret that I cannot allow . . .'

Margaret Beaufort used her outstretched hand to wave him to silence. 'My lord,' she said, 'there is nothing in this world which would make me less comfortable than to have you the subject of comment. But, as to what can be allowed . . .' She stopped, and her eyes went past him to me. But I was moving away, so that she nodded quietly and turned back to him. What was said between them afterwards was not my concern, although I could have hazarded a guess. But even for hazarding guesses there was no time, for other members of the King's Council were emerging and Christopher Urswick was making for me.

He came with quick steps, the sandy hair on his head no higher than my chin. His eyes, dull as the blade on an ancient sword, were narrowed with anxiety. 'Ah, Morane,' he said, 'it is as well you are here.' He put a hand on my arm. 'Come with me. Sir William Stanley is making certain accusations against you, which it is right you should hear.'

'Is he, by God? Then I think I know what they are.'

'Indeed?' He clicked his tongue. 'What has been happening?'

'It would take too long to tell at this moment.'

'Then I trust you have the explanations,' he said, leading me to the door. 'The King will wish to hear them.'

'The King?' I hesitated.

'Who else?' he demanded. 'Sir William does not deal in trifles, especially as far as you are concerned. Come.'

Joseph Anderson moved his weapon to let us pass. I saw that he had been listening, for his face was a-frown. I winked at him with a confidence I did not feel and followed Christopher Urswick into the Painted Chamber.

Those who had remained there looked round as we came in, or I would have had more time to marvel at the room, at the walls with their brilliant pictures of English kings, and the coloured windows guarded by statues of the Saints. There was not even an opportunity to glance through the distant arch at the chapel beyond, next to which Edward the Confessor himself had placed the royal bed to be right close to his place of worship.

John Morton, Archbishop of Canterbury, near seventy years of age, and still ambitious for the Cardinal's hat from Rome, looked me up and down with eyes that were nearly lost in folds of skin. King Richard's implacable enemy, it had been his smooth tongue which had turned Buckingham against Dickon, his best friend, persuading that duke that he had an equal right to the throne, the only other obstacles being of little importance — such as the two young Princes in the Tower. The rebellion had failed; Buckingham had lost his head, and the two boys had disappeared. John Morton was now not absolutely sure that they had been killed, and it had been I who had planted that doubt in his mind. Thus he was no friend of mine, either.

Of the others, Jasper Tudor, uncle of the King, and his closest adviser after Morton, regarded me with a half-smile on his owl's face and nodded. And then there was Sir William Stanley himself.

Whereas his brother, whom I had just left bickering with his wife, had a girth that was increasing with the years, Sir William retained a shape that was as angular as the designs drawn by Euclid in his dissertations on geometry. A pointed beard covered a sharper chin, and when the mouth above it opened it disclosed teeth that immediately brought to mind a rusty trap. Grey, uncoloured eyes, as of an eagle disappointed in its prey, narrowed at my approach.

'Hah!' he said, swinging round to the King. 'Here is the fellow himself, Sire. The one who instigated the rumour of your defeat at Stoke Field, intending treason.'

King Henry Tudor put the quill down beside the ink-bottle and brushed aside the open book of accountings in front of him. The pale face moved upwards and the green eyes came to rest on me.

'Indeed?' he inquired. 'And what have you to say to that, Master Morane?'

As I went down on one knee I saw Jasper Tudor put his hands on his hips. 'What?' he asked. 'A clerk such as he? Who would listen to him?'

'It seems that many did, my lord,' was Sir William Stanley's reply. He was in haste to press his charge, for he could not know what evidence I had or witnesses I might bring to point to him as the real instigator. A prior attack would dispose of their credibility.

King Henry waved me to my feet. 'Well, Master Morane?'

'Your Grace,' I replied, 'after two years this sudden accusation comes as a surprise.'

'No doubt,' Bishop Morton agreed sardonically. 'He would have thought the business was forgotten.'

The Tudor eyes glanced at Morton, then came back to me. There was speculation in them, for this was the very matter I had spoken of not long before. Then he turned to Stanley. 'There is some new evidence of this come to light, Sir William?'

'It has only just come to my attention, Sire.'

'Has it, Sir William? How?'

'The Lieutenant of the Tower has informed me that this man Morane brought the false rumour himself. He was overheard bragging of it to Thomas Howard . . . er, now the earl of Surrey, it seems.'

A quick frown crossed King Henry's face at the last two words, but it was gone in an instant. He turned back to me.

'Bragging, Master Morane?'

I shook my head. 'With humble respect, Sire, but Sir William must have been misinformed. I was in fact congratulating my lord of Surrey upon his new title, and took the opportunity of reminding him that his loyalty to you had not gone un-noticed . . . that is to say, when he had refused to believe the report that you had been discomfited at the battle.'

'Ah!' Morton said. 'So you knew of his refusal?'

I turned to him. 'As all London did. And as all London today rejoices at the King's generosity towards him.'

Morton scowled. 'A smooth tongue,' he muttered.

If King Henry heard the remark he made no sign. He eyed Sir William Stanley. That magnate was struggling to conceal his rage. 'It may be that you have been misinformed, Sir William,' he said gently. We shall have the Lieutenant questioned. Master Urswick,' he said without turning, 'see to it, and report your finding to me.'

'Aye, let us have the truth of the matter,' Jasper Tudor said. 'And let us hear what Thomas Howard has to say.' He scratched his head. 'Although I cannot see that it is of much importance any more. As I recall, Morane seized the boy pretender, that . . .' he stopped to think '. . . that Lambert Simnel, and brought him to us alive . . .' He swung round on Stanley. 'What reason could he have had, unless he was plotting with . . . but all the rebel leaders were killed.' He stopped, puzzled.

'Except Lord Francis Lovell,' Sir William Stanley pointed out.

'He was drowned while crossing the Trent,' Christopher Urswick said. 'Or so it was reported. Whatever the case, he has not been heard of since.' His dull eyes examined me. He still had his suspicions of my part in Lovell's disappearance.

'Enough of this,' King Henry said, getting up. 'Master Urswick will discover the truth of your information, Sir William. There are more pressing matters.'

'Aye, my lord,' Morton boomed. 'And one not fully discussed at your council. The insurrection at York over the new taxes.'

I had not heard of any insurrection at York, and neither was I to hear any more just then, for Christopher Urswick led me from the room. I could feel Sir William Stanley's angry eyes on my back as I went.

CHAPTER 4

' I T would be better to question the Lieutenant first,' I said as soon as we were outside.

'It seems to me,' Christopher Urswick said, pursing his lips, 'that it would be better to question *you* first, Henry Morane. What has brought this matter to light again?'

'I cannot guess,' I said nonchalantly, nodding at Joseph Anderson as he stood to attention beside the doorway. 'Maybe Sir William sees another opportunity for my discredit, being jealous of the favours shown me by the King.'

'Jealous?' Urswick made a noise that would have been a snort if it had not come from someone in Holy Orders. 'The most powerful man in the country jealous of someone such as you?'

I gave him an amiable grin. 'An ant that takes even one grain of corn from a rich man's store incurs the risk of being crushed.'

'Enough of parables, Morane,' Urswick said irritably, 'what . . .?'

Queen Elizabeth had come into the hall, and was crossing to the Painted Chamber. She smiled when she saw us, and stopped abruptly, causing her ladies nearly to bounce into her.

'How now, Master Urswick?' she said. 'Was all well with your journey?' As tall as I, with fresh cheeks, and fair hair tumbling from under her blue cap, she was a picture to compare with the finest of the portraits in the Chamber ahead of her.

Urswick forced a smile. 'Well enough, madam,' he said.

'Then my husband . . . the King will sleep better of a night.'

She must have seen the look on my face, for she coloured slightly, smiled again, this time at me, and then glanced back at Matilda, who had remained with her other servants. I bowed low to hide my embarrassment. Elizabeth of York, even though now crowned as Queen, and mother of an infant prince, was still the same wide-eyed girl who had walked the battlement of Baynard's Castle with me six years before, exclaiming at the sights of London.

As she moved into the Painted Chamber Urswick turned back to me. 'And why by Sir William Stanley? He could as easily have had you murdered as press the matter with the King.'

The same thought had already occurred to me. 'Maybe it proves his guilt,' I said artlessly.

'You mean that it *was* he who sent the false report?'

'It seems to have been.'

Christopher Urswick clicked his tongue with impatience. 'Come now, Morane. Do not be evasive. If you have any evidence . . .'

He was interrupted for the second time. 'He has no evidence,' Matilda said, and we turned round. 'That has been the danger,' she went on. Then she lowered her voice. 'Because if Sir William knew that Henry Morane was the only one who heard it I should have no husband.' She smiled sweetly at Christopher Urswick. 'I therefore had to arrange otherwise.'

I looked at her with astonishment. 'What . . .?' I began.

'Good sir,' she went on, ignoring me, 'it seemed to me that Sir William Stanley should be made aware that if any mishap occurred to Henry Morane there were others of higher station who would consider it proof of his desire to suppress evidence of his treason, and forthwith speak of it to the King.'

It took Urswick a moment to digest that. Then, 'Treason?' he exclaimed. 'Sir William Stanley? Mother of God!' I had never seen him so agitated before. 'Quietly, madam, please.' He waved a hand at her. 'But how do you know of this?'

'Because Henry Morane told me,' she replied simply.

'Oh, no!' He put a hand to his forehead. Then he sighed. 'Well, then, madam, what did you do?'

Matilda smiled again. 'I let it be known that others knew . . .'

'Yes, yes. But how?'

28

'I did not mention Sir William Stanley by name, of course. But I spoke of it so that Mistress Belknap could overhear.'

'The Mistress Belknap who accompanied the Queen just now?'

'The same, sir. She is Sir William Stanley's woman.'

'What?' It was some moments before Christopher Urswick could say any more, then it was merely an echo. 'The Mistress Belknap is Sir William Stanley's woman?'

Matilda nodded. 'Why yes, Master Urswick. I thought you would have known that. He has his spies every-where.'

'Great Heavens! Does the Queen know of this?'

'Faith, no! She is too sweet a person to be plagued with such matters.'

'Then no one knows of this?'

'They do now,' Matilda laughed. 'Christopher Urs-wick, master of the King's spies.'

I began to laugh. But Urswick was not amused. He recovered his composure and asked Matilda, 'And who, madam, are these persons of higher station who are supposed to know of it as well?'

She shrugged. The dark hair that came down to her shoulders contrasted with the brilliant green she was wearing. She pulled up the fullness of her sleeve and pointed at the sentry. 'Why, now, Captain Anderson will do for one, will he not?' That black-bearded worthy grinned. 'He is of higher station than Henry Morane, for sure, now that his wages are eleven pence a day.'

I made as if to smack Matilda on the buttock. But the movement died, unborn. The Lady Margaret Beau-fort and Lord Stanley were watching us from across the hall.

'It seems to me,' Urswick said after a few moments, 'that my questioning will have to be conducted with care. Sir William Stanley is held in high esteem by the King. I dare not shake it without firm evidence.' Then he smiled. 'But that business can wait. Affairs at York engage the King's attention, in spite of Morton's fears to the contrary. The city is reluctant to pay taxes for a war to preserve Brittany from the French. And the earl of Northumberland has been commanded to march south to enforce collection.'

'Northumberland?' I echoed. 'It will take him more than a week to march there. And when the Scots learn that their border is unmanned . . .'

'You forget that their king has recently been murdered. The new James the Fourth is a minor, and the nobles quarrel amongst themselves. Besides, there is no one else with force enough near York. And,' he added, as if an afterthought, 'the earl of Northumberland's oath of loyalty has not yet been put to the test.'

It was no afterthought, of course. It was the real point. Henry Percy of Northumberland was another of those who had betrayed Dickon. And Henry Tudor, while being the unwitting benefactor of it, could not fail to notice the defection. Also, the domains of Northumberland were so far away from the authority in London that the earls thereof had become a law unto themselves, following their own desires and resenting any interference in their affairs. The collection of the new tax in York was to be a test of that high-and-mighty earl's loyalty. Yet the squat, hairy little Henry Percy, for all his power and prestige, was not going to find it easy to carry out. He had no friends in York, for the citizens had not forgotten his conduct towards their beloved Dickon. I spoke of this to Christopher Urswick.

'Precisely, Master Morane,' he said. 'Precisely. But you have friends in York, do you not? Your forthcoming visit will be of interest to the King.'

Joseph Anderson, by the doorway, gave a loud chuckle. Urswick turned round. 'Aye,' he said, 'and the King thinks it well you go too, Captain Anderson.' The smile on the black-bearded face disappeared as quickly as it had come.

I gave a loud groan. 'And that means,' I said, 'that there is someone required to be disposed of, is that it?'

'There is no question of that,' Urswick snapped. 'What is required is to know whether the insubordination is spontaneous, or whether there is an instigator.'

Insubordination? Spontaneous? Instigator? I watched Anderson's frown. Then it cleared and he nodded. 'Ah! Then if there is no instigator we are to find one, eh?'

For a moment Christopher Urswick was taken aback. Before he could reply, Matilda cried, 'But has not Henry Morane already done enough to have earned the King's leniency of his bond?'

'Speak not so loud, madam,' she was told. 'The King has acquired some trust in Henry Morane. His previous loyalty to Richard of Gloucester has not been to his disadvantage.'

'But how can that be?' she asked.

'It might have been different if Dickon were still alive,' I said grimly.

'Precisely,' Urswick said again. 'In his eyes loyalty to one master implies loyalty to the next. When the first is dead, that is,' he added quickly.

I understood. In his devious way he was telling me that the opposite was also true. Once a traitor, always a traitor, was what the King thought. And he wanted to know if the discontent in the North was being stirred up deliberately and, if so, whether is was by someone near the seat of power. There was some suspicion of a plot, it seemed, and Henry Percy of Northumberland was to be used as a cat's-paw to drag it into the open. I started to speak, but Urswick was addressing Matilda.

' . . . no one knows of Morane's destination, madam. Not even Morton, not even the Queen,' he said.

'Queen Elizabeth? Why ever not?' she asked.

'Because that is the King's wish. And have you not just told us that there are those around her to whom, in her innocence, she might let slip the matter?'

'And if she inquires of me regarding my husband?'

'That has already been seen to, madam. Morane is about the King's business. There has been discontent in Bristol, too . . .'

'Bristol?' I said with surprise.

'Aye.' He turned to regard me. 'The mariners there complain of their difficulties in the Northern seas, where Iceland lies. There has been sea-fighting, and consequent lack of trade, especially in the catching of fish thereabouts. It has been put about that you are journeying to Bristol to ascertain the details.'

Matilda shrugged. 'So long as any lies that are told are not told by me.' She took me by the arm. 'Come,

Henry, we have some time together before your departure. Tomorrow, Master Urswick?'

He pursed his lips. 'I regret, madam, it must be forthwith.'

We stood, eyeing him, our anger rising. Then Anderson cleared his throat noisily. 'Ah, well,' he said with resignation. 'Better York than the frozen peaks of Iceland.'

I turned on him. 'Are there any in Iceland?' I asked him. 'Or are you sure the King will not send us there to find out?'

CHAPTER 5

IN early spring the blood quickens, and nature unfolds. The woodlands bear a bright new raiment, seeming to shiver with ecstasy in every passing breeze, and the traveller finds himself able to cover greater distances between dawn and dusk each day. Inns, shuttered for the winter, show their newly painted signs, a medley of colours confusing to those inexperienced of the road, for the welcome and comfort of a night's lodgings does not always depend upon the brilliance of the design. And the highways of England carry many travellers; retinues of noble lords, and of important churchmen, are always on the move, their fore-riders clearing the way and their musicians following behind in carts.

Traders from all over Europe with loaded packhorses come to sell their cloth, wine or other commodity at a profit. Others, whose packs are empty, seek to buy wool, grain, timber or other products to be transported to the great storage houses of London before being shipped across the water. There are those who sell their services in construction and repair; stone-masons, carpenters, mill-wrights, tinkers and so on. Others are musicians, mumming-actors and jugglers moving on to the next town, or perhaps to the manor of some great lord. And then not only are there thieves, cutpurses and coney-catchers, but others who prey on the unwary such as tooth-pullers, blood-cuppers and surgeons. Neither should I omit the Abraham-men, playing upon the sympathy of the untutored rustic, who will fall to the ground in a fit, violent or inert at will, which only money can cure.

Early on the second day we fell in with a family of cloggers making their way to North Wales for the summer, where they would move from village to village, felling the nearby alders and turning them into the heavy footwear which was all the countryfolk could afford. They were happy people, making much noise with the flutes whittled from the alders of a previous year, and containing more holes than they had fingers to stop. And even though their women kept their eyes downcast, the men made much conversation with us, telling us of their trade and their travels to remote villages where the inhabitants had never moved more than a furlong from its boundary. Sometimes, they said, they would buy women from such places, for although they might be hanged for it if they were discovered, those women made the best wives, being industrious and faithful, not like the free-bosomed townswomen whose husbands had ceaselessly to be on the watch. I glanced at Anderson as this was said, and saw him try to repress a smile.

At the inn by the village of Barnet the landlord took me aside and asked if I were Henry Morane. I agreed, somewhat surprised, when he told me that it fitted a description given to him; a man with pale eyes, much scarred about the face, accompanied by another with a black beard and bald of pate. When I asked who had given the description he replied that it had been a lad, fully grown, but as yet not in need of a steel blade to his chin more than once a week. It seemed that the lad was in some haste, and had gone farther along the road to make more inquiries.

I shook my head, puzzled. The only lad I knew near to that description was my nephew, Matthew Coombe, of Kingstone-on-the-Thames. Yet Matthew was in London, apprenticed to a silver-smith in the Strand. Matilda had asked me to visit him, for he had begun to show discontent with his work. It seemed that some sea-captain lodged in the same house, and young Matthew had become seized with a desire to make an ocean voyage. I would have spoken with him, had not Christopher Urswick sent me away so quickly. But if it were Matthew Coombe inquiring for me I could not think what business brought him all the way to Barnet to search for me. However, I soon forgot the matter when we came to the old battlefield where Warwick the King-maker had met his end eighteen years before. Joseph Anderson stopped his horse to point at the clump of trees where Warwick had tethered his horse to fight on foot, and had been slaughtered when he was trying to run back to it after

34

his men had been routed. He laughed, remarking that anyone who dismounted, wearing eighty pounds of armour-plate, could not expect to escape if the day went against him.

'He was advised to fight on foot,' I told him. 'The same as his men, who needed the encouragement. Besides,' I added, 'it was a close thing. If Oxford's men had not gotten lost in the fog we should have had the worst of it instead.'

He turned round in his saddle. 'You were there too?'

'Aye. But only a boy, and frightened out of my wits.'

'Your first battle, eh? It is an experience never forgotten.'

'Neither were Tewkesbury, nor Bosworth. The fear was no less.'

'That's true. Sometimes it is the greater because of the recollection of previous occasions. Yet,' he went on, 'in such great battles there are always numbers of one's comrades close by. While you, Henry Morane, since I have known you, seem to prefer more private affrays.'

'Prefer?' I laughed. 'What is thrust upon me is not my preference. I am a scrivener, not a man of war.'

'Ohoho! Then it was a strange scrivener that I first met, who carried a sword and daggger in place of ink-horns, quills and a box of sand!' He turned to look back at a body of four or five men who had been following us, and we had been late enough, sleeping off the night's carousal. It was a time when there were no other travellers in sight, and I looked at them with interest.

They were determined looking fellows, seeming in more haste to reach their destination than to pass the time of day. Three of them rode on ahead while their leader, swarthy and with a cast in one eye, slowed to inspect us. I raised a hand in greeting, when there was a sudden yell from the clump of trees and a crowd of village urchins came swarming out at us.

'There he is!' shouted a tousel-head, some ten or eleven years of age, and taller than the others. 'There he is! The black-bearded sheriff of Nottingham! Let us put the villain to flight!' There were yells of 'Robin Hood! Robin Hood!' and a shower of sticks and stones flew at us.

The man beside me stopped and swore at them as a

35

stone hit him squarely in the chest. But Joseph Anderson took it in good part. He gave a bellow of simulated rage, wheeled his horse, and charged at the urchins. Seizing one of them, a lad with strips of red cloth attached to his ragged shirt, he held him aloft.

'Come on, Will Scarlet!' he roared. 'Go and get your quarterstaff and we'll fight it out, man to man. I will avenge the insult of being likened to the wicked sheriff of Nottingham, when I am the Lion Heart's very own man, sent to arrest that same sheriff.' He laughed and set his captive down.

The lad wearing the guise of Will Scarlet looked up at him, his little face a-frown. Then he pointed at me. 'Is that King Richard himself, then?' he asked reverently.

'Oho, and who else?' Anderson roared. He opened his purse and threw some farthings on to the grass. 'And that will prove it to you, my friend.' Then he wheeled round and rode back towards me, a huge smile all over his face.

But there was no smile on mine. The stone which had hit the man beside me had not sunk into his clothes and fallen away as such a missile would do. It had bounced off. And the noise it made spoke of something harder than wool under that stained shirt. I looked at his companions. Those ahead had ridden on to where the road curved round a hillock. The trees were thicker there, well laced with bushes and brown winter undergrowth. They were peering ahead, as if to see if the way was clear. Behind, two others, now dismounted and less than twenty paces away, stood with bows drawn back to the ear, the arrowheads pointed straight at me.

'In there,' the swarthy fellow said, waving his sword towards the hillock.

I saw Anderson's dark eyebrows go up. He began to reach for the mace at his saddle, only to let his hand fall away again when he saw where the longbows were aimed. He shrugged, and rode on ahead of me, slowly.

We went in, bramble stems tugging at us as we passed, until we came to a space between the trees where the winter wood had been felled. I would have made a dash through the undergrowth, but the two archers were close enough behind to have made it too much of a hazard for both of us to escape. And I was curious. Neither of us presented an aspect of wealth that would attract a band of rogues like these.

Ordered to dismount, we stood while the others did the same, the archers being careful to keep at least one of their bows trained on me. Then the leader put his sword at my throat. He seemed about to kill me without explanation, and I held up a hand.

'Wait,' I told him. 'What . . .?' And then I saw small faces peering at us through the matted brown stalks and fronds of last year's bracken. My expression must have warned him, for the sword-point left my throat as he swung round. One of the others had seen them too, and growled a warning. Then, all of a sudden, there was a great shout, and the crowd of urchins rushed into the clearing, waving sticks and screaming, 'Rescue! Rescue! Rescue the Lion Heart!'

I did not hesitate. As the blade moved from me I jumped forward and gripped the man's arm, twisting it as hard as I could and throwing him to the ground. I would have kicked him in the ribs had I not remembered the steel under his shirt. Instead, my boot found him in the neck, and he rolled aside with a choking gurgle.

As I picked up his sword and swung round to attack the next man I saw that Anderson had dived under his horse and come out the other side, somehow with the mace in his hand. He swung it as the nearest of his captors, hitting him in the middle. There could have been no armour under that one's shirt, for his chest caved in like a broken egg. But then one of the others brought a club down over Anderson's head, and he fell to his knees with a groan. I was about to bury the sword into his attacker when I stopped suddenly, appalled. Young Will Scarlet's urchin face was a twisted mixture of disbelief and horror as he stared down at the quivering feathers on the shaft that protruded from his stomach. His little mouth went square as he tried to cry out, but the blood came first, choking him, and he rolled away into the bushes, clutching at his middle. A red mist of rage came over my eyes and I made a wild leap at the archer who had done it. But before I could reach him the club came down on me as well and the red mist

37

changed into stars and flashes of light. The trees began
to rotate round me and the brown floor of the forest
came upwards slowly to meet my face. I saw with sudden clarity that the dead leaves were being pushed aside
by innumerable shoots of tiny, white bracken fronds
unfolding in the spring, and then another blow took
that vision away too.

38

CHAPTER 6

A T least we were alive, was my first thought as my senses returned and I saw Joseph Anderson sitting propped against a tree, his bloodstained face glaring at the swarthy, swivel-eyed leader. That villain, sword in hand again, was waving it at his companions. They held spades, and two of them were stamping down newly-turned earth. Poor little Will Scarlet had found an early resting place. I hoped that the other children had escaped without hurt. The body of Anderson's victim was missing, too. They had been busy while we slept, it seemed.

'Come on, come on!' Swivel-eye urged. He pointed the sword at us. 'There's two more holes to dig yet before those brats get back to their hovels and raise the Hue and Cry.' He spoke with difficulty, and I saw with satisfaction a great red weal under his chin.

One of the diggers threw down his spade. 'I've had enough of this,' he said truculently.

'No more for me, neither,' the other said. 'You told us when we came that two were to be dug, no more. I'm a soldier, not a sod-turning sexton.'

Swivel-eye glared at them. 'You'll do what you're told,' he growled. 'And quickly. Because if the Hue and Cry comes before you've finished you'll hang for sure.'

'Yerh!' the first one agreed. 'Those foresters' brats'll find the way here well enough. Let's take these two farther on and bury them somewhere else.'

'It'll be dark before we find a place. And it'll be done the quicker the less time you take with talk.'

'I'll do no more digging,' the other said. 'Let them make their own holes.'

The leader turned round and inspected us. Then he nodded. The two spades were thrown across. I glanced at Anderson as I picked up mine. The fellows might be soldiers, but they had not seen how the Irish fought at Stoke Field with farm implements like these. We had a chance now, but how an opportunity might arise I could not see. But Anderson gave me a quick nod.

39

He would await my signal.

One of the men had ridden down the track to watch for the Hue and Cry, but there were still two bows aimed at us as well as the leader with his sword. I began to dig slowly, watching them as I threw aside the earth. A bow cannot be kept fully drawn for long, and perhaps these fellows, being experienced in battle at longer ranges, did not realise that a half-drawn bow is equally deadly at close quarters. I waited to see if, when they grew tired, they relaxed their strings fully.

There was little hope of rescue from the Hue and Cry, though. No sheriff would stir himself on the testimony of village children who had been acting a game, even if one of them was missing. A missing child was no rarity in these turbulent days. Abductions might be uncommon, but they still took place. And once the abductor was out of the parish the Hue and Cry would end. It would be several days before any credence was placed in poor Will Scarlet's disappearance, and even if the children persuaded the sheriff to visit this glade the growing fronds of spring would have covered the evidence. Besides, would they think to bring spades?

Spades? They were not implements commonly carried by retainers such as these. They had come prepared. We were to be disposed of without trace. From what Swivel-eye had said their orders had been explicit. And there was little doubt who had given them. No one knew of our destination, not even John Morton in spite of his anxiety about York. Christopher Urswick had assured me of it when he had spoken to me privately before we set out. Then he had added, his eyes without any expression, that it would be 'accidentally' let fall to Sir William Stanley. And when I had protested angrily he had replied that if that magnate now attempted my demise it would be proof as far as Urswick was concerned that what I had said about the false rumour from Stoke was correct. In any case, he went on, now that I was warned of a possible attack I would be on my guard, would I not? And, he concluded, with a thin smile on his face, had not my past adventures shown that I was able to protect myself? I swore as I dug at the earth. Whatever guard I might have taken had been broken

40

down by a pack of children at their games.

The ground was soft, but we did not hurry, making ourselves out to be more sorely hurt than we were. It was a matter of judgment, though, for if we were too slow the leader would lose patience and have us disposed of, and force his men to do the digging. I watched him carefully between each stroke, but his attention did not slacken. It would not be long before we came to the point where we would have to take our chance and try conclusions with our implements before the arrows tore us apart. And I could see by his expression that he knew it as well as I.

Then the chance came, as often such things do, whether for good or evil, in an unexpected manner. The bushes behind us parted, and a young man stepped into the clearing. He held what appeared to be a short iron tube in one hand, while from the other dangled a length of cords bound tightly together, a thin plume of blue smoke coming from one end. I knew what it was straightaway, although such things are rare in this country.

His appearance caused the archers to move their bows in his direction. The leader, mastering his surprise but still watching us, walked across to him, sword-point at the ready. Joseph Anderson and I stopped digging and waited.

'Who're you?' Swivel-eye demanded, looking the youth up and down. I, too, was eyeing him with astonishment. Then, suddenly, I called out to him.

'Quick, Matthew! Quick! Give it the fire!'

He glanced at me, and nodded. I saw that the weapon was pointed at Swivel-eye's chest. But there was armour under that shirt. Then, as Matthew pressed the match to the top of the tube, Swivel-eye lunged forward. I saw his blade slice Matthew's arm, but he held on. There was a sizzling noise and a tiny puff of smoke. I stood, taut as a drum, for what seemed an eternity. Swivel-eye ducked, the better to lunge again. Then there was the mother of all explosions and the leaden ball, no bigger than a pea, hit him right on the bridge of the nose. His face disappeared in a spatter of brown and yellow as if it were a cake of cow-dung under a heavy boot. A thick black cloud rolled over him and billowed across the glade. I leapt through it at the two archers who had been covering us. One blow from the edge of my spade severed an arm from its shoulder before the man knew what had hit him. But the other had time to release his bow. I heard the thrum of the string and felt the wind of the arrow as it passed my ear. Then I had him. With all the blood-thirst that was in me for the murder of little Will Scarlet I brought the edge of the spade across his neck with a blow that even the royal executioner would have been proud of. His head spun clean into the air, slowly, like the dying circles of a child's spinning top, the tongue leaping out and the eyes opening and closing as if it were a fair-ground doll.

I moved aside quickly to avoid the fountain of blood and almost collided with Anderson as he came striding through the smoke. He nodded briefly as he surveyed the scene. Then he handed me the mace and reached down for the arm I had severed from the first archer. It lay apart from its owner, the fingers still opening and closing around the bowstave. Anderson put his boot on the wrist and prised the weapon loose. As he began to cast around for arrows he growled at me, 'Look to it, Henry Morane. There's still one of them down the track.'

I shook my head violently. I had forgotten about him. I ran to the path, swinging the heavy weapon. There were still scraps of bloodstained cloth sticking to it. Then I heard the sound of hooves and the man was coming towards me, sword at the level. I fell flat on the ground straightaway, for a mace is no match for shrewdly pointed steel when its owner is mounted. But then a man flat on the ground is no target for a sword from horseback. Only a long spear will reach him, and even a well-trained mount will not tread on a man lying inert. The blade sliced above my head as the man rode by, and I got up quickly to clout him before he could turn. But instead of straightening up for another blow, he continued leaning sideways and then began to topple slowly from the saddle, a yard-long arrow right through him from one side to the other. He hit the ground with a crash, one foot still in the stirrup. I grabbed the reins and put my hand over the nose of his frightened beast. But it was a soldier's horse, for it stood quite still, although all

42

a-tremble, so that I was able to disengage its rider's boot.

'God's Hooks!' Anderson said, wiping his brow and grinning at me. 'That was the battle of Barnet all over again, eh? And much more close-run.' He cleared his throat, spat on the ground, and surveyed me. 'Aye, Henry Morane,' he went on, 'and one of these days your private wars will run that much too close . . .' he snapped his fingers '. . . and if Jesus is my Saviour He will see to it that I am not present.' Then, to my astonishment, he crossed himself.

I turned back towards the other side of the clearing and saw Matthew Coombe sitting back against a tree, cradling his arm and trying to wipe the vomit off his face with the other hand. He got up when he saw us and gave a shamefaced grin.

'I am sorry, uncle Henry,' he said ruefully, 'but I have not been in such an affray before and could not master my sickness. Neither did I know what effect this would have on a man, as I had only fired it once before.' He held out the weapon.

I gave him a reassuring smile. Neither had I been in an affray where four men had been killed so quickly.

'Uncle Henry?' Anderson's eyebrows went up. '*Uncle* Henry?' He began to laugh quietly. 'God in Heaven! Are there more of the Morane clan?'

The pistoia, from the Italian town of that name, was one I had seen before. In fact it was the very one I had bought for Matthew some six years previously, almost immediately to be plagued with anxiety lest he shoot all his father's chickens at Kingstone-on-the-Thames. I blew the burnt powder away from the touch-hole and put it in my pocket. 'Only fired it once before?' I asked him.

'My father confiscated it forthwith,' he smiled.

I grinned back at him. 'Now, Matthew Coombe,' I said, 'before you tell us how you came to be here there is much work to do. First we will bind up your arm . . .' the wound was not deep as I· thought '. . . and then we have to bury all these men before any hue-and-cry.'

'Why not leave them where they are?' Anderson said.

'Because if they are found the children will tell of our appearance, especially that of a black-bearded man. Or

43

would you shave off that forest of sea-coal that hangs from your face?'

'But is it of importance to bury them?' Matthew Coombe asked. 'We were defending ourselves. The children would testify to that.'

Joseph Anderson spat on his hands and picked up a spade. 'Anything to do with the law is better avoided,' he growled. 'Bind up your arm, boy, and do what Morane . . . *uncle* Henry says.'

I had little fear of any hue-and-cry for the reasons I have already stated, but I wished to have the bodies of his men completely concealed in the same way as Sir William Stanley wanted them to dispose of us. It would cause him much anxious cogitation if they were never seen again.

While Matthew Coombe and Joseph Anderson were at their tasks I collected the horses, examining their furniture. One of the saddles bore the mark of the Hart's Head, which confirmed whose retainers they had been. I considered whether to bury it with the other equipment or carry it away to show Urswick as proof of Sir William Stanley's hand in the business, but after searching the body of the leader, I had no need to keep the saddle for evidence. The paper I found on him I put inside my coat for later scrutiny. There was still much to be done in that forest glade before nightfall.

*   *   *

It was not before we had found an inn and were seated at trestles with ale-pots in front of us that I questioned Matthew Coombe.

'I had been searching for you along the road,' he told us, 'when I encountered a motley of village children crying that Will Scarlet had been killed by villains while he was trying to rescue King Richard the Lion Heart and his black-bearded henchman. I did not know what they meant by Will Scarlet, but it was the black beard that gave me thought. I therefore went to where they pointed to see for myself. A few moments within earshot told me what was happening. And so I primed the gun and stepped forward to inquire further.'

44

'You stepped forward to inquire further?' Anderson said. He cleared his throat. 'It is as well you did, then, for that tiny firepot makes a brave noise . . . even if it can only do so once at a time. Well then, Matthew Coombe . . .' he grinned at me 'and praise be to God that it is not Matthew Morane, anyway, once you learn to use the longbow you will make a formidable soldier.' He clapped the lad on the back.

'But you will not become a soldier, Matthew,' I said to him. 'For I see that your hair is cropped in the manner of an apprentice, so that your indentures are not yet finished, indentures to Master James Herring, silver-smith of Charing in the Strand.'

'That is so, uncle Henry. It was because he knew you that he gave them to me.'

'Well then, now tell me how you came to be searching for us.'

Brown eyes examined mine. He was as tall as I, but thinner, and the innkeeper had been right about his chin needing steel only once each week. 'I came to warn you against being waylaid, but it seems I came too late.'

'Yes, yes,' I said, 'but who sent you?'

'Oh. But it was my aunt . . . Mistress Matilda, of course. She begged James Herring for leave to allow me to go. She told me where you would likely be, and described Captain Anderson here. But I would have recognized you in any case, uncle Henry, even though you have aged somewhat since we last met.'

The remark was made with the innocence of youth, and I would have ignored it had not Anderson given a loud guffaw. I glared at him.

'But why?' I spoke as if to myself. 'Why did she choose you? There must have been others who . . .'

'Master Herring asked her the same question,' Matthew Coombe said quickly, 'but she told him that there were many spies about the court, and if she were observed entrusting another man with the message he would likely be intercepted and forced to disclose it. Whereas I, being her nephew, and an apprentice withal, would not be suspected. Also . . .' he drew himself up a little '. . . I would not prattle of it afterwards. She said that your destination was known to the Lord Chamberlain,

45

and that he was sending retainers to prevent it.'

'She told Master Herring that?'

'No, no. Only to me, later. Master Herring is a kindly old man, yet, for all his regard for you, he would be afraid to dabble if he knew that such high-and-mighty names were concerned.'

'And did she say how she came by this information?'

At that he smiled. 'She said you would ask that. I am to tell you . . .' the smile faded and he eyed me curiously '. . . it is something I do not understand. But she said that you would.'

'What was it?'

'That it had been by carrying oats to Saint Uncumber.'

CHAPTER 7

I F there were means of keeping cattle alive through the
winter then there would be fresh beef for breakfast in
the spring. But until the Lord in His goodness sends pas-
tures that will survive the cold, the beef in April will taste
as dry as sand, and remain as thickly impregnated with
salt as the barrel in which it has been kept since the
wholesale slaughtering in the autumn. Pigs there are, and
sheep too, but beef is the meat for an Englishman. And
if hard with salt, why, then the more ale is needed to
slake it down. Thus when we had ridden no more than a
mile from the inn, in the damp, morning mist we had to
dismount to relieve ourselves, making clouds of steam
to rise and join the fog. Then it was that I bade Godspeed
to Matthew Coombe, enjoining him not to talk of what
had happened, not even to Matilda, but to tell her that
he had found us, and that we were on our way to York
in safety.

He closed his breech and smiled. 'You need have no
concern, uncle Henry,' he said, 'for I am not returning
to London.'

'Not returning?' I stared at him.

'No.' He shook his head firmly. 'To learn to be a silver-
smith has its merit, but this journey has given me a better
opportunity. The chance of another way of life.'

Anderson laughed. 'Why not?' he said. 'Who would
want to be a silver-smith when the life of a soldier . . .
now take his longbow, for instance . . .'

I cut him short. 'You're using this mission to break
the indentures your father made for you? Is that it? You
will break his heart as well, you know, lad.' Edward
Coombe was a tanner, who had worked hard to amass
enough money in his iron-bound chest at Kingstone for
his son to acquire a craft. And Edward Coombe was a
man I had come to like. I sighed. Such was the thought-
less ingratitude of the young.

'My father may be sad at first,' Matthew Coombe admitted. 'But when he learns of my achievements he will

be proud, more proud of me than as a master silver-smith.'

'Your achievements? And what will they be?'

'Why . . .' he waved a hand at the horizon '. . . as a mariner, uncle Henry. I will explore the distant oceans, the far-away lands.'

'God's Hooks!' Anderson muttered. 'He wants to go to Iceland!'

I ignored him. 'What distant oceans?' I demanded. 'Where have you learned all this . . .' I was going to say 'nonsense', but thought better of it. It would encourage the natural obstinacy of youth.

'There is a man,' Matthew Coombe said, 'who pays rent to Master Herring for a room above his shop. All through the daylight hours, and often afterwards with the light of a candle, he draws maps and charts of the seas round Europe. From Muscovy in the north to the Pillars of Hercules . . . yes, and beyond through the In-land Sea to the ports of the Saracens, to Constantinople and to Syria. He has been to all those places. Aye,' he turned to Anderson, 'even to the Iceland you speak of.'

'And he is to take you with him?' I inquired, scenting the coming seduction of this youth into a career of madness.

'Well, no,' Matthew Coombe admitted. 'But he has told me of them, and shown me his maps. His advice, in fact, has been to wait till I am older, but first to gain experience with fishermen. That, uncle Henry,' he added, drawing himself up, 'is where I am bound. And as this journey has taken me towards the northern ports, that is where I will go. To the sea, and to learn its ways.'

'A laudable ambition,' I said after a moment. 'But who is this man?'

'He is from Italy. A sea port. It is called Genoa.'

'I have heard of it. But why has he come here, to England?'

'To show his charts to the King.'

'Then why doesn't he do it? Cannot he gain audience?'

Matthew Coombe shook his head. 'He cannot as yet. Because on his voyage from Lisbon his vessel was set upon by pirates off Cornwall, and all his charts were lost. He must draw new ones first.'

48

'And what does he expect King Henry to do?'

'To lend him money, of course. So that he and his brother can hire ships to sail westwards across the ocean to Cathay and Japangu.'

Anderson burst into a roar of laughter. 'Ask King Henry for money? Your friend must have fever of the brain! Does he not know that the King wouldn't even pay to ship one salted eel from Hull?'

'A moment,' I said, eyeing the youth. 'You say he plans to sail *westwards* to Cathay? Westwards? Across the Great Ocean?'

'For sure, uncle! The Great Ocean laps the shores of Europe all the way from Iceland to Cadiz, and, as the world is round, it must also make its tides on the coast of Japangu and Cathay at its other edge. And that is what Master Bartholomew draws on his maps, you see.'

'Quicker to walk to Cathay across Asia, as Marco Polo did,' Anderson observed. 'And safer, too. No monstrous sea-creatures like the seven-headed Hydra, or the Kraken that gobbles up Christians but spews back Turks and Jews. And the Monk-fish, a devil with horns and the body of a man joined to a whale . . .'

But I was thinking. The lad was convinced, I could see. I said, 'And you would go with him if King Henry provided the means?'

He nodded vigorously. 'I would, uncle.'

'Then,' I said slowly, 'I could see that he gained his audience.'

Matthew Coombe drew up his horse. 'You could, uncle?'

'But only,' I said, 'after you have returned and finished your apprenticeship. How long have your indentures to run?'

'A year. Maybe a quarter more.'

'That is little enough. By then you will have made your master-piece and be admitted to the guild.'

'Or only be a journeyman not able to afford his own shop.'

'No matter. You will be of the Craft anywhere. In Bristol, for instance, where there are many smiths. And mariners,' I added significantly. 'There are even more of them. And, as master of a trade you can make acquaintance of the masters of theirs. While now, to beg your bread until some fisherman makes a belly boy of you . . .'

'A belly boy?' Anderson said. Then he understood and laughed.

Matthew Coombe looked doubtful. 'And,' I added, 'by then I shall have spoken with your friend from Italy, and if what he says has merit I shall see to it that King Henry hears of it as well. You say this Master Bartholomew has a brother? Is he a chart-maker as well?'

'No, no! He is a mariner, the most skilful of them all. He has sailed every sea, and knows each one's rocks and shoals. He remains in Portugal, awaiting the King's pleasure to hear his request, and if that fails he will go to Spain to plead with Ferdinand and Isabella. Yet he would prefer the support of the King of England if his brother can secure it.' The brown eyes regarded me seriously. 'He and Bartholomew are very close. Almost as twins, Bartholomew says.'

'And this brother?' I said. 'This mariner. What is his name?'

'The same as Bartholomew. But he is called Christopher. Christopher Columbus.'

CHAPTER 8

W H I L E the countryside farther south had been as-
tir with the urgency of spring, once across the Trent
it seemed that Nature was not yet fully awake.
The forests still stood brown and silent, and there
were even thin plates of ice to snap under our horses'
hooves. I drew my cloak close about me and cursed
the wind.

'Ah!' Anderson said. 'It comes from those frozen peaks
that your nephew wants to see. That fellow Columbus . . .'

'A man with fever of the brain,' I said shortly, 'which
Matthew will soon discover for himself.'

'Maybe,' he agreed doubtfully. 'But it is as well you
persuaded him to return, for his father's sake, at least.'

If there was a state of insurrection at York the city
bore no sign of it. There were no new corpses on the
Tyburn gallows, a mile outside the walls. Those that
hung were so rotten with age that even the crows had
gone, leaving the maggots for the smaller birds.

At the barbican before the Tower Gate, sometimes
called the Mickle-gate, there were no more than two sentries, one on each of the circular bartizans that flanked
it. A bearded one hailed us and said that the gates were
closed for the night. I told him that I came for John
Sponer, Sergeant of the Mace.

'At this time of the evening he will be at the Bull,
I think. Do you know it?'

'Aye. If John Waterhouse is still the landlord.'

'You know York, then, sir?' The sentry eyed me with
a new respect.

The tavern was so full that we had difficulty pushing
our way through all the folk to the trestles at the back.
But they were good humoured, although I heard a voice
say, 'They must be Midlanders, thirsty as their draught-
horses.' One fellow was leaning against a corner, supported by his forearms and the top of his head, the
better to peer downwards at what he was doing. I

51

slapped him on the back as we passed, disturbing his aim.

'At least we do not piss like them,' I said, which brought some laughter. And then I saw John Sponer, Sergeant of the Mace, seated at a trestle, with two other men. I recognized John Nicholson, the Sergeant's Messenger, but the other I did not know.

It was John Nicholson who looked up, and when he saw me he covered his eyes. 'God's Balls!' he groaned loudly. 'I should have heeded that dream I had last night, and stayed away from here!'

'What dream?' I inquired amiably.

'Of you, Henry Morane. Your body was hanging from the battlement of Harwood Castle. It was a dream I woke from with some regret.' He punched me gently in the middle. 'But,' he went on, 'perhaps it will come true. Meanwhile,' he looked at the others, 'as you are here, with that same black-bearded shadow close behind you, we had better not let it be said that York does not welcome visitors, whoever they are.'

John Sponer, tall and ungainly, with tousled fair hair and steady blue eye, looked at us and laughed. He turned to the other man, shorter and darker than the other two, and with hair cropped close. He said, 'You recall the commotion at Harwood Castle some two years back, at the time of the Simnel rebellion?'

The dark one nodded, eyeing me. 'I do. It was reported that a body of men stormed the walls, killed a sentry, and were driven off after a sharp fight.' His eyes took in Anderson. 'Are these two of them?'

'Two of them?' Nicholson said. He pointed at us. 'That was all of them.' He groaned again. 'Ah, well. Here they are again. And that can only mean trouble, especially after my dream.' He turned to me. 'And who are you going to kidnap this time?'

I put a finger over my lips with mock secrecy. 'Can it be told in front of your friend?' I whispered loudly.

'Oh, yes,' John Sponer said, holding up his ale-mug at the serving wench and indicating us, 'John Vavasour is an officer of the City, too. The Sword-Bearer, no less.'

At that Joseph Anderson gave a loud guffaw, and pointed at them in turn. 'John Sponer, John Nicholson, and now John Vavasour! Three Johns! York does not lack for pisspots, it seems!'

'And moreover of gold,' I said, pointing at their gilded badges. 'Even the one to which King John gave his name was only of silver.'

'I will not have you calling my friends pisspots!' It was the wench, black eyes aflame and bosom heaving. She emptied the ale mugs she had brought over us. A roar of laughter went up all round us as we sat gasping and spluttering. Anderson gave a bellow and started to get to his feet, but his head came up against her huge bosom, and he subsided again, grinning. 'For that,' he said to her, 'for that you'll bring us twice as much.' He reached out for her, but she eluded him and ran off through the crowd. A moment later there was a yell of pain from the barrel-room. Anderson got up and rushed in there. The yelling stopped, and he reappeared with an ale-mug in each hand and a wide smile on his face.

'The landlord was berating her,' he explained, 'I had to . . .'

'Oh ah,' Vavasour said, 'we know what you had to do. It is her way with strangers.' The three of them smiled. 'First she insults them, then seems to be berated for it, so that she needs comfort. How much did it cost you?'

But Anderson was not put out. He waved the mugs he was carrying. 'These cost nothing,' he said.

'Now,' John Sponer said, his blue eyes on me. 'We will hear what brings you to York again.'

I waved an airy hand. 'We were passing by on our way to the North country, and could not miss greeting you for the sake of old times.'

Nicholson sniffed. 'An explanation as convincing as a lawyer protesting his sincerity.'

'The last time,' Sponer persisted, 'you came to kidnap the pretender, the boy called Lambert Simnel. Who is it this time?'

'Whom would you have me take? Henry Percy of Northumberland?'

There was a sudden silence. Then John Vavasour leaned forward on the trestle. 'Is that a jest?' he asked quietly.

Before I could reply, Nicholson spoke. 'He was

53

Dickon's man, for sure. We know that. While Dickon was still alive, that is.'

'See here,' I told them straight. 'My loyalty is bonded to the authority of the realm, which today is Henry Tudor. But to Dickon I was also bound by affection and, even if he is dead, it still remains for his memory. And I am the only man still alive who fought for him and saw him cut to pieces before my eyes. And for that to me his blood calls out for vengeance.'

'Ah!' Sponer said. 'Then we are all of the same mind.'

'In part,' I agreed. 'But Sir William Stanley is the most to blame. It was his men who killed Dickon.'

But, as on the previous occasion, he would have none of it. He cleared his throat and spat on to the sandy floor. 'If Northumberland had not witheld his men when Dickon called for aid Stanley's louts would have been scattered like the Cheshire hogs they are.'

'Nevertheless . . .'

'Enough of this,' John Vavasour said. 'Old battles are never the better for being re-fought.' He raised dark eyebrows at me. 'But you are here to take Northumberland?'

'Then if you need assistance . . .' Nicholson began.

'Great God!' I exclaimed. 'I would not dare! Take Henry Percy, Lord Warden of the Eastern Marches, the King's Lieutenant of the North, Chief Justice of all the Forests-beyond-the-Trent, Steward of Knaresborough, Constable of all the King's Castles in Northumberland, Sheriff of that county for life, and fourth earl of that name? What chance would I have, an ordinary scrivener, of revenge on him for Dickon's death? No, my friends, even King Henry himself would think twice before commanding such a thing. All the Border Counties would rise in revolt.'

'Then why are you here?' Sponer persisted.

'Because,' I said slowly, 'it has been said that York has refused to pay the new taxes, and that the city is in revolt.'

They sat and eyed each other. Then Vavasour said, 'At least you do not mince words, Master Morane. But look . . .' he waved a hand round the inn '. . . does it seem that York is in revolt against the King?'

'Aaaah,' Anderson growled. 'It is those hangdog priests round the King who have put this about. Chancellors, Archbishops, Secretaries and the like, creeping like moths along the walls and muttering curses against men who dare to enjoy the sunlight that God sends us.'

I waved a finger at him, but his eyes had gone towards the serving wench. 'Nevertheless,' I said to Sponer, 'the taxes have not been paid.'

'Not yet,' he agreed. 'But that is because we have sent a petition to the King's Tax-collectors asking for his forbearance in allowing the country-folk hereabouts time to pay. There is no question but that they will pay, yet they are poor and cannot find the money all at once. And if, as we hear, that Henry Percy of Northumberland has now been appointed the Collector, then he had better not try to collect the tax before we have an answer to our petition.' He looked round at the others, and they nodded emphatically.

'Then,' I said, 'I will tell you this. And it is for your ears alone. I carry a sealed package addressed to Northumberland. And it is from the King.'

There was a long silence until John Sponer let out his breath in a sigh. 'You know its contents?' he asked quietly.

'As I said, it is sealed.'

But seals can be eased and pressed down again if one has the implements and takes great care. And the abbot of the Cistercian monks at Roch, near to the village of Rotherham, had remembered me from two years earlier, when I had used his Scriptorium for a similar purpose.

'Maybe we should lock you up before you deliver it,' John Nicholson said.

But I did not smile. 'Then those same hangdog priests would call it treason,' I said. 'No, John . . .' I put a hand on his arm '. . . I came to warn you to treat Northumberland with circumspection. Who knows, but events may turn so that he pays for his betrayal of Dickon.'

'I cannot see how,' Vavasour said.

'Neither can I, as yet,' I agreed, but I was thinking of the paper I had taken from Swivel-eye's pocket. 'But . . .' I got up '. . . in any case, my friends, I leave tomorrow for the North and Henry Percy.'

55

'You will not have to go that far,' Sponer told me. 'He is no more than twenty miles from here. At his manor near Topcliffe, with a hundred men, all armed. It is close to Boroughbridge, of which he is Bailiff.' He smiled. 'A title you forgot.' Turning to Nicholson, he said, 'Show them the way, John.'

John Nicholson shrugged at him. 'The last time I showed them the way somewhere there was trouble at the end of it.' He turned to me. 'Maybe there will be trouble again . . . this time for Northumberland.'

CHAPTER 9

T H E Roman road, now known as Leeming Lane, passes through Boroughbridge on its way north, near to the battlefield of that name, where, in the previous century, Edward the Second had broken the power of the barons. That made us wonder whether King Henry Tudor would be able to keep a restraint on his own over-mighty subjects, such as Northumberland, the Stanleys, the earl of Oxford and others, who, not able to impose their will on the Yorkist kings, had promoted the cause of the Tudor in the expectation of being able to dominate him and thus improve their own position. For, no matter how much wealth and power a magnate acquires, there is always more to be gained from an acquiescent monarch and, should he be weak enough, that magnate might even be able to seize the crown for himself, as Henry Bolingbroke and Edward of York had done. But it did not seem to us that any of the existing nobility were man enough to make for that glittering prize, preferring to let Henry Tudor carry the responsibility of government while they used him to further their own ends. At least that was what John Nicholson thought. I gave it as my opinion that this new Tudor king was of much stronger will than was generally considered.

It was when he mentioned that Boroughbridge had been fought with spears that Joseph Anderson joined in the discussion. 'Neither side used the longbow?' he asked incredulously.

'So it was said,' Nicholson replied. 'Edward the Second had not long before been defeated by Scottish spears at Bannockburn. Thus, to him it was a more decisive weapon.'

'Decisive?' Anderson laughed. 'Not so decisive as the red-hot poker up his backside that finished him off a few years afterwards.'

Some three miles north of Boroughbridge the way to Topcliffe lies along another Roman road, this one not being kept much in repair. Over the centuries many

stones have been removed, the walls of the nearby peasants cottages being the better constructed as a result.
Other paving stones lay in heaps, long overgrown with
moss and sturdy weeds. And from where they had been
taken lay deep pools of mire. At the Swale, which was
not in flood in spite of the season, the timber bridge was
firm, recently reinforced by great oaks from the forest
of Galtres which covered the land on the other side.

Topcliffe village was built round the market square,
with the ancient church of Saint Columba on the side
nearest the river. Few people were to be seen, for it was
nearly dusk, and when John Nicholson suggested we
went inside and pray for Aid in our mission Anderson
demurred.

'What aid do we need?' he asked. 'There is a letter to
deliver to Northumberland, that is all. A man who
whines for help too often must serve no purpose but to
cause God impatience, so that He might withhold it
when it was most needed.'

With a homily like that thrust at us we decided to
enter the tavern instead and seek mattresses for the
night. The place was full; of waggoners, sheep herders
and other country folk, and the landlord told us we
should have to wait until dark, when they had gone and
we could throw our mattresses on the floor. He was a
sly looking fellow with eyes that were never still, and
spent much of the time flickering across towards a
group of four men at the other side of the room. I saw
that they kept to themselves, were better clad than the
others, and all wore daggers.

I asked him how far it was to Cock Lodge, Northumberland's manor house, and he answered quickly and
without much thought, saying that it was little more
than a mile along the edge of the Swale. Then his eyes
flicked back to me.

'What do you want with Cock Lodge?' he demanded
in a voice loud enough for the four men to hear.

It had its effect. One of them disengaged himself
from his companions and pushed his way across to me.
A well-built fellow, he was, with short brown hair and
trimmed beard, and eyes of the same colour. 'And what
do you want with Cock Lodge, my friend?' he reiterated.

58

'I asked the way,' I said mildly. 'Would you know it better?'

He looked me up and down with a sneer. Here was a country bumpkin to be taught a lesson. His left hand came out to seize me by the jacket and pull me on to the point of the dagger held close beside him in the other. Afterwards he would claim that by the nearness of the weapon to him he only just had time to draw it before stemming my rush. It was a well-worn trick, and he should have known better, but I did not wait to consider the matter, nor why he should want to kill me.

The hand that reached out for me suddenly became a fist clenched in pain. The hilt of my own dagger was right up against his forearm, three inches of steel protruding through his sleeve on the other side. He gasped, and I saw the bearded face screw up before I pulled him towards me with the blade, as one uses a trident to draw an eel from the mud. But he was heavier than an eel, and it was not until my weapon grated between the two bones of his forearm that he came willingly. Then I reached out and took the dagger from his other, unresisting hand, and pushed it into his midriff. He gave another gasp, and his business was settled.

It had been too quick for his companions to see exactly what had happened, for they had been watching with contemptuous grins until they saw him fall. Then weapons came into their hands and they moved forward together, to be brought up short by the point of John Nicholson's sword. It was then that I noticed that the tavern had emptied, and that Joseph Anderson was nowhere to be seen. But a moment later he was behind them, his teeth showing behind his black beard, and the battle-mace dangling from his wrist.

'Since you had control of that one,' he said, indicating brown-hair squirming on the floor cradling his wounded arm against his torn belly, 'there was time to get this iron club. I'll clout the middle one while you two deal with the others.'

That brought them swinging round, and when he saw the mace the 'middle one' retreated quickly from the threat of its murderous spikes. He backed away so fast that he came right up against me, and this time I had a

59

dagger in each hand. That finished the affair, the other two dropping their weapons and holding their arms out in submission.

'Now,' I said to them, 'you can take your two sawdust heroes back to Henry Percy of Northumberland and tell him that I carry a letter for him from King Henry the Seventh of England, Ireland and France. And,' I added, 'I also have the King's Writ which entitles me to deliver it in person.' I pointed the daggers at them for emphasis before I went on. 'And if any harm should come to me before it is delivered the hundred archers that follow me will see to it that the same Henry Percy, earl of Northumberland or no, will be arrested. And you, my friends, and all those that guard him will not live long enough to make explanations of your conduct this night.'

They stared at me, ashen-faced. 'A hundred archers?' one said.

I stared back with all the assurance of a coney-catcher. 'And now you will tell me what you are doing here in Topcliffe.'

'His Grace the earl sent us to see if there was any trouble from the countrymen over the new taxes. And if we encountered their leader, one John a Chambre, he was to be disposed of. We thought that you were him,' the second one added.

A voice spoke up suddenly from behind us. 'Oho!' it said. 'So I am to be killed, am I?'

We turned to see a huge fellow, with eyes set wide apart in a head with little top to it, somewhat in the shape of a pear. His hair had been red, but now was streaked with grey, and his eyes were the colour of rusty nails. 'I am John a Chambre,' he announced unnecessarily, 'Chief Forester of the King's forest of Galtres, and tomorrow I lead a thousand of my countrymen to Cock Lodge to protest to your same Henry Percy against the tax. And you, fellow,' he said to me, 'whoever you are, will give me that King's Writ so that I can kill these louts here and now to show our Henry Percy that we are not afraid of him.'

'The tax will be collected peaceably,' I told him, 'and neither you nor anyone else will read the King's letter to Northumberland before he does.'

'And what if I and my fifty men outside take it from you?'

'Then you will do it over the body of the Sergeant's Messenger from York,' John Nicholson said.

'The Sergeant's Messenger is it? An officer of the city. Then what are you doing here? And on whose side do you fight?'

'I am on the side of the law,' Nicholson said. 'And there will be no fighting . . .'

'Besides,' I put in quickly, 'the letter from the King might command leniency. And then where will you stand if you make trouble first?' But I knew that the letter commanded no such course. Northumberland had been ordered to collect the tax in full, and 'those that whine the most will be pressed the hardest'. King Henry was deliberately stirring up trouble for Northumberland.

John a Chambre scratched his head. A few small insects fell wriggling on to his shoulders. 'Oh aye,' he said after some thought. 'It might offer leniency, at that. Then that dog's-son Northumberland will not be able to gainsay us. So . . .' he began to turn away '. . . we shall all be at Cock Lodge at noon to hear what he has to offer.' Then he put a finger against his nostril. 'And as to your hundred archers, Master King's-Writ, I wonder where they are at? Still in London, maybe?' His loud laugh echoed round the tavern even after he had gone.

I turned back to the other two. 'Go,' I told them. 'Leave your friends here.' I pointed at the innkeeper, who had been a cowering spectator all this time. 'As this fellow seems to have been in league with you, he can do his part in burying them.' I thrust a dagger into the wooden beam beside him. 'This is now yours,' I told him. 'And if you do not dispose of the two bodies properly I will have it said that you killed them with that very blade, which will fit the wounds if tried. And,' I added, 'my friends here will swear to it as witnesses, while your two . . .' I waved the other dagger at Northumberland's men '. . . will, if they have sense, not show themselves here again until the matter of the taxes has been settled.'

'Aye, that we will, sir,' one of them asserted vigorously,

61

'and more. For if the King's letter you carry does not allow leniency in the tax collection, then we will be too few to face Chambre and his thousand angry farmers. We shall not stay, whatever his lordship commands.' He glanced at his companion, who nodded his agreement. 'And neither will any of the others when we tell them of this night's work,' he added as they went out.

CHAPTER 10

L I T T L E more than a mile, the innkeeper had said,
and true enough, Cock Lodge was visible in the distance,
standing on its mound like a light-house erected for the
benefit of mariners. Neither was I unlike a mariner, for
the way along the edge of the Swale was covered with
deep pools of mire, and I had to guide my nag from
one clump of turf to the next. As I came nearer I could
see, beyond the Lodge, another, higher mound on which
stood the grey ruins of Maiden Bower, erected by the
Conqueror himself in the Norman motte-and-bailey
style. But Maiden Bower had belied its name, being a
strongly built castle, whereas Cock Lodge had been
erected within the last hundred years as a manor house,
a residence in no need of fortification in more settled
times. It was the favourite home of Henry Percy, fourth
earl of Northumberland, for his others were up in the
wild border country, where there was no comfort nor
respite from eternal vigilance against the marauding Scot.
Standing in the junction between the Swale and the Cod
Beck, it is in truth a pleasant situation, even at that time
of year before the trees wear their greenery and the
forest grows alive with birds and the other sounds of
spring.

On one side were the kitchens, and on the other the
hawk-mews and stables. Between them, the courtyard
was a sea of mud, with huge bales of straw lying about,
each one steaming with the heat it somehow generates.
Compared with the other dwellings thereabouts, the
manor was a palace. There was even clear glass in the
windows at each end of the great hall, so that one could
look out over the Cod Beck or the Swale without being
buffeted by the weather. Inside, so John Nicholson had
sworn, the coloured floor-tiles and the carpets on the
walls were renewed each year, and the vast fire-places,
set in alcoves against the walls with chimney holes above
them, were of real brick.

He himself, with Joseph Anderson, had remained

behind in Topcliffe. I thought it better that no official of York should be seen to have a hand in my mission, which I would now complete on my own.

'Have a care, Henry Morane,' he had warned, 'for this business has a smell about it. It would go very ill with our city, and the people of this county, if any harm should come to Northumberland.'

'Why should it?' I had replied with a confidence I did not feel. 'No one, not even this John a Chambre, would dare it against such a high-and-mighty lord. His thousand farmers, if indeed there are so many, are no more than borrowed for the occasion to impress the earl, and perhaps to influence him to re-consider the hardship he might inflict on so many folk. They are steady, simple people, of your own county, known to keep their temper.'

He had smiled at that, and I asked him what he knew of John a Chambre.

'He is chief forester of Galtres, as he told us. It has been said that he was given the post as a reward for his services to the Tudors at Bosworth.'

'He fought against us, then?'

'Yes. But he is not a Yorkshireman. He is from Denbigh, a town in North Wales.'

But I knew where Denbigh was. It was also in the domains of Sir William Stanley. The pieces of the business were beginning to fit together.

There were some twenty or thirty men-at-arms on the lawns outside Cock Lodge who eyed me as I approached. Our assailants of the night before must have apprised them of my mission, for no attempt was made to question me until I reached the guard at the doorway. But he knew of me as well and, after inquiring my name, took me inside straightaway.

Henry Percy was seated at a vast oaken table at the other end of the great hall, the windows behind him dancing in the morning light rippling on the Swale. The smell of the early-spring flowers and scented herbs that had been strewn over the floor instead of the more usual rushes was fragrant to my nose.

It was not until later that I discovered the necessity for them. The earl looked up with a frown when the guard thumped in, dropped the butt of his pike-staff to the tiles and announced my name, adding that I brought a message from the King.

'Morane?' he inquired. 'And who are you?' He waved his secretary away. That scribe, thin, and with a lined face, picked up his tablet, quill, ink-horn and pounce-box, and then dropped them on the floor in his haste to be gone. Northumberland waited, his fingers making hoofbeats on the table, until they were all collected. He was fatter than when I had last seen him at Bosworth. As he stood no higher than my shoulder, and was as wide as he was tall, with very little neck, the increase in his girth coupled with the mat of grey that sprouted all over his face and head, gave him the likeness to a hairy frog, if there could be such an extraordinary creature.

'Now then, Morane, put the letter on the table and step back over there.' He waved a round hand at the fireplace as he looked me up and down. 'And take that weapon from your belt when you are in my presence.'

I put the dagger on the table and moved across the room, to feel my buttocks warming from the logs that burned in the alcove. It would have been pleasant to stand there for a while, had not the smell been so grievous. It was in the fireplace that the noble earl had been performing his defecations, a custom not uncommon even in manorial residences where the garde-robes are some distance from the house and the weather is unkind.

He read the letter quickly, then took it over to the window to read it again, as if he were unable to believe its contents. Then he turned to me. 'Henry Morane, eh?' he said, frowning. His face was as grey as the hairs that sprouted from it. 'You have read this?' he inquired, waving the paper.

'Sir!' I said, drawing myself up. 'The package was sealed!'

The frown disappeared, and a look of relief came

into his face. I knew at once that he was not going to carry out the King's command — yet. He would temporize with John a Chambre and his mob while he sent for reinforcements from the North. And then the slaughter would begin. I knew Northumberland's reputation.

'Nevertheless, my lord,' I said, giving a slight bow. 'I am aware of the King's desire that you should show no mercy to those that plead they cannot pay. The tax is to be collected in full.'

'You think so, eh? Well, Master Morane, it seems you have too much impertinence for my liking.' He jerked his head towards my escort. 'Take the fellow outside and hang him,' he ordered.

The retainer gripped his weapon and hesitated. 'My lord,' he said, 'he has told us he carries the King's Writ.'

'Then take it away from him and burn it. I will not have Writs waved at me by any Tomdick the King chooses to send.'

'A moment, sir,' I said quickly. 'There are others who await me at Topcliffe, and who know of my mission. They are also aware of the contents of that letter,' I added, almost as an afterthought.

Henry Percy's eyes narrowed. Without taking them off me, he waved the guard away. The latter wasted no time. He had bad news for his fellows.

Northumberland walked back to the table and sat down again. 'Do they indeed?' he inquired, an unpleasant smile on his face.

'Aye. And one of them is an officer of the city of York.' I bared my teeth, but it was no smile. Seeing him sitting there had suddenly brought back the recollection of Bosworth; Dickon, sitting his horse, the vizor on his helmet pushed up almost to obscure the golden battle-crown, and the clash of arms all about us. 'Send to Henry Percy again,' he had called to his esquire above the din. 'Tell him not to waste a moment.' He had pointed with his battle-axe towards Surrey's men, still fighting bravely. 'Tell him to attack down there.' It had been the second message to Henry Percy and, as the esquire spurred his horse, Dickon watched him go. As he lowered his vizor, he had added, 'His men will turn the day if he does not tarry . . .' But Northumberland had not come at all.

I inspected him, my rage mounting. 'He waits for me,' I assured him, 'for King Henry does not lose his suspicions too easily, my lord, as you should well know. I recollect that you spent a year in the Tower after Bosworth.'

'By God!' Northumberland shouted. 'I'll have you hanged for that impertinence, no matter who waits for you at Topcliffe. As soon as I have dealt with that rabble . . .'

'Then you had better do that now . . .' I pointed at the window '. . . for I can hear a commotion outside, and . . .' But I did not finish, for two men came rushing in. They wore the dress of servants, stained as if from the kitchens.

'My lord, my lord!' the first one shouted. 'There is a fellow called John a Chambre outside, demanding audience, and he says he has a thousand men behind him!'

'A hundred, more like,' Northumberland said scornfully, reaching for his cap. 'Have the men-at-arms keep them at their distance while I speak with the fellow alone. And see to it that he is divested of any arms he carries.' He was unlacing his tunic a little, and I saw the hilt of a small dagger concealed inside his belt.

'There are no soldiers, sir. Only us. And your secretary, who cowers in the cellars.'

'No men-at-arms?' Northumberland looked incredulous. 'Where are they, then? Speak up, man!'

'They went, sir! They went! They shouted that they would not stay and face a thousand men over a matter of taxes . . .' The other servant began to pull at his sleeve to drag him away. They made for the doorway.

Henry Percy looked at me. It was easy to see what he was thinking. He could deny the commands in the King's letter . . . provided I were not alive to refute it. Then he would be able to make his escape. His hand began to move towards my dagger on the table.

I stood my ground. 'Remember, my lord,' I said as calmly as I could, 'that your guards overheard our conversation. The contents of the Kings's letter is now known to all, including John a Chambre and his farmers.

And,' I added with emphasis, 'it is known that you are aware of them too. To deny them would now be useless. You will have to go out and face them with whatever explanation you can summon up. There is no escape this time.'

'This time . . .?' Henry Percy sat down again. His eyes met mine, and I saw the realization come into them. His treachery to Dickon was at last going to be paid for. The Jaws of God were closing on Northumberland.

CHAPTER 11

THE news of the murder of the earl of Northumberland reached Topcliffe more quickly than I did. I had of necessity to return by a more circumspect route along the Eldmire Road, and arrived at the inn to find Anderson and John Nicholson drinking melancholy mugs of ale-and-mead as a gurgling requiem for the departed soul of one Henry Morane. My appearance terminated the proceedings with John Nicholson letting out a long, exasperated sigh which ended in a belch.

'Ah,' he said, examining the finger with which he had prodded my chest to see why it had not gone straight on through. 'I might have known, of course. But you were absent so long that we finally were cheered by the thought that the Devil had at last got his own.'

Joseph Anderson crossed himself, but as he still clutched his mug, most of its contents spilled over his tunic. Then he looked me up and down and began to laugh. 'Aye,' he agreed, 'it seems he failed, even if he did have to daub him with pigshit and straw. A pity,' he went on, calling on the landlord to fill our mugs, 'because now my expectations of returning to London, to a life of ease with unlimited ale and complaisant morts, have gone.' His eyes went to the ceiling beams and he gave a great belch. 'Oh Lord!' he called out, 'even though Morane has returned, deliver us from any more battle, murder and sudden death.' He paused, as if waiting for his message to reach its Destination, then turned back to me. 'And how did you get away? We heard that all at Cock Lodge were killed.'

I tore off a piece of the rustic smock I was wearing and wiped mud from my face. The damp straws in my hair were more difficult to dislodge. 'By taking the guise of one of John a Chambre's peasants,' I told them. 'There were so many, swarming about the lodge, that it was not hard to lure one aside and relieve him of his pitchfork and smock. And, as I had seen that the courtyard was all mud and piles of straw, I daubed myself so that my own mother would not have recognized me.'

'God's Hooks!' Anderson said with reverence. 'He had a mother! The poor woman must have died early after breeching one such as him!'

'Aaaah!' John Nicholson was thoughtful now. He asked me to recount what had taken place, and then gave another sigh. This time it was not one of mockery. 'This will be a dreadful thing,' he said. 'For a high-and-mighty earl to be murdered by the common people will bring great trouble to us all.'

'I do not think it will,' I said, 'for I will testify that it was John a Chambre's hand that struck him down. Those that followed him were but simple folk, making their protest for mercy, and not out for violence.'

'You will do that?' He looked relieved. 'It is a long time since such a deed took place. What happened then I do not recall hearing.'

'It was some forty years ago,' I told him, 'when the duke of Suffolk had his head struck off on board a rebel ship, but he was fleeing to exile and was not considered of great account. A lesser noble, Lord Say, was killed in Jack Cade's rebellion not long after. But that was a rebellion, although it was also about taxes.

'But there is no reason for this to lead to a rebellion. These are only a few simple peasants as I said, whereas at the time of Jack Cade the whole country was disaffected, and not only with taxes. The colonies in France had been lost, and the English who had settled there had to return, leaving all their estates behind them. When Cade's rebellion failed they began their own war with the crown, and against each other, York and Lancaster. Now there is no like situation. The nobles have lost no colonies across the sea. There is a stronger king than the half-witted Henry the Sixth. This one will see to the enforcement of the law and the stability of the realm, which all men, especially those of great wealth, will insist upon. Besides,' I concluded, 'the great nobles are much fewer in numbers than in those days, and have less power.'

'Hah . . . urk!' Anderson belched. 'A lesson in history

from the er . . . erud . . . learned Henry Morane.' He put a finger to his nose and regarded me carefully. 'So there is to be no rebellion once this John a Chambre has been hanged, then?'

'And who is to see to that?' We swung round to see the fellow himself, the top of his head only missing the beams because of its flatness. He was smiling cheerfully. 'You, Henry Morane?' he inquired.

I saw the sword in his hand and shrugged. 'So you know my name? You found the King's letter to Northumberland, then?'

'Aye, and now I've found you.' He looked me up and down, taking in the smock. 'So that's how you got away, is it? Well now, that can be corrected.' He waved the steel at me. 'Come outside, so that I can watch my men hang you.'

Anderson got up unsteadily. 'You think to take him, hey? Then let's see your men come in here and do it, first stepping over your body.'

Chambre swung on him. 'Wait,' I said quickly. 'I heard you tell your men they would be pardoned for this deed,' I said to him. 'What makes you certain of it? Or was it a lie just to soothe them?'

'It was no lie, my friend. I have the assurance of a great lord.'

'You think so?' I began to smile at him, and he did not like it.

'This I know . . .' he began, but I cut him short.

'What you know,' I told him, 'is what you were told by that great lord. But he has since changed his mind. Do you know one Randolf Eu?'

That set him frowning. I saw Anderson's puzzled look and John Nicholson's stare of incomprehension.

'Randolf Eu,' I repeated. 'Retainer of Sir William Stanley? You would know him by sight, or better?'

'What has Randolf to do with this?'

'What he has to do with it,' I replied slowly, 'is that he carried a letter from that same Sir William Stanley addressed to you, which countermanded previous instructions. More, he specifically abjured you from causing trouble over the new taxes and molesting the earl of Northumberland.' I took a paper from inside my shirt,

71

and heard Anderson grunt his recollection. It was what I had taken from the body of Swivel-eye, now lying buried in the Barnet forest. I gave it to John a Chambre, adding, 'It is not signed or sealed, which is to be expected, but its authenticity was to be proved by Master Eu.'

Chambre snatched it from me and read the few lines. His eyes came back to me. 'Then why did not Randolf Eu deliver it himself?' he demanded.

My smile was grim. 'He thought better of it,' I said.

'I do not believe it!' Chambre shouted. 'The letter is false!'

'Then consider it as such,' I urged him gently, 'until you are put on trial for the murder of Henry Percy. Then see if your great lord supports you.' I turned my back on him, making a sign to the terrified innkeeper for more ale.

John a Chambre stood there, his wide set eyes glaring at us. After a while he said, 'If I am put on trial for murder I will plead the Benefit of Clergy.'

'Aye,' I agreed, turning back, 'do that. And because you can read you can claim to be a cleric and be tried by the Church. But . . .' I waved a finger at him '. . . the same parliament that approved these new taxes also brought in a new law as to Benefit of Clergy. A man now may no longer claim immunity as a cleric more than once. Now,' I went on slowly, so that he could understand, 'if you are convicted of a murder, and escape by making that claim, you will be branded on the thumb with the letter 'M'. And no man, clergyman or otherwise, bearing such a brand, can make the same plea again. If condemned, he will be hanged forthwith.'

'Great God!' John Nicholson said, 'is that the case now?'

'It is,' I assured him. 'And when you return to York you will hear of it, for no doubt by now the sheriff and the pulpits will be proclaiming it.' To John a Chambre I said, 'Think on it, my friend. For if you escape the charge of murdering Northumberland by claiming Benefit of Clergy, you will be branded for life, and how long will that be if you murder me as well?'

John a Chambre's rusty eyes grew speckled with rage. He took a step towards me, saw the point of Nicholson's

72

sword in the way, thought better of it, and went out of the tavern muttering to himself.

Joseph Anderson began to laugh. 'Aye,' I said to him, 'but you, black-beard, cannot read at all, and so no one could accept that you have Holy Orders.'

'Haw, haw,' he said. 'But I can read the Neck Verse.'

'Recite it, you mean. Having learnt it by rote.'

'Of course. If the law is stupid enough to give a man the Holy Book and always demand that he read the fifty-first psalm, then everyone to be charged with felony quickly learns it by rote. I know it well.'

'And used it many times, no doubt.'

'And how many 'M's' will be branded on your thumb, Henry Morane, after that affair in Barnet forest?' he laughed.

'Whatever you two are talking about,' John Nicholson said, 'it seems better that I do not know. But how did you come by the letter? And how did you know it was from Sir William Stanley?' He saw the look on my face and gave a shrug. 'Perhaps I had better not ask that, either. Yet,' he went on after a moment, 'if you had that letter why did you not give it to John a Chambre last night? But for that, Henry Percy of Northumberland might still be alive today.'

I turned slowly. 'But,' I said, giving him an innocent stare, 'I thought you men of York also wanted him to pay for Bosworth Field?'

John Nicholson's eyes grew wide. 'Jesu!' he said quietly.'You mean that you held that letter back deliberately? You killed him, then!'

'Not I, my friend,' I said, and my smile was quite serene. 'It was the Vengeance of the Lord. For I never laid a finger on that treacherous, hairy earl.'

CHAPTER 12

T H E pattern of events was now becoming clear. Sir William Stanley, his nose for the scent of political upheaval still as keen as ever, had been observing the situation in the north since the murder of King James the Third at Sauchieburn the year before, and had drawn his own conclusions. With the new Scottish king, a lad of fifteen, controlled by his lawless barons the threat to the Border was already acute; now the removal of Northumberland had made it worse, especially as his death was the result of a rebellion. Who better than Sir William Stanley, with his three thousand well-trained Cheshire levies, to step in, restore order and hold the bastion against the Scots? Once in possession, he would be strong enough to make his own demands on Henry Tudor, not only for the earldom of Chester but possibly for the estates and title of Northumberland as well.

Yet Sir William Stanley's conclusions were the wrong ones, for he was a man more of cunning than sagacity. Certainly the demise of Henry Percy would cause the Tudor no great sorrow, but Stanley had failed to realise that Percy's heir was a minor too, a boy of only eleven, so that the wardship of all the estates and their revenues would revert to the crown until he came of age. More, King Henry was unlikely to cede territory, vital for the defence of the realm against the Scots, to another powerful magnate whose loyalty might be no greater than that of Northumberland.

Thus it was that Sir William Stanley had connived with John a Chambre to raise the peasants in revolt, not only to demonstrate that Northumberland could not control the situation, but also to have that earl's life terminated during the disorder. And then he had suddenly countermanded his orders to John a Chambre.

It was, as I could see now, because he had taken fright at the unexpected revelation of his treasonous plot after the battle of Stoke. This was embarrassing enough, but it would be much more difficult for him to deny *two* alleged acts of treachery at the same time, if his plans for Northumberland miscarried.

His concern must have been all the greater when he discovered that the King had secretly changed my destination to that of York. The secrecy could only be aimed at himself — Christopher Urswick would, in his devious way, have made that clear — and therefore John a Chambre must be restrained immediately. There was no time to send messages to summon the man and tell him so. A message must go direct, and his retainer, Randolf Eu, would carry it. He would take an escort of sufficient strength to overwhelm any that I had, and dispose of me once and for all. My demise would not only hinder the allegations of his treachery at Stoke, it would also satisfy Sir William Stanley's long-standing grudge against me. More, it would stop the delivery of any royal letters I was carrying to York, which letters he would be interested to read for himself when Randolf Eu brought them back.

Another point then occurred to me. Archbishop Morton had shewn anxiety over events at York. Yet those events had not then taken place. Someone had stirred his anxiety, and the only one who was about to set those events in train was Sir William Stanley. I sat down in the scriptorium of York Minster and wrote all this down for Christopher Urswick. It took much of the day to compose, for the kindness of the monks caused them continually to interfere by making sure that all my wants were satisfied, thus interrupting my train of thought. But in the end the letter was finished, and I had Joseph Anderson depart with it for London straightaway.

Not long after he had left news came that the whole countryside was in a state of revolt. The peasants had seized whatever weapons they could and had followed John a Chambre into the forest. There they were gaining more adherents and were threatening to march on York itself. A new leader had appeared, displacing John a Chambre. It suited that tall forester well enough, for his was the task of inciting the people and bringing them together, while Sir John Egremont, for that was his name, commanded the enterprise by virtue of his higher station.

'Who is this Egremont?' I asked John Sponer.

'We know him well enough,' was the reply, 'although it is a long time since he was seen in the city. His estates are to the north. His father was Thomas, Lord Egremont, of the Percy family, uncle to the recently murdered earl.'

'His cousin, in fact?'

'Aye, and heir to the earldom if there had been no surviving son.' John Sponer shook his head. 'Some say that he was behind the murder. If so, then the son will need to look to his own protection.'

King Henry will see to that, I thought. He will not care to lose his wardship to the earldom now. I wondered what measures he was taking, and hoped that Sir William Stanley would not be permitted to march in and restore order. My letter should reach Urswick in time to prevent that.

John a Chambre and his men duly appeared outside York. Their numbers had much increased since the affair at Cock Lodge, and now there seemed to be many more than the thousand he had first claimed. Sir John Egremont rode along Goose Lane, outside the wall, and at Monk Bar demanded the keys of the city.

The demand was ignored. York was well provisioned, and unlikely to fall to a crowd of unarmoured peasants, however numerous. Each day they would have to forage farther from the city, and each day there would be more who did not bother to return. Indeed it was only five mornings later that we could tell that most of them had drifted back to their homes. Then news came of the King's advance guard marching up from the south, and Egremont raised the siege, taking his motley army to meet it.

But the peasants, even if untutored, were not witless. It was one thing to kill a tax collector, even if he was a nobleman, but quite another to take up arms against the King himself. And while those north-countrymen were not cowards, they had more sense than to match pitchforks and clubs against armoured men on horseback. Thus, when the royal forces appeared there were no more than fifty or sixty countrymen to meet them. A slight skirmish scattered them, leaving a dozen or so to be brought captive into the city. One of these was John a Chambre, but Sir John

Egremont, being well horsed, made his escape.

The King's advance-guard was only of two hundred men, but they were fully armed and on great war-horses, supported by fifty archers riding on drays. The captain of the latter was easily recognized by the black-bearded face under the bowman's helm, and when he took off the steel hat to wave it at the crowd there was no mistaking the bald pate underneath. But it was when the commander rode out from the darkness of the barbican and stopped for his esquire to remove his battle-helm that the roar of welcome seemed to shake the very stones of that ancient work.

'Surrey! Surrey! Thomas Howard of Surrey!' The roar went on and on. The citizens rushed towards him, and his escort was hard put to keep the crowd back. I, too, was not ashamed to admit to a lump in the throat at the sight of him.

King Henry Tudor had been very astute to send Thomas Howard to put down the rebellion. His release from the Tower and the restitution of his titles had given much satisfaction to York, for his affection and loyalty towards Dickon were well known. I learned later that Archbishop Morton had warned King Henry against sending him, as York still had a somewhat sullen acceptance of the new regime, and Surrey could command a large following there. But Thomas Howard justified King Henry's confidence, letting it be known straightaway that, for all his affection for Dickon, he would not tolerate any disloyalty to the new authority. And when King Henry himself arrived in York a few days later he went further, announcing that the Council of the North, which Dickon had created, would be re-constituted, this time with his own son, the prince Arthur, as Lord Warden. But, King Henry had continued, as that Prince was not yet three years of age, Thomas Howard, earl of Surrey, would be his Lieutenant. Whatever else he was going to say was drowned by a tremendous yell of acclamation that continued for several minutes, so that in the end he gave up, his thin face smiling, and lifted his hand in acknowledgement as he stepped down from the platform. Even that gesture brought more cheers, and it was clear that in those few moments King Henry had gone further to gain acceptance in the north country than any quantity of edicts and proclamations from West Minster would have achieved in years. But to speak of his visit to York is somewhat previous, for in the meantime order had to be restored in the countryside.

Immediately Surrey arrived they built a tall gallows and hanged John a Chambre the same afternoon. They built it wide enough to hang three of his fellows as well, but him they set higher than the others, so that I had some difficulty finding a ladder long enough to climb up and talk to him. By the time I reached him he was in a sorry state, with eyes and tongue protruding as he choked. I spoke loud, hoping for him to hear above the noises he was making, telling him that I was empowered to offer him leniency if he would testify as to his involvement with Sir William Stanley, but whether it was through obstinacy or because he was too far gone, he gave no sign of understanding. As I descended I seized his bound feet and jerked them down with my weight, terminating his struggles, afterwards running away quickly to avoid the indignation of the remaining spectators at being cheated out of their viewing of the whole, slow process. But then I bore no particular animosity towards John a Chambre.

CHAPTER 13

THOMAS Howard, earl of Surrey, looked at Anderson and then at me. 'From what I have heard,' he said, 'there has been some connexion between your activities and the death of Henry Percy. It is as well that it has not been established, or I should have had to hang you on the same scaffold as John a Chambre and the others.' I knew he meant what he said, for Surrey was not one to baulk at hanging anyone where the death of a fellow noble was concerned, whatever his feelings about Northumberland. 'The innkeeper at Topcliffe,' he went on, 'at first came forward and said that you, Henry Morane, were present at Cock Lodge while the murder took place. But now,' he added, his iron-grey eyes on mine, 'it seems he has thought better of his assertion.'

The smirk on Anderson's face brought Surrey round to him. 'So it was you that persuaded him, hey?' The smirk changed into what Anderson tried to make an innocent stare, so that Thomas Howard snorted and turned back to me. 'And as for you, Morane, it seems you have friends in this city, and if I were to listen to these stubborn Yorkshiremen I should believe that you were never within ten miles of Cock Lodge, aye, and more, that it is doubtful if you were ever even in York itself.' He got up to examine the wooden carvings on the walls, speaking as if to himself, 'So that when I see you standing here, in its very Guild Hall, I am not sure whether I am in a dream or not.' He swung round at me. 'And I am curious to hear the explanations you give to the King when he arrives.'

I did not know then that King Henry was to come to York, but I said, 'My Lord, it is better you do not hear them. For the King will surely say that I have been to Bristol, not to York.'

At that Surrey looked astounded, then wiped a hand across his brow. 'Now I think I must have a fever of the brain.'

'No, no, my Lord,' I said quickly. 'But I know that

His Grace will be pleased if my visit here is not spoken of. These are matters on which I have been charged not to discuss. But if the King comes to York will the whole court accompany him?'

'The court? Oh, I see!' He smiled. 'You can rest easy, Morane, for the Lord Chamberlain has been given leave to visit his estates for the audit of his stewards.'

It was as I had thought. Sir William Stanley had gone to muster his men in case the situation in the north got out of hand. Then Surrey came back and put a hand on each of our shoulders.

'And you can both rest easy,' he said, 'as to the matter of the false report from Stoke Field. I myself questioned the Lieutenant of the Tower, and he now admits that he cannot properly recall what the fellow told him of our conversation that night.' His face became bland. 'It is unfortunate that the fellow himself cannot be called to account either. Not long after my talk with the Lieutenant his body was found in the Tower Moat, and . . .'

He was interrupted by a loud guffaw from Anderson.

'And,' Surrey went on, trying to ignore him, but unable to keep a smile off his face, 'the matter is now closed. On both sides, Morane,' he said to me, 'so that it would be unwise to pursue your allegations.'

'I never had any intention of it, my lord,' I told him. 'It was Stanley who brought the charge against me, you will recall. The matter was only raised in conversation that night between us, as a reminiscence, as you were directly concerned. Besides, as I was the only person who overheard his plotting, my word as a scrivener would have carried no weight against Sir William Stanley.'

Surrey nodded. 'I thought that had been the case.'

'Ah, well,' Anderson said, 'at least we can prove his complicity in Northumberland's murder. You have his letter to John a Chambre?'

'It will prove nothing,' I told him. 'It is neither signed nor addressed to him. Chambre, who might have confirmed its origin, is dead, and so is the man who carried it.'

'A moment, my friends,' Surrey interrupted. 'Am I, as the King's Officer in York, to know what you are talking about?'

'No sir,' I said quickly. 'It would embarrass you.'

'Then,' he grinned, 'I would prefer not to be. But if you in fact possess a letter from Sir William Stanley, once he learns you have been in York he will make inquiries as to its delivery.'

'But sir!' I protested. 'I have not been in York.'

He laughed at that, then became serious. 'But take care, Henry Morane,' he said. 'For God help you if Sir William Stanley gets his hands on you again.'

CHAPTER 14

THE wild daffodils in the meadows of Sheen were beginning to fade, those in the forest beyond already being mostly devoured by the goats of the villagers or rooted up by hogs. Yet each year they rose again to nod their yellow trumpets together in the breeze, an effort of survival that was always a wonder to me. Perhaps the rooting pig had some instinct that made him leave one shard from each cluster to spread again, ensuring his food for next year. It seemed to me that man was the only creature caring nothing for his own survival. The thoughts came to me as I rode past a group of village children aiming pebbles from their slings at fledglings in the trees. Yet, to judge from the infantile curses that floated across the grass, perhaps God Himself was ensuring the survival of the young birds by the poor aim He was giving the urchins. I waved at them as I rode round by the river and entered the Manor by the drawbridge at the Water Gate.

The buildings were strong and would endure, having been rebuilt only seventy years before. Materials had come from such diverse places as the quarries of Yorkshire and the brick-fields of Calais, as well as from manors that had been demolished at Byfleet and Sutton. While it had cost the enormous sum of six thousand pounds, it was an amount that King Henry the Fifth, after his victory at Agincourt, had well been able to afford for a hunting lodge only six hours rowing from West Minster.

Sheen Manor had come into the hands of Elizabeth of York from her mother, Elizabeth Woodville, the now discredited Queen of Edward the Fourth, but the present king had taken a liking to it too, and spent as much time there as possible with his wife in the peaceful surroundings of river and forest.

I went on through the River Court, exchanging cheerful insults with the guards, who were hoping to obtain their revenge on me at dice from a previous occasion.

Her Highness the Queen, they told me, was at her devotions in the chapel with her mother-in-law, the Countess of Richmond.

The habit of referring to the Lady Margaret Beaufort as the Countess of Richmond infuriated her third husband, Lord Stanley, as much as her continued resistance to him in matters of the flesh. While as to the latter he had long ago made other arrangements, and already had sons of his own by a previous marriage, the fact that his wife, consort to his new earldom of Derby, was always called the Countess of somewhere else, irritated him beyond measure.

Yet Margaret Beaufort had been the wife of Edmund Tudor, earl of Richmond, when she had given birth to the present king, and the Countess of Richmond she would always be called. In part is was due to the affection in which she was held, because of her unswerving loyalty to her son through all his vicissitudes, and in part it was because little was known to Lord Stanley's credit. His earldom of Derby was considered to be no more than a payment for his defection from Dickon, and the English have little respect for one who changes his coat for material gain.

The sergeant of pikemen suggested throwing a few dice until the royal devotions were concluded. But I had other plans. Putting on a stern face, I reminded him of his duty, which was to guard the manor against invasion from the river. At that he laughed and inquired if the boat that lay out there could be considered to have any belligerent intentions. I had to agree that it seemed unlikely, for it was tied by a rope to a tree on each bank, allowing the current to fill out the net that trailed behind it. A pleasant way in which to catch young salmon on a spring afternoon, especially as the crew of three lay fast asleep beside an empty ale-barrel. I promised the sergeant his chance that evening, and moved on towards the chapel.

Queen Elizabeth of York and Lady Margaret Beaufort knelt at the wooden rail, their ladies close behind them, while Reginald Bray ministered to their devotions. Bray had been Margaret Beaufort's secret agent during the days of Dickon, carrying messages to her son in Brittany.

83

But that son was now king, there were no more secret letters to deliver, and Bray was back at being Confessor again. I watched him as he intoned the chant like a mournful hound, and saw a flicker cross his face as he saw me come in and kneel at the back, behind the Queen's other women. In front of me a pair of feet protruded from under a green skirt as their owner knelt to hear the chant. I put my hand on one of them, walking my fingers a little way along the leg. There was a twitch, and a fierce whisper came at me, 'Remove your hand, sir!' before Matilda turned round. So did some of the others, and I heard a suppressed giggle.

When she saw me, Matilda smiled, and I shuffled forward alongside her on my knees. The floor stones were harder than I had expected.

'I should have known who it was,' she muttered.

There was no time for a reply as the ladies by the altar were rising, and those around us were moving aside to let them pass. The Queen and Margaret Beaufort came by, arms linked, then the Queen saw me and stopped.

'Why, Master Morane!' she said. 'We welcome your return, and trust that all is well in Bristol.'

'Well enough, your highness,' I said, bowing low. 'But I cannot yet make my report on it, as I am told that the King is in York.'

One of the ladies beside her was staring at me. Mistress Belknap seemed to be surprised at my presence. I inclined my head in acknowledgement of her gaze, taking in the brown eyes, curling hair and the separate bosoms that, once released from the restraint of her clothes, would bounce like baskets at the strawberry fair. She was well disposed elsewhere too, and, once the astonishment had left them, there was a light in her eyes that even a monk would find hard to ignore.

'He will be returning within a few days,' the Queen said, 'when he will rest here before returning to West Minster, I hope.' She lowered her voice a little. 'There has been some rioting in York, we hear, Master Morane. Perhaps you have heard of it?'

'Indeed, madam, the whole country has, I think. But they say it is finished, with those responsible either hanged or fled to the Dowager Duchess of Burgundy.'

84

'Ah, yes, aunt Margaret,' Elizabeth of York sighed. 'It would be pleasant if she would forget old animosities.'

Her mother-in-law took her arm again. 'Come, Elizabeth,' she said, 'it is time you attended your baby prince.'

Elizabeth of York smiled at me as she moved away, the allusion to the heir to the Tudor throne bringing her back from reminiscence. Behind her followed her sister, the Lady Anne of York, who glanced at me inquiringly. Surrey's son would have given much to have seen her face when I told her that all was well with that young man.

'Hah!' Matilda said, when they had gone. 'At least you seem to have returned unscathed. Or are there any pieces missing?'

'None that would incommode you,' I grinned, and received a slap across the face. 'But I would hear how Matthew Coombe came to find me.'

'What?' she smiled up at me. 'Would you hear all that first, Henry Morane?'

'Well, if it were of more importance . . .'

She put her arms round me and kissed me. 'Could anything be?' she whispered in my ear.

*   *   *

I sat up on the bed and watched her as she walked across to the arras to get her clothes. 'Now,' I said, 'what was that about Saint Uncumber you told Matthew Coombe of? If I thought you were carrying oats to that Bearded Virgin of yours, I . . .' But she was not listening. She was picking a paper off the floor.

'Faith, and what's this?' she said. 'A love letter in the nice round hand of a woman that you dropped in your haste to strip and bed with me?'

'I would forego any woman to bed with you,' I replied. But, beyond a swift, contemptuous glance at me, she was more interested in the paper. She read it, slowly to herself at first, then out loud:

'Randolf Eu brings this letter which he cannot read. But he will tell you it is from me and carries my new commands. The commands are that the Earl must not now come to any mischief or suffer any harm. You will see to it and burn away this paper.'

'And what does that mean?' Matilda asked.

I told her that it was Stanley's letter to John a Chambre; how it had come into my possession, and what had happened afterwards.

'Jesu Mary!' she exclaimed. 'Then it was as well I sent Matthew Coombe to warn you!'

'He told me you had sent him. But how did you know to do so?'

'It was Master Urswick.' She came back to the bed and sat beside me. 'He was in a great state. He clicked his tongue and rubbed his hands together so often that I knew something was amiss. He said that Sir William Stanley had learned that you were for York, and not for Bristol as was supposed, and was sending men to way-lay you. Urswick could not send any of his own men, as they might be recognized and come to harm, for they were only clerks. Then I thought of Matthew Coombe. He was not known to anyone, and had wit enough to find you. I did not know he would meet such a risk . . .' She saw my expression and stopped.

'It was all simulation,' I told her. 'Sir William Stanley had learned it from Urswick himself. He let it fall deliberately.' I put an arm round her and held her tight, for her face was shocked, and told her of Urswick's conversation with me before I had set out. 'He was trying to prove to his own satisfaction that Stanley was guilty of sending the false report from Stoke. But then, it would seem, Master Urswick took fright, because the affair was bigger than he had anticipated. He discovered that Stanley, instead of hiring ordinary country ruffians, had sent no less than five of his best military retainers to dispose of me. At least, that is the only explanation I can think of. And I intend to demand one when I see him.'

'Jesu!' Matilda said. 'He would play with you like that?'

'He would play with anyone,' I replied. 'If it suited him. He was not with the King at York. Is he at West Minster then?'

She shook her head. 'He went with an embassy to Spain, carrying proposals for the marriage between the

Prince of Wales and Catherine of Aragon.'

'And neither of them three years of age,' I observed.

'It is only to make an alliance against France, Lady Margaret says. That same Prince Arthur will be calling for me to read to him those books printed in great letters by Master William Caxton, and there are pictures which the Prince would fain see. Queen Elizabeth says he prefers my reading to all the others.' She got up and went to the arras.

'And this?' I said, picking up Stanley's letter. 'It is not in his hand, of course, and so dictated to one of his secretaries.'

'Aye, and carefully worded,' she called back. 'So that its message would not be understood by Randolf Eu, but he could confirm its authority.'

'That is not what I meant,' I said. 'You said it was in the hand of a woman. How then could it have been written by a secretary?'

'I did not say it was written by a secretary,' she replied. 'It was you who said so. Surely even Sir William Stanley would not be so foolish as to dictate such a letter to a scrivener who would be the first to be put to the question if there were suspicion of his activities in Yorkshire?' She began struggling to get the green dress over her head without dislodging the pins in her hair. When I had finished helping her she smiled. 'No, no, Henry Morane. Do you not understand? The letter needed to be written by someone who was not a paid scrivener, and thus whose hand would not be known.' She took the paper from me. 'This was written by a woman, and I have seen her handwriting before.'

'You have?'

'Aye, indeed! Many times. She writes accounts for the Queen. It is Mistress Margaret Belknap.'

CHAPTER 15

THE Lady Margaret Beaufort sat in her favourite place by the windows, at the distant end of the great hall of Sheen Manor. It looked out across the tiled courtyard, through the blossoms of the fruit trees on the other side, and beyond them to the reed-bordered waters of the Thames. The panes of glass beside her were of lozenge shape, some of red, others of blue, yellow and purple. And as she was clothed in her familiar brown, as well as being seated below one of the mulberry-wood carvings that adorned the walls, she merged with her surroundings like a doe in autumn. I strode across the panelled floor and, being of high spirits, took off my cap and flung it at an antelope whose carved wooden horns stuck out as if challenging me to hang my headgear there. My attempt was successful, but only for a moment, then the cap fell away and, to my horror, I saw that Margaret Beaufort was sitting beneath the animal. The cap fell straight on to the book which she was reading.

She gave a quick exclamation and looked up. I was on my knees straightaway, but at the look on my face she smiled.

'Why, Master Morane,' she said, 'there might have been some trouble for you if it were known that you had set your cap at the King's mother.'

I looked at her open-mouthed, which made her laugh outright. She held out the cap and I took it, too bemused to speak. It did not seem possible that the Lady Margaret Beaufort could make such a jest.

She held up the book. I saw that it was the same one she had been reading on the previous occasion. 'Do you know, Master Morane, what William Caxton says?' she inquired. But she did not expect me to tell her, for she went straight on, 'Look at what has been lost to English life,' she read, following the printed words with her forefinger. She glanced up at me and went on, 'Look at what has been lost since the days of the Black Prince, and of Henry the Fifth. O, ye knights of England, where is the chivalry of those bygone days? What do you do today but go to the baths, those warm stews brought back from the degenerate Turk, and play at dice . . .' She stopped and frowned. Mistress Belknap was standing there. 'Yes?' she inquired, the austerity back in her pale eyes again.

'It is the Queen,' the lady said, making a curtsey. 'She asks for you, madam. She wishes you to inspect a new rocker for the Prince of Wales. The woman asserts that she was once rocker for your own son, and would do the same for the cradle of the next king. Her highness thinks you could vouch her story.'

'Well, in faith!' Margaret Beaufort said. 'What state of affairs are we coming to when the Queen herself has to ask me to judge her rocker!' But she got up. To me, she said, 'Master Morane, I would have you hear the rest of what William Caxton writes.'

I bowed. 'As you say, madam. Although, as I recall, what you have read so far was addressed to Dickon himself . . . er, that is to say, Richard the Third . . . it was published in his time . . . when he was . . .'

'I know very well to whom it was addressed,' she replied with some asperity. 'Does that make the sentiment of any less moment? Or perhaps, Master Morane, it might even increase it in your eyes, eh?' Before I could make any reply she had gone, her brown skirts swirling behind her.

'Well, well, well!' Mistress Belknap said. 'It seems that Master Morane had better reconsider his loyalties. Some of the affection that still exists in York for Richard of Gloucester seems to have brushed itself on to you during your recent visit there, or the Lady Margaret would not have reproved you for it.'

'It is possible, madam,' I said, and saw her brown eyes narrow. 'Although I do not think she is yet old enough for her memory to be failing, so that she would consider my visit there two years ago as recent.'

'Oh?' She looked disappointed. 'I had understood you were there within the last two weeks.'

I gave a shrug. 'I might have to go to Yorkshire, madam, it is true. King Henry desires information of his seaports. But Bristol was the more pressing, as conditions . . .'

'Then you do not know why Henry Percy of Northumberland was killed?'

'I have heard accounts of it. Was the earl kin to you, then?'

She laughed, shaking her brown curls at me. 'Not precisely, Master Morane. I was once his woman, that is all. And thus have an interest in his fate, although he cast me aside.'

I looked her up and down appraisingly. 'He was always known for a fool,' I said.

'Perhaps,' she sighed, not taking her eyes off me. 'How was he murdered? And who was responsible?'

'A knight called Sir John Egremont led the rebellion, they say. And when it was put down he fled with but one retainer to Burgundy, leaving three or four of his chief supporters to be hanged in York.'

'Three or four? Do you know who they were?'

'I have heard that the chief ruffian was known as John a Chambre. Once one of Northumberland's own retainers,' I added, the lie coming as a sudden inspiration.

'Ah yes!' she exclaimed, clapping her hands. 'I recall the name at Northumberland's court. He and another man were close friends. Perhaps he was hanged too.'

'Perhaps,' I agreed. 'Their names have been announced.'

'You may have heard it then. He was called Randolf Eu.'

'Randolf who?'

'Eu.'

'Me?' I shook my head. 'Madam, you become confused.'

A small foot appeared under her skirt and stamped petulantly on the wooden floor. 'I do not! It is you, Master Morane, who make sport of me!'

'I might, if I dared.'

There was a long silence while she eyed me. Then she smiled and took my hand. 'Forgive me, Master Morane. It is because you speak as if you have been in York recently . . . or at least,' she added, 'as if you have had much information from there.'

'Aye,' I agreed. 'I have friends who send me news. Gossip, too, although it is often of little interest as I do not know the folk concerned. For instance . . .' I brushed some dust off my cap '. . . it seemed to have been a matter of amusement because the retainer Sir John Egremont took with him to Flanders had but one eye. But I have no acquaintance with that knight, and so do not know what there is to laugh at.'

She took the bait like a carp in a monastery pond. 'No,' she said with as much nonchalance as she could muster. 'But I would hear more of that joke.' She looked anxiously about the hall. 'They will send for me soon. And this is the first place they will look, knowing I came to call the Countess of Derby.' I glanced at her, and she smiled. At least she had been schooled to use the proper title. 'Come!' she laughed, swinging our hands together. 'There is time to walk out there in the orchard before they find me. I would have every piece of news from York, Master Morane.'

'But I have told you all I know, madam,' I protested, yet making little effort to hold back as she pulled me along.

The apple-orchard was filled with blossom and the steady hum of a million insects hard at work. Each flower had its intruder, those of the crab trees more than one, for their nectar was of a strength to drive the honey-bees mad. They seemed not to be able to stop filling their tiny bellies until their weight brought them down helpless to the grass below, squirming with pain and ecstasy among the bright green blades. Yet there was one tree which attracted less of them. It was of the same height as the apple-bearers, but stood on its own, holding up clusters of purple flowers somewhat as a chestnut does, but with leaves of a different shape.

'That one,' Mistress Belknap said, 'once grew in London, but Henry the Fifth had it dug up and brought here when he built the manor.'

'I have seen no others in London,' I said.

'There may not be. It is from Persia, beyond Araby they say, where it is called a Lillack or some such name . . . taken by the Crusaders from those same Turks of whom the Lady Margaret spoke.'

'For a tree to have lived these three hundred years it must have come from the moon,' I said. 'You brought me here to show me this?'

'And other things, Master Morane,' she smiled, taking my hand and putting it inside her dress. 'I am no Turk whose castle needs to be taken by assault.'

'The draw-bridge is not raised, then?'

'It never was,' she murmured in my ear. 'But first tell me of your journey to York and if you encountered Randolf Eu.' She began to pull me down on to the grass beside her.

'It would take too long to recount,' I told her.

'Then the draw-bridge might have to be pulled up again.'

'That would take even longer. Six men winding pulleys might not be enough.'

A frown came between her eyes. 'Are you a fool, Henry Morane, to make idle chatter at a time like this?'

'The chatter is not idle,' I assured her. 'I wait for the bees in the grass round you to go away. One inside your skirt just now . . .'

She got up quickly. 'Over there,' she said, breathing hard. 'Under the Lillack tree. There are none there.'

'The ants will have driven them away.'

'Ants? You think so?' She eyed me in sudden fright. She was a child of the couch, not of the countryside. Then she saw my face and began to smile. 'You still make sport with me, Henry Morane, do you?'

'The sport has not yet begun,' I grinned at her.

CHAPTER 16

T W O days later the royal barge brought messages on the morning tide for Queen Elizabeth. King Henry had returned from York, and he sent his respects to his wife together with his regrets that, due to the many affairs of state that awaited him, he could not yet find time to visit Sheen Manor. He prayed her indulgence, and that she would bring her court to West Minster, and that the Countess of Derby would accompany her. There was also a letter for Queen Elizabeth in the King's own hand which, when she broke the seal and read, brought a smile to her mouth and a redness to her cheek, as Matilda told me, but after that she had torn the paper into little pieces and thrown them away.

'A pity,' I laughed, 'or you would have read it for yourself.'

'I would have,' she replied defiantly. 'A letter from a husband that can bring a blush to the cheek is one to be shared.'

'Even if that husband is the king of England?'

'Why not, Henry Morane? One husband is much the same as . . . well, perhaps not. But could *you* write a letter that would bring a blush to *my* cheek?'

'Give me pen and paper and pounce box, and . . .' I reached towards her. 'But it is easier to bring the blush another way.'

'There it is!' she said with mock resignation. 'As William Caxton says, there is no romance left in England today.'

'Mother of God!' I said, holding her at arm's length. 'Has the Lady Margaret been reading Caxton to you too?'

She laughed, then put a hand to her mouth. 'Jesu! I had forgot! I have to attend the Queen to carry her reply to the Barge Master!' She kissed me quickly and pulled up her skirts to run.

'Ask her if you can read it,' I called after her.

Robert Savage, short, spare and grey of head, had been Master of the King's Barge for Dickon, and to his brother Edward the Fourth before that. He had sworn his allegiance to the new king after Bosworth, and had been confirmed in his office. There were many others like him, from the judges on the King's Bench to the humblest scavengers of the court, who had made haste to take their oaths to the new authority. They had sworn freely, not being in danger of life and limb, but nevertheless in fear of losing their appointments. And who could blame a man, especially with a family, for hazarding his livelihood? While it was true that some had done so, fleeing to Duchess Margaret in Burgundy, they were mostly those without kin on whom vengeance could be taken. For no one knew with what ferocity the Tudor king would impose his rule.

I found Robert Savage in the Guard-House by the inner moat, rolling dice with the sergeant. They groaned good-humouredly when they saw me, and we soon got to business, assisted by the contents of a barrel from the Royal Barge. He had brought the vessel's sand-glass, which stood over in the corner by his cloak, and I saw that the brown grains still had nearly half an hour to run. Robert Savage was not one to miss the tide back.

A little while later the sentry admitted Matilda. She carried a rolled parchment, ribboned and waxed with the Queen's seal. Robert Savage took it from her and threw it on to his cloak, where several other letters were lying. The superscription on one of them caught my eye. I picked it up and gave it to Matilda.

'It would be better if you took this one back to be properly addressed,' I told her. 'Have the secretary write it better.' I glanced at the sand-glass. 'There is enough time.'

She gave me an uncomprehending look, then, seeing the writing, composed her face quickly, nodded, waved at the others, and departed.

The sergeant laughed without looking up. 'None of the secretaries seem to be able to write properly these days,' he remarked. But Robert Savage was frowning at the other papers on his cloak. I spoke quickly.

'Well,' I said, smiling at him. 'The sergeant can't write at all. But he sets himself up as a judge of others.'

'Aaah!' the man grumbled. 'It's not my trade. Come

94

on, Master Robert, don't dally when I'm winning. It's for you to throw.'

'Aye,' I said, 'and while I'm on my feet I'm for the river to piss. Shall I take those letters to the boat in case you forget them?'

He nodded, intent upon the dice now. 'And have your wife take that other one straight there when it is ready.'

Matilda was waiting for me, the opened letter in her hand. 'Listen to this,' she said, beginning to read.

'Written at Sheen Manor this June day to my dearest knight, Sir William of the pointed beard!!! On a matter of importance which calls for precedence even though my undying affection calls for requitement by your loving caresses . . .'

Matilda looked up. 'She wastes ink,' she observed, then read on:

'The matter is that the fellow called Morane has come here from the King's business in Bristol. He has not been to York as we expected, and thus has not encountered Master Eu. I have interrogated him at length, my dearest lord, for your sake, but it has not been easy for whatever shallow intelligence Morane possesses was quickly overcome by his regard for those charms which I have promised you are for your delight alone, and which I put to good use, although at no time were they in danger to the fellow . . .'

'Indeed?' Matilda commented, eyeing me.

'But Morane has many friends in York, it seems, who have sent him messages about the insurrection. John a Chambre has been hanged, as you must have surely heard, and the other leader, Sir John Egremont, a knight whom I do not know, has fled to Burgundy, taking with him a fellow who fits the description of Randolf Eu. It is clear therefore that Master Eu has betrayed your trust, my dearest. I would have waited to tell you this while lying in your arms at London, but as it will be more than a week before the Queen's court is ready to move to West Minster I pen this now in order to apprise you quickly.'

Matilda folded up the paper and eyed me.

'The letter drips with honey,' I observed.

'It drips with more than that,' she said icily. 'I wait to hear, Master Morane, your description of the charms that were used to entice you.'

'Being of shallow intelligence makes it hard to remember,' I smiled. 'But it seems that at no time were they in danger to me.'

'Aye, so *she* says. But what do *you* say.'

'I say that if that letter reaches Sir William Stanley it will be her death warrant.'

'Her death warrant?' Matilda stared at me. 'How?'

'Because it shows the connection between Stanley and John a Chambre. The risk of such a letter falling into the wrong hands is something that Stanley will ensure does not happen again. He will dispose of Mistress Belknap before she can commit any further indiscretions. As he did with Alice in Dickon's time.'

Matilda shuddered. 'Jesu Mary!' she whispered. 'You think so? Cut her to pieces as I saw him do to Alice?'

'He will certainly kill her. We cannot allow the letter to be sent.'

There was a long silence while she studied me. 'And yet,' she said, 'she will tell Sir William Stanley of the letter when she sees him, for she is of the kind that will expect appreciation of her effort. Thus in any case Sir William will realize she has been indiscreet. And if he does not receive it he will make inquiries of the Barge-Master, and then suspicion will fall on you, Henry Morane. No!' She shook her head firmly. 'I will not have you take the risk. Mistress Margaret Belknap must take her own. The letter must go.'

'I could not countenance submitting her to such a risk . . .'

'You could not countenance it?' Her eyes blazed. 'You would protect the woman? A well-fleshed frump like that? A frump who would seduce you to gain her

96

favour with Sir William Stanley?' She seized my arm. 'Now listen to me, Henry Morane. When Sir William reads this letter his suspicion of you being involved in the disappearance of Randolf Eu will be quietened. He will have no need to concern himself with you, a mere scrivener, any more.' She waved the paper. 'You will be the fish that has slipped from the hook.'

'But Margaret Belknap will remain on it.'

She made a noise that sounded like 'Pah!' 'And what if she does? She is no kept woman like Alice. She is one of the Queen's ladies. Sir William Stanley will not dare any harm to her. And even if the letter were to fall into other hands he could wave it aside as the imaginings of a foolish woman. But to murder her would lead to too many inquiries.'

I gave up. 'Maybe you are right, sweet apple. Perhaps,' I added, keeping my face without expression, 'I concern myself too much for a frump who would have seduced me with her well-fleshed charms.'

'Yes, Henry Morane. I have yet to hear more of that.'

'You have?' I inquired. 'Even before this letter is sealed again and returned to the Barge-Master before he sails?'

She sighed. 'I should have known that there might be some delay in your explanation.'

CHAPTER 17

THE movement of the Queen's court between Sheen and West Minster was by now a well-rehearsed operation. Travel by water is in any case easier than by road for so many hundreds of people; retainers, ladies, musicians, priests and all the different servants. Apart from the noisy, chattering crowds of people there are also the chests, barrels and boxes with the equipment, harnesses, wardrobes and valuables of those to be transported. It is true that to move from one royal residence to another no furniture has to be moved, and so it is less complicated, especially than by road where unwieldy wagons have to be driven at a pace kept down to that of the slowest ox-cart. Such travel is uncomfortable and bears no comparison to that of barges on a smooth river, all keeping to the same swift pace, and without the need to halt for the travellers to relieve themselves. This necessity, when acceded to by the women, brings ribald comment from the oarsmen, but then it is the oarsmen who work the hardest and are therefore entitled to extract whatever they can from their wearisome occupation.

While Margaret Belknap's statement that it would take more than a week before the court would be ready to move was an exaggeration, it was a surprise to all that, the very next afternoon, there was a great fanfare of trumpets out on the river and a long line of barges came into view. The vessel at their head, larger and more sumptuously covered than even the Queen's barge, carried a banner outstretched on a wire frame. Its device was that of a Hart's Head, and I knew it for Sir William Stanley's. The Lord Chamberlain himself had come from West Minster.

He jumped ashore, ignoring the salutes of the guards, and made straight for the great hall, I and many others following as closely as we dared. But the hall was empty, save for the Lady Margaret in her favourite seat. The Queen, I knew, was occupied elsewhere, being bathed by her women.

The clack of his boots on the tiles brought a frown to Margaret Beaufort's face, but when she saw who it was her expression changed to one of surprise. She folded the book over her thumb and looked up at him.

'How now, Sir William?' she said. 'What brings you here so suddenly? There is nothing amiss at West Minster, I trust?'

'Suddenly, madam?' Sir William Stanley bent to kiss her hand. 'Should I have sent a herald to announce myself?' He gave a thin smile. 'And cool my heels on my barge while I waited?'

'Ah!' Lady Margaret smiled back. 'Then perhaps the suddenness could not be avoided. But all is well with the King, I trust?'

'All is well with your son, madam. I come here at his request.'

'At his request?'

'Well, with his consent, shall we say? To give assistance to the Queen for her journey to West Minster.' He waved a hand at the windows. 'And to bring some baskets of strawberries from my gardens there for her, and for yourself, madam.' He bowed again.

'The strawberries will be welcome, Sir William,' she smiled. 'For those of West Minster are even better than those of London. But as to assistance I do not understand. She has managed the business well enough by herself on previous occasions.'

'There is no question of it,' Sir William Stanley agreed, his beard pointing at her again. 'But it has been after each of those occasions that His Grace, your son, has chided himself for his lack of consideration as a husband.'

'Has he indeed?' Margaret Beaufort's grey eyes regarded her brother-in-law. 'He must have chided himself severely then, to have sent no less than his Lord Chamberlain, when a knight or other gentleman would have been acceptable to the Lady Elizabeth, I am sure. Or . . .' she laughed gently '. . . perhaps the sun shines so well today that the Lord Chamberlain himself preferred to take to the river and leave the cares of court behind him for a while? And indeed,' she added, the smile coming back again, 'could anyone blame him for that?'

But Sir William Stanley was not amused. 'He had better not try,' he said in a voice approaching a snarl as he looked around, but I was well effaced. 'Where is the Queen?' he demanded.

The Lady Margaret Beaufort, Countess of Richmond and Derby, lost her smile. She handed the book to one of her ladies and got to her feet. 'I think, Sir William,' she said, 'that you forget this is the Queen's residence. She will no doubt grant you audience when she is ready to do so. Meanwhile I suggest that you consider if the King himself would have been so impolitic as to demand her presence in so peremptory a manner.' With that she left him and walked out of the hall.

It was while they were all taking their supper in the great hall, as we thought, that Matilda and I walked by the river. The sun was low in the sky over the forest of Middlesex, and its rays danced through the leaves, making golden sprites on the water. We did not speak of anything for some time, then Matilda stopped and took my hand.

'Henry Morane,' she said, 'this visit of Sir William Stanley has me afeared. It is not natural that he should . . .' Her hand tightened. There was someone in the apple orchard.

We moved quickly from the path into the bushes. Then Margaret Belknap's voice came from under the fruit trees. 'My lord, Sir William!' she said.

I tried to lead Matilda away, but she would have none of it, making signs that she wanted to see what was going on. I gave a shrug of resignation as we moved closer. Margaret Belknap was in Sir William Stanley's arms.

After a while he disengaged himself and sat down, pulling her to the grass beside him. He picked up a small basket and gave it to her. 'These are for you,' he said.

She looked inside, then clapped her hands together. 'Strawberries!' she exclaimed with delight. 'Just like those you brought for the Queen!' She took one out and bit at it. 'I am indeed in your favour, my lord,' she said, her eyes round and big at him.

'Jesu!' Matilda breathed beside me. 'He means to poison her!' She made a move as if to interrupt, but I held her back.

'Wait,' I whispered. 'How can you be sure of that?' And when Margaret Belknap held out another fruit to Sir William Stanley I heard Matilda's breath ease out slowly.

But Stanley no more than took the fruit in his moustache before spitting it away and kissing her. 'This is much more sweet, my Margaret,' he said.

Matilda turned and looked at me with wide eyes. I shook my head and put my lips against her ear. 'Come away,' I told her. 'There is nothing we can do. If Stanley should learn that we had watched him poison her it would be the end of us both.' I took her firmly by the arm and led her away.

'Oh, God in Heaven!' Matilda cried when we were out of earshot. 'We must go back, Henry Morane! We cannot let him kill her in front of our very eyes!'

'I have told you,' I said sternly, 'there is nothing we can do.'

'There must be! Yes! I will tell her that the Queen requires her attendance immediately. She cannot have eaten too many yet.'

'Then Stanley will know you have seen him feeding them to her.'

'What does that matter now?' She shook herself free and ran off.

There was nothing left for it. If Matilda interfered it would be the end of her. Sir William Stanley would have to be killed first. He would have to be killed at once, in spite of the dagger he must carry. I swore, for I did not carry a weapon at court, and cast around for something to use. A stout branch would do. I found one and ran after Matilda. Sir William Stanley must be dealt with, even if Margaret Belknap gave evidence against me afterwards . . . then a cold rage came over me. She would of course be dead of the poison before that . . . Then, almost before I could stop, Matilda was running back, tears streaming down her face, to throw herself into my arms.

'Henry! Henry,' she sobbed. 'He was taking his pleasure of her!'

'Ah!' I said, somewhat relieved. 'Then he did not see you?'

101

'No, no!' she cried. 'But he had poisoned her first!'

'I know,' I said, throwing away the branch and holding her tight. ' I know, my poppet. We saw him . . . but
. . .'

'But you do not understand!' Her tear-swept face turned up towards me. 'Oh Jesu Mary, Henry Morane! He was still feeding her with those poisoned fruit while he took her!'

CHAPTER 18

MATILDA took my arm to steady herself against the motion of the barge. I laughed and told her she would be no sailor on the Ocean.

'Maybe so,' she smiled, 'but it brings to mind our nephew, Matthew Coombe. Will you see this fellow Columbus?'

'As promised,' I assured her, 'and persuade him from seducing the lad from his master-piece.'

'If you mean to use force, Henry Morane, be careful.'

The oarsman beside us looked up quickly and spat into the water. I said, 'No, no. I will see to it that the Italian's project is brought before the King. Then, when it is turned down, the fellow will have to go elsewhere, perhaps to France, to peddle his wares, and Matthew will be left alone.'

'But if the King shows sympathy for it?'

'He won't,' I laughed, 'if it means parting with any money.' The oarsman looked up again and grinned. 'But even if it does,' I added, 'it will mean Bartholomew travelling to Lisbon to fetch his brother.'

'He could send messages instead.'

'He could,' I agreed, contemplating the fishermen's nets spread out over the grass by the village of Putney. 'But . . .' I turned back to her '. . . who better to carry those messages than I? And King Henry would want to know more of this Christopher Columbus, and who better to report on him than I? And it would take me as long to find him as it would for Matthew Coombe to complete his master-piece.'

She smiled at that. 'Aye, Henry Morane, I think it would.' The deep blue eyes were mocking. 'Even though you might be disappointed to find that all Portuguese women have pimples, which I have on good authority.'

'Is that so?' the oarsman inquired. 'Well, English morts are good enough for me.' He watched his spittle float away behind us.

I was about to reply when there was a whistle from

one of the boats ahead. The Queen's barge had moved aside, signalling the others to overtake. When we drew level we were ordered to stop rowing, and soon we were tied to the royal vessel.

Queen Elizabeth waved at us. 'Mistress Morane,' she called, 'we have all taken our fill of strawberries and . . .' her face became sad '. . . would not have a surfeit as poor Mistress Belknap did. Here are some for you and your husband, should you wish.'

Matilda's hand tightened on my arm as she forced a smile. 'You cannot refuse,' I murmured to her as she curtseyed her thanks.

The basket was passed across. Queen Elizabeth smiled at me. 'They were uncle Dickon's favourite fruit, Master Morane.'

'I know it, madam' I said gravely. 'And for that reason I do not care for them so much today.' It was a remark that could be taken in two ways, and I saw the Lady Margaret Beaufort watching me. Then Sir William Stanley's boat came swirling round us.

The pointed beard moved up and down as he inspected me. The look in his eyes showed regret that the basket being passed to us was not poisoned. He addressed the Royal Barge. 'Your Highnesses,' he said, 'this is no time to dally if we are to reach West Minster before the tide changes against us.' He did not wait for a reply, but waved at his crew to begin their strokes again, and his barge pulled away.

'I could not eat these,' Matilda said when our boat was alone again. 'Even though I know they cannot be poisoned.'

'Poisoned?' the oarsman said. 'How can they be if Queen Elizabeth herself has been eating them.' He almost paused in his stroke. 'You think someone means to poison her? By God's Very Balls! She is Dickon's own niece! Nobody had better harm her!' This time he did lose his stroke and there was a yell from the bargemaster at the stern. He came striding forward as the boat lost way.

It took a few moments to pacify them. No one was trying to poison the Queen, I assured them. But it had first been thought that the fruit had been tainted because

Mistress Belknap had screamed before she died that it had been the strawberries. But then, I explained to them, Sir William Stanley had pointed out that she had eaten the contents of one whole basket, which, coupled with the great quantity of wine she had been drinking, was enough to bring anyone to a fatal seizure.

'Aye,' Matilda whispered to me later, 'maybe I had done better to listen to you, Henry Morane, and not allowed the letter to be sent, for I had not expected her to be killed before my very eyes.'

The tide was turning as we reached West Minster, and vessels were beginning to find their way up-river more easily. Among them were fat barges bringing red bricks from Calais for Archbishop John Morton's new palace at Lambeth by the marshes on the other side of the stream.

'I must confess to some interest in meeting this Bartholomew Columbus,' I said to Matilda, 'because there seems to be some foundation in his brother's project. However far it is to the Indies across the great ocean, there is at least no other way by sea.'

'You think not?' she inquired.

'For sixty years the Portuguese have been sailing farther and farther along the coast of Africa, and there is no way round it. They will soon find that the continent ends in the great southern ice.'

'You think so?' Matilda inquired, more demurely this time, so that I turned to look at her. 'But was it not said before Prince Henry the Navigator sent his mariners to explore the coast of Africa that beyond the equator line the sea boiled into a green foam and no man or ship could survive in it?' At my expression she began to laugh. 'Is not a woman to know of such matters, then, Henry Morane?' She paused, then added, 'Especially as the Lady Margaret Beaufort would discuss them with anyone who would listen.'

'The Lady Margaret? Her interest is confined to the writings of William Caxton.'

'Faith, no! She is interested in every science, from the stone of the Philosopher which turns iron into gold to the venom that snakes keep under their tongues and the dewdrop which the oyster opens to receive before

105

making the pearl. Everything is of interest to Margaret Beaufort . . . especially now that it has been proved that what you say about Africa is wrong.'

'Wrong? How?'

'Why, that it has no ending before the southern ice.' She smiled with delight. 'Which is something you do not know, Henry Morane.'

'I do know,' I growled. 'It is swallowed up in the great ice.'

'Ha, ha!' She laughed and pointed a finger at me. 'But while you were away in York news came from Lisbon that a navigator, another one called Bartholomew, Bartholomew Diaz, had found that Africa ends in a cape pointing at the southern ocean. His ships sailed right round it and found a warm current flowing from the north. The current can only be from the Indies, he swears, and so the way to them lies open.'

'There have been many headlands found in Africa by the Portuguese. Why should this one be different?'

'Because it is the very last one,' Matilda insisted. 'Beyond it Diaz reports that there is nothing but open sea, and the coast turns to meet the warm current. He has called it the Cape of Storms, but King John of Portugal will have it that, as the Indies lie beyond, it will be called the Cape of Good Hope.'

I shrugged. 'And you believe these rumours from Lisbon?'

'Everyone does so. Especially as they have been vouched for by Sir Edward Brampton.'

I knew of Sir Edward Brampton. He commanded great respect. An English merchant, resident in Lisbon since Dickon's time, the King's agent, and the only Jew ever to be knighted for his services. I shook my head in wonder.

Matilda laughed and snapped her fingers at me. 'So much for *your* Bartholomew, Henry Morane. The Portuguese have found the way instead!'

CHAPTER 19

HAVING left the affairs of the north in the firm hands of Thomas Howard of Surrey, and confident that his military experience would keep the Scots in check, King Henry was able to turn his attention to more pressing matters overseas.

The immediate question was the security of Brittany, a country whose relationship to France could be compared with that of Scotland to England. Now that its duke had died King Charles the Eighth was claiming that the duchy reverted to him, and, to lend force to his argument, was threatening to invade that country and marry the duke's heir, the fourteen-year-old Anne. The latter threat probably frightened the young girl more, as the French king was no subject for a court painter, being stunted in body, with an over-large head, and halting in speech through lips the size of a purse. Since I had spoken of it that night to Thomas Howard in the Tower a treaty had been made with Anne of Brittany. Six thousand English soldiers were to be sent to help her, she in turn handing over two towns as surety. She also promised not to make treaties with, or marry anyone without the consent of Henry Tudor and, as was to be expected in any agreement with that monarch, the entire cost of the English expedition was to be borne by Brittany.

Another treaty had been made with Maximilian, Archduke of Austria, heir to the Holy Roman Empire, and Regent of Burgundy. Regent, that is, of those parts of the Netherlands which did not belong in dowry to the Duchess Margaret, sister of Richard the Third. While the new agreement bound Maximilian and Henry Tudor to make war on France together, the latter was heard to remark to his uncle Jasper that even if it did no more than prevent Maximilian from making a private bargain with France the treaty would have served its purpose.

Approaches had also been made to Spain, and Ferdinand of Aragon had been receptive. A treaty with the

107

English king could be used to bargain with Charles of France for the return of his two provinces north of the Pyrenees, the price for their return being the repudiation of that treaty. Not for nothing was Ferdinand known as The Fox. Yet Henry Tudor, himself no new pupil in the school of deception, had suggested to Ferdinand that, while his army was preoccupied in turning the Arabs out of Granada, the French king's eyes might be moving towards Italy, and to Naples in particular. The seizure of Naples would be a direct affront to Ferdinand, for its king also came from Aragon.

However, the basis of any treaty with Ferdinand and Isabella was a marriage between their daughter, Catherine of Aragon, and Prince Arthur, heir to the English throne. To ensure it King Henry required that Catherine be sent to England forthwith for her education, and to be accompanied by a dowry of no less than 200,000 crowns at a value of four shillings and two pence each. Ferdinand countered with the demand that the jewellery and plate which she took with her should be counted as part of that amount, but he withdrew that demand when King Henry agreed to make over to Catherine one third of the entire revenues of Wales, Cornwall and the county of Chester, and to postponing her departure for England until she reached the age of twelve.

It might appear that Ferdinand got the better of the bargain, but it served King Henry's purpose in that it demonstrated to the rest of Europe that England, small as she was, could stand up to the might of Spain, and was a power to be reckoned with. And when Ferdinand's remark that it would be eight years before Catherine reached the age of twelve and anything could happen in the meantime was reported to King Henry he merely smiled. The same thought had occurred to him too.

Meanwhile relations with France were kept very correct, for to send soldiers to Brittany was not to declare war, it was merely to reinforce an ally, and there was still that fourteen-year-old treaty of Picquigny between King Edward of York and Louis the Spider by which the French king sent an annual tribute. King Henry Tudor was not one to risk a treaty being repudiated where money was concerned.

It was the treaty with Maximilian which was first called upon to be honoured. The cities of Bruges and Ghent had revolted against him while he was away in the east fighting the Hungarians. Four thousand men sallied out from those cities and laid siege to Dixmude, which sent urgent messages for help from the English in nearby Calais. Lord Daubeney, its captain, learning that the besiegers were in turn seeking help from France, inquired of King Henry what he should do. The reply came back at once. Lord Daubeney was to raise what men he could in Calais and its neighbouring bastion of Guisnes, commanded by Sir James Tyrrel. Another force of a thousand archers under Lord Morley was being despatched across the Channel forthwith. Within a week of Dixmude's appeal for help there were two thousand archers, a thousand pikemen and sixteen guns moving along the coast, their left flank watched by half a dozen ships.

The relief of Dixmude, hard fought along the causeway into the town, was achieved before the arrival of the French. The revolt against Maximilian was over. And most important of all, the speed and decisiveness of King Henry's response was not lost on the courts of Europe.

Of some significance at Dixmude was the death of Lord Morley by a shot from a hand-held gun, the first English noble to have been slain in such a manner that I could recall. Sir James Tyrrel, too, had been hit by a crossbow bolt, but recovered. He was that Tyrrel who, much against his will, had been sent by Dickon to guard Calais against the French during the Bosworth campaign, and who was later to be forced to confess, after a long and elaborate suffering, to murdering the Princes in the Tower at Dickon's instigation.

Then, six weeks after the relief of Dixmude, Maximilian signed a treaty with the French agreeing to take no further interest in Brittany in return for Charles ceasing to interfere in the affairs of Burgundy. The independence of Brittany seemed lost. Yet Charles was reluctant to engage in open war with England, for the Pope was now pressing him not to concern himself with Brittany when the invasion of Italy would be more profitable. But whether it would be more profitable to Charles the Eighth or to the Holy Father was open to question, for while the French had their eyes on the wealthy northern cities, the Holy Father intended to use their army to seize Naples for him. This report stirred Ferdinand of Aragon into cementing his alliance with his kinsman in Naples, and to send a thousand Spanish soldiers to Brittany. Henry Tudor for his part made a treaty with the powerful city of Florence against the duchy of Milan, thus forcing its duke to appeal to France for protection, and so delaying any attack upon Naples. It was a monstrous game of chess, played by five sovereigns under the surface of a murky pool, stirring up the mud with their bishops, their knights and their castles, with only the duchies as pawns.

CHAPTER 20

F R O M West Minster it is no great distance to the village of Charing, where the stone cross to Queen Eleanor stands squat and solitary on the grass, a target for stones and other missiles from the village urchins, and a meeting place much favoured by dogs. It is there that the Strand begins, a strand that belies its name for the space between it and the river is taken up by the palaces of the rich — bishops of Norwich, of Lincoln and of Carlisle, and the Savoy, once the London home of John of Gaunt, but now a burned and blackened ruin, the nesting place of thieves, cut-throats and other ruffians. But while that noble duke and his Savoy Palace have long been gone, the line of bishops survives without interruption to their revenues.

On the side opposite those palaces the ground slopes gently upwards through orchards and the Convent Gardens to the fields of Saint Giles and the manor of Bloomsbury. From these open lands two streams run down to the river, crossing the Strand some quarter mile from each other, and each boasting a narrow stone bridge on that roadway. It was at the first, the Ivy Bridge, that I encountered the battle.

It had not rained for some time, and the dust at first obscured what was going on. Then I saw that at least a hundred youths, most of them apprentices to judge by their cropped heads, were fighting in and around the tunnel made by the stream under the bridge. They did not have weapons, though, using arms and feet, the latter being in greater use to deliver savage kicks at their opponents with loud oaths, and even greater cries when the boots found their mark. At that I realized that it was no riot, merely the young disporting themselves at the game of foot-ball. It is a game known well enough to country folk, where an inflated pig's bladder, encased in leather for its own protection, is propelled towards its target by the foot, the inhabitants of one village challenging the next, the targets being the church doorways

111

of each. In this case, however, the targets were the Charing Cross at one end of the Strand and the vestry of Saint Clements' church at the other, a distance of more than half a mile. The first was defended by the lads of that village, who had withstood a determined attack by the London apprentices, and were now driving them back. The bladder itself was somewhere in the mud of the stream under the Ivy Bridge and, as it was not permitted to withdraw it by hand, rival players from each end were trying to butt it out with their heads. As I watched one of them was dragged out unconscious and flung aside so that another, perhaps with a harder head, could resume the contest. When the unfortunate bladder finally appeared the air from it was gone, and there was an interval while enough peas and beans were collected from the nearby fields to stuff it into its former shape.

This game of foot-ball is forbidden in the City of London, and indeed in all cities, not for the wounds received by the participants, but due to the diminishing skill shown by young men today at archery for lack of practice at the butts. Likewise, King James of Scotland had banned a game using curved sticks to smite a small wooden sphere. When I had been scrivener to King Edward of York I had seen a copy made of the Scots' parchment roll forbidding that game, but the transcriber had been unable to decide whether the practice was called 'gowf' or 'goff'. I smiled at the recollection. Whatever the Scots did was likely to be incomprehensible in London.

I made my way past the contestants when one of them detached himself and called out, 'Uncle Henry!' It was Matthew Coombe, cap and face all dusty, and with blood on his shirt. 'It is good to see you. And to know that you are safely back from York.'

'Do not discuss that,' I said, taking him aside. 'It is the King's wish. He has put it about that I was in Bristol.'

Matthew Coombe's eyes opened wide. 'Oh!' he said, impressed. 'The King's business, eh? Then we must talk of other matters. How is the black-bearded archer captain, or is that . . .?'

'His health is not a matter of secrecy,' I laughed. 'His duty is the protection of the Royal Body, but when those duties are relaxed he finds bodies of a more attractive nature to attend upon. I came to see your Italian friend. Does he still lodge with Master James Herring?'

'Yes, uncle. I will take you to him.'

'No need for you to stop your game. I know the place.'

Matthew Coombe waved towards the crowd of youths. 'They do not need my help now,' he smiled. 'There are still forty and more of us, enough to drive the Londoners back to their walls.'

I took his arm. 'Come on, then, and let us see if he can impress me enough to gain him audience with the king.'

James Herring, short, fat and whiskered in white, had already put up the shutters of his shop. He was standing in the sunshine examining a kind of wheel which another man was holding aloft. He looked round as I approached, smiled, and clapped me on the shoulder. But his expression lost its amiability when he saw Matthew Coombe.

'You idle boy!' he snapped. 'With your master-piece not yet begun you waste your time in useless sport.'

'Come now, Master Herring,' I laughed. 'Was every moment of your own apprenticeship spent working? Or have you forgotten that you were once young enough to make sport?'

'I might have done,' he grumbled. 'But not at this children's game of foot-ball. We engaged in more manly contests.'

'Aye,' I agreed. 'Rowing.' Seeing his puzzlement, I added, 'Across the river after curfew to South Wark to swive the pretty little Winchester Geese that flutter there all night. Why, I recall . . .'

He cleared his throat quickly and looked behind him. 'Enough, Henry Morane. My wife sits behind those shutters. She is in no mood . . .' he rubbed a red mark on his nose '. . . my tongs,' he explained. 'She threw them at me.'

'Goldsmith's tongs?' I queried. 'They are not heavy enough to make such a mark.'

'They were red hot at the time,' he grumbled, and made us all laugh. 'Come,' he said after a moment. 'The back of the shop. There is a barrel of ale there, and . . .

bring that idle nephew of yours . . .' at which that young
man grinned '. . . and you, Master Columbus,' James
Herring went on, turning to him, 'there is wine from
Bordeaux if that Genoese throat of yours cannot carry
good English ale.'

The man he had called Columbus brought his attention away from the wheel and turned towards us. As he
stood upright he was taller than I had first supposed,
and I saw that his cap covered reddish hair, his beard being the same colour. The eyes that met mine were pale
green and very steady. 'The English ale,' he said after a
moment, 'is very good. It will give me pleasure.' He spoke
slowly, picking his words as if he did not have many of
them. And indeed that was true for he had not been in
the country long.

'See that, uncle Henry,' Matthew Coombe said, pointing at the wheel Columbus held. 'It is an astrolabe. Used
for navigation.'

'Be quiet, boy!' James Herring said. 'Navigation diverts
you too much. It is a business for mariners, not silver-
smiths. If it is of no interest to me it should be of less to
you.'

'I would see it,' I said to Bartholomew Columbus,
holding out my hand. I spoke in Latin, and his expression
cleared instantly.

'Good!' James Herring said in the same language. 'It is
easier to converse with him this way. Although he speaks
Spanish and Portuguese as well. Here,' he went on, taking
the astrolabe. 'You hold it up towards the sun thus . . .
then the shadow from this arm at the side falls across an
angle mark . . . there! And now I read off the mark so
given . . .'

'It seems no more than an ordinary sun-dial held in
the hand,' I said, with a quick wink at Columbus.

'An ordinary sun-dial? An ordinary sun-dial!' James
Herring was appalled. '*This*,' he spluttered. '*This* is an
instrument that informs the mariner of his exact position on the ocean, when he is so far from land that it
cannot be seen . . . when he is far from any port . . .
why,' he went on, 'without it he would sail to the edge
of the earth and over it.' James Herring drew himself up
straight. 'It is a machine of great precision, Henry Morane,

114

learnt from the Arabs, and this one . . .' he held it high
'. . . this one has been constructed by Master Columbus
in my house with his own hands! Is that not so?' he concluded, turning to the mariner. When he saw the latter's
face he swung back to me, then Matthew Coombe. But
that young man had had time to compose his features.

CHAPTER 21

T H E maps drawn by Bartholomew Columbus were nearly complete, and though I knew little of the craft, their aspect was impressive, not only with their outlines of the sea-coasts and tides, but also with the fearsome monsters which adorned the empty parts of the Ocean. There were whales spouting great columns of water, ferocious serpents which he assured me could bite off the end of a ship, and vast, spider-like creatures whose tentacles could entwine a sailor to his doom. Yet they were more than mere adornments to the maps, and no sailor will deny their existence, for they serve to increase the respect for his bravery and the difficulties he has to encounter beyond those of wind and tide.

Then news came from Spain that the armies of Ferdinand and Isabella had taken the Arab sea-fortress of Malaga, and were preparing to move northwards on Granada, the Arab capital, and their last stronghold in Spain. Granada was not expected to hold out for long, and once the war was over Bartholomew's brother Christopher would be able to obtain the closer attention of Queen Isabella, who had already shown interest in his project. Thus Bartholomew wished to postpone his interview with King Henry as it might conflict with his brother's ambitions and, he added wryly, the resources of Spain were much greater than those of England for such a venture.

Yet the siege of Granada took many months to prepare, and when it became evident that the Arabs would be able to hold out for at least a year Bartholomew Columbus grew restive. He would approach King Henry forthwith. But by then the audience had to be postponed. Queen Elizabeth was with her second child, and the King had no ears for anything but news of her progress.

The child was a girl, and at first, so Matilda told me, the Queen was much concerned that her husband would be disappointed. But Matilda also overheard the maternal tones of Lady Margaret Beaufort in conversation with her son, so that we were not surprised to hear that King Henry had comforted his wife by pointing out that they already had one son, and without doubt the next child would be another. Neither was it surprising that the infant was given the name of Margaret, and when she was baptized with as much ceremony as if she had been a prince Queen Elizabeth's cup of happiness was full. It was plain to all that the affection of the King and Queen for each other was growing with the years, and that the union of the houses of Tudor and York was complete. It seemed as if there would never be another cloud in the sky over the realm of King Henry the Seventh.

Even when a great outbreak of the sickness known as the Measles swept London he was not dismayed. The courts would have to move to Sheen, that was all. The fact that the manor in its forest by the river could not provide for over a thousand people descending upon it at once was not the King's concern. A matter of greater moment to him was that a musician had disappeared.

Among the many presents sent to the new princess was a lute, gilded and set with precious stones, from the Archduke Maximilian of Burgundy. That duke, so addicted to music that he had three grand horse-drawn carts of instruments playing to him on his travels — one of them even holding an organ — had sent the lute on one of his own ships from Flanders. The instrument, in a specially made wooden box, had been safely delivered and was now on Three Cranes wharf, but the player who had brought it had not been seen since. It was a matter of some importance in view of the uncertain disposition of Archduke Maximilian, whose displeasure at that particular time was better avoided.

King Henry himself had instructed me to find the lute-player, and inquiries soon showed that he had definitely arrived in London. More eyes than usual had followed the movements of the ship after it had passed through the Great Bridge. This was due to the commotion its master had made over the fee of six pence for raising the draw-bridge. He had refused to pay on the ground that his was no ordinary trading vessel, but belonged to the Duke of Burgundy himself. The Bridge

Warden, as stubborn as all city officials are, had never-theless refused to let him through. Whether the vessel belonged to the Duke of Burgundy, the Holy Roman Emperor or Saint Peter himself the bridge would not be raised until the fee had been paid. The City of London owed no allegiance to dukes, foreign kings or any saint in the Calendar, and would resist any attempt upon its sovereignty. In the end an Alderman had to be sum-moned, and it was finally agreed to let the ship pass through as it carried a gift for the new princess. Then, as it was passing through, the Alderman shouted down that notwithstanding this concession the fee would have to be paid on the way back. At this the shipmaster raised his fist and roared back a stream of Flemish oaths that would have undoubtedly sounded magnificent had they not been drowned by the cheers of the crowd.

The fee was in fact paid very soon afterwards, for the shipmaster, learning of the measles sickness, wasted no time in argument. The box was manhandled on to the wharf by his own crew, along with the reluctant musician and, as the tide was already turning, the vessel put about and made for the Bridge. The crowd, seeing what was happening, hastily re-assembled, this time armed with sticks and other missiles, as well as buckets of ordure and not a few piss-pots, so that any oaths the mariner shouted this time were muffled by the coat over his head as he steered through the gap. And then, when the show was over, it was noticed that the lute-player had disappeared.

Inquiries at the nearby churches brought blank stares from the priests, those that were not bemused by wine, that is. And when I swore that the man was not sought as a felon but that King Henry would even pay a reward for him the stares changed to disbelief and I was waved contemptuously away. In the ale-houses and taverns my suggestion that King Henry would actually pay out money for a lute-player brought only ribaldry, and had I not been known to the tavern-keepers I would likely have suffered more than ribaldry before I left.

Neither was any information forthcoming from Andro-meda's House. That lady, as formidable as her name, dis-claimed all knowledge of the fellow. 'A reward from the

118

King, you say?' she laughed. 'A likely story, Henry Morane. But . . .' her smile grew more fixed ' . . . I would take a reward from you. Come . . .' she took my hand ' . . . over there on the paliasse. For the sake of the old days of Dickon. It has been a long time since we saw you here.' I had some difficulty in assuring her that my business was pressing and must take my leave. It had indeed been a long time, and the rust on her teeth measured it. Besides, several of her geese wore peculiar maps of red spots on their cheeks which no amount of chalk could conceal.

Along a narrow lane near London Bridge, where the balconies of the houses leaned across so close that their palings seemed to nudge each other, and where the gathering darkness brought cut-throats scuttling like crabs among the rocks after the tide has gone out, I found the entrance I sought.

A wax candle gleamed through the holes in a moth-eaten arras. I pushed it aside and stepped in. A hand immediately came round my neck and I felt the sharp edge of steel against my throat. I stood very still and said my name as well as I could. The blade moved away and its owner came out from behind me.

'A thousand pardons, Morane effendi,' he said, bowing low. 'A thousand pardons. Had I known it was you . . .' A smile penetrated through the nest of hair under his huge Saracen nose.

'It is nothing, Mehmet, my friend,' I replied, waving at the rolls of silks and cottons that lay around us. 'It could well have been a thief. And why are you not shuttered and bolted for the night?'

'Alas!' He gave a mighty shrug. 'I cannot make the door fast as my dissolute nephew has once again failed to return before darkness. I therefore have to watch with great diligence in case a villain enters.' He put the knife back into his belt. 'But it is my nephew you came to see?'

When I agreed he rubbed his hands together. 'Alas, Morane effendi, only Allah knows when he will return. Meanwhile I would offer you the solace of wine or ale, but my Faith forbids me to keep such a concoction in the house.'

'A pity.' I gave him an innocent smile. 'Because the last time I was here there was a certain leather bottle over in that corner which contained a powerful distillation of grapes, and which was neither wine nor ale. In fact . . .' I pointed ' . . . there is such a bottle there now, but no doubt it contains water for the horses you stable at the back.'

'Water, effendi? Ah yes, my horses have need of water. But that bottle does not contain water for horses. It is the property of my nephew, and what it contains I do not know . . .'

'To have an uncle who tells such lies,' a voice said from the doorway, 'causes me great sorrow. When his very beard reeks of the distillation.'

It was Ali, his brown face a-smile, the golden tooth gleaming in the candle light. 'Master Morane!' he said, throwing his arms round me. 'I have prayed to Al . . . to the great God on High that you were well and that my crime has been forgiven by the King.'

'Crime?' I laughed. 'Oh yes, it has been forgiven.'

'Crime? Crime?' Mehmet wanted to know. 'What is this? Is my house to be sullied by a crime committed by this spawn of my incontinent sister?' He aimed a blow at Ali, which the latter dodged. But I could understand his anxiety. For a foreigner, especially a Saracen, to live in London without molestation from its citizens he must be scrupulous in being seen to keep within its laws.

'Let your mind return to its former tranquillity, Mehmet, my friend. What your nephew refers to as a crime took place more than three years ago, was forgiven at the time, and has long been forgotten. He did no more than arrange for the return to their homeland of the Germans who survived the battle at Stoke Field.'

'Germans?' Mehmet's anxious eyes gazed at us in turn.

'Aye. They were mercenaries brought here by those who supported Lambert Simnel, some two thousand of them. While King Henry would have hanged the leader had he not been killed in the battle, he pardoned the rest provided they left the country forthwith. But they had no means of doing so. They did not know their way, neither did they speak the language. Yet they had been well paid by the Duchess Margaret of Burgundy, and your nephew arranged their shipment at a price which left them little to show for their adventure.' That was not strictly true, for Ali had hired the ships some time before the men were pardoned.

But Mehmet knew his nephew only too well. 'So you made a profit from the King's enemies?' he accused, his eyes protruding like ripe plums. Then he groaned and threw his hands in the air. 'You could have been hanged for treason, and I should have been eternally disgraced.'

'You would not have been disgraced, uncle,' Ali grinned. 'For our relationship is not known.'

'Ah.' Mehmet sucked in his beard. 'And the profit you made? Where is it?'

'It was little enough,' Ali said placatingly. 'The demands of the ship-masters were excessive, for they were reluctant to give aid to the King's enemies.' I could not help smiling at that, for the ship-masters had been Yorkists to a man.

'You lie!' Mehmet yelled. 'You fearful little camel! You lie as readily as the creature that bore you, and who dared to call herself my sister!' He stuck out his hand. 'Give me half,' he demanded.

'It was no more than a pittance,' Ali protested. 'And it was spent in furthering your interests in the docks at Bruges, uncle.'

'Interests? What interests have I in the Flemish whore houses where you squandered it?' This time Ali failed to dodge the blow, and went spinning across the room to bounce up against the leather bottle.

'Look at what he has done!' Mehmet wailed. 'He has split the bottle! My precious liquid, what shall we do?'

'Drink it up as fast as we can,' I suggested, slapping him on the back. 'Then you will be able to forgive your nephew, who has your interests at heart at all times.'

'Now,' I went on, when peace had been restored. 'I have a commission for you, and the reward will be split between both.' They stopped glaring at each other and turned to me. 'A musician has come from Burgundy with a gift for the new princess, and . . .'

'A lute-player?' Ali asked. 'Yes. I saw him when his ship was at the Bridge.'

121

'You did, eh? Then you know where he is now?'

'Assuredly, Forane effendi. He had much money in his purse, and wanted to go home.' He drew himself up with satisfaction. 'And, accordingly, I arranged his passage this morning on a ship to Calais. He will be found there if you wish to question him.'

'And the money from his purse, nephew?' Mehmet said, smiling fiercely. He held out his hand, palm upwards.

CHAPTER 22

MEHMET'S nag liked the cold no better than I. She would have moved faster had she dared, but she was a city horse and not used to the icy unevenness of country roads. Neither did she like the biting wind that, unobstructed by buildings, howled up her tail. I could have taken a boat to Sheen, but they said the edges of the river were frozen by Brent Ford, and there is no man more ready to raise his price than a London boatman. Besides, the King would never have recompensed the extra price, and Mehmet had lent me his nag for a pittance. And in that inclement winter weather there are not likely to be footpads lurking in the bushes.

Down the short slope into Wandsworth, and crossing the narrow sparkle of the Wandle stream, I was comforting myself with the thought that even if I hadn't found the lute-player I knew where he was, when my head began to swim about me and I had difficulty in keeping in the saddle. A violent shiver seized my body, to be followed by an exhilarating heat. I prodded the nag, as it was only half a dozen miles to Sheen, where comfort from the fever would await me. A second prod took her mind off her business and she stumbled to her knees, projecting me into an icy pool. It was no great fall, but I rose unsteadily, and then discovered that I had been wrong about footpads.

They must have seen my condition as I rode through Wandsworth, and followed me. A blow on the back sent me stumbling, and I saw one of them making for the horse. I tried to reach my dagger, but my mind was not clear, and I was clubbed again, then felt myself being dragged into the bushes. Dimly, I realised that they were experts in their business, and they would leave no mark on me, for a frozen body excites less comment than one damaged by wounds. Then my senses left me.

There they were, three thousand red-coated horsemen, spears gleaming in the sunshine, each wearing the badge of the Hart's Head. I told Dickon how Sir William Stanley had secretly pledged himself to Henry Tudor the night before, but he had laughed. 'Aye, Morane,' he had said, 'but whatever his pledge, he will see which way the battle goes, and as it will go to us, he will come in at our side.' Then the cry went up that John of Norfolk had been killed and his son, Thomas Howard of Surrey, a prisoner. And Northumberland had not come.

They had pleaded with Dickon to leave the field and raise fresh forces for another day. The Duke of Suffolk, for instance, still awaited his call. But Dickon would have none of it. He was King of England, and as King of England he would live or die that day. A sudden charge across the flank at the Tudor bodyguard would settle the issue. It might have done, at that, had not Sir William Stanley joined in. I saw Sir Richard Ratcliffe die quickly, John Kendall writhing on the grass, clutching at the spear under his breastplate, and then Dickon overwhelmed by those same red-coated horsemen, stabbed and smashed to pieces inside his armour. I woke up suddenly and cried out loud.

'Aha! So you think to live, eh?'

I tried to rise, but could see nothing but river-reeds, shiny with damp, that made a roof above me. I put out a hand and felt sheepskins which had been cast over me, their stench announcing that they had not long been vacated by their owners. Then a bucket of water was dashed into my face, so that I gasped and fell back wheezing.

'Jesu Saint! What a horrid countenance,' the same voice said. 'As red as the Bollocks of God, and bleeding like a wounded rat. Yet you breathe, my friend, and so you may yet live until the redness goes and the fever mounts.'

'Fever?' I muttered. 'I have no fever . . .' My voice changed into a snarling cough as I lifted my head a little. I was in a stone hut, reed-roofed, with a brazier showing a dull gleam in one corner. Its occupant was a tall, thin greybeard, with patches of brown and pink where his hair had once been, and one ear hewn right off.

He came over and looked down at me, then began to laugh quietly. 'You think to recover soon, my friend? When the whole of your body is the same as your face,

124

laced with weals and spouting blood? I should pray for you, as once I had the right to do, but perhaps this will be better.' He held up my head and put a bowl of soup against my lips. It was a mouthful of such marvel as a man would never forget. 'You have the London sickness, my friend,' he went on, the grey eyes inspecting me carefully. 'It is of the worst kind, the black, bleeding measles. The black measles . . . bleeding measles . . . black . . .' And then I was asleep.

It was warmer when I woke. The reeds above me were dry, and I could hear the cries of marsh birds. Although the brazier still burned in one corner there was no sign of the grey, mutilated man. I crawled to the low doorway and parted the reeds outside. The frost was gone and there was sunshine. I would have got to my feet, but had not the strength, so that when he returned he made clucking noises of disapproval and dragged me back to where I had lain. 'What day is it?' I asked him.

'Of what importance is that?' he replied. 'The winter has gone and for you, my friend . . . why, you are still alive and likely to stay so now. Does else matter but to be alive?'

'Yes. The matters of food, and wine . . . and maybe women.'

His face cracked into a smile so that I thought the skin would peel away. 'You are nearly well, my friend, if you can talk of such things.' He turned to the brazier. 'There is soup, fresh made from the river ducks, salmon from there also. And, when you require a woman, then there is a slut in Putney who will pleasure you for the price of half a dozen blackbirds ready for roasting. But as to wine . . .' he spread his hands out '. . . it will mean a journey across the river after dark to rob a tavern, and you are not yet well enough to help me with a barrel, for all I can carry with these old bones of mine is a small leathern bottle.' He stopped and pointed a finger at me. 'I take nothing from this side of the river, you understand? The men of Surrey let me live here in peace. It was the Middlesex men who shaved my ear, and so I make them provide for me.'

'Although they do not know it,' I smiled. 'I will not ask who you are,' I went on, 'for that would offend your privacy. But I may ask why you brought me here and cared for me. And why you have not been afraid of the measles sickness, especially the black, bleeding kind?'

He eyed me gravely. 'As to your last question, my friend, I, too, have suffered the bleeding measles and, so the Holy Father assures us, to suffer it once is to have no fear of it again. But as to why I brought you here I would in turn ask you if you were to encounter a man, stark naked in the frost, waving a dagger and shouting vengeance for Dickon, would you not give him aid?'

While I was considering this, he went on, 'As to my name, it is nothing now. No more than the men of Putney call the brain-crazed hermit by the river. Once it may have been Martin, Father Martin. Martin Caillou . . .' he smiled reminiscently '. . . now no more than a pebble on the beach of time.' Then the smile left his face. 'But once I was a chaplain to my lord of Surrey's men, seized at Bosworth by traitors who came from Middlesex and said they came to fight for Dickon . . .' He stopped. 'But enough of that. It must be that my lord of Surrey has died of tedium after all this time in the Tower.'

'He has been pardoned and now holds the North for King Henry Tudor.'

'He does, hey? You mean he has betrayed his allegiance?'

'Allegiance?' I said. 'Dickon is dead and, like mine, it has to be given to the new authority.'

'Yet you did not cease to shout for Dickon in your fever.'

'You said it was for vengeance that I shouted.'

'Yes! It was. You also swore at Stanley and Northumberland. I heard men say that Northumberland is dead. And you would be too, my friend, if Stanley heard what you said of him.'

'He has tried it,' I said, and then told him who I was and much of what had happened since Bosworth. He remained silent for a long time.

'Ah!' he said in the end. 'For a man who possesses nothing, no clothes, no money, except for a dagger . . .' he waved across to a corner where I supposed he had put it '. . . it is a wild tale. But . . .' he put up a hand to stop any protest '. . . I do not disbelieve it for I have seen the scars on your back and chest where you say Sir William Stanley ran you through. And if a man can survive such a dreadful wound then God must surely be preserving him to take His vengeance on the man who made it. I will find you clothes, Master Morane, from Middlesex of course, and in a few days you may be on your way to wherever you will.'

'I would repay you if I could,' I told him. 'But not with money or the like to insult you. But Thomas Howard is at York. He would be pleased to see you again. A letter from me telling of your kindness . . .'

'No, no!' He held up a hand. 'My life is here and I am content.' Then he smiled. 'But,' he said, 'if you insist on repayment, then it would be enough for you to return one day with the news that Sir William Stanley has met his deserts.'

CHAPTER 23

'WHY, Henry Morane, you look as if you have been swiving all the pimply whores in London! Is that where you have been?'

'I have been sick. The measles sickness.'

'All this time?' Matilda's deep blue eyes regarded me.

'All this time. It was the black measles.'

'Faith, then it was as well you did not come to Sheen with it. There would have been much concern, especially for the baby princess.'

'And my absence caused none? Not even to you?'

At that her face broke. She put her arms round me. 'Oh, Henry, Henry Morane!' she sobbed. 'The world was ending when you did not come . . . I . . . I tried to convince myself that Sir William Stanley had not gotten to you at last, privily somewhere, because I was sure he would have bragged of it to me . . . but when the lute-player came, and you did not, my fears grew . . . I did not know what to do or who to ask . . . Christopher Urswick is still at the French court . . . and Joseph Anderson could not offer more comfort than to say that you have always been able to look after yourself, up to now at least . . . for a while I believed him, but you still did not come . . .'

'Shush!' I said, kissing her to stop the flow of words. 'I came as soon as I could, poppet. There was no way of informing you. Caillou the priest would not journey to a place such as this.' I told her of the hermit and the care he had taken of me, then, 'The lute-player, you said?'

'Aye. One came. But not the first one. Another one.'

'Then he was braver than the first,' I smiled, smoothing her hair.

She smiled a little, too. The change of subject had eased her. 'He had no choice,' she said. 'When the first musician returned, Archduke Maximilian flew into a rage, saying that King Henry had been insulted. The man's left hand was cut off, and a second player

128

despatched forthwith. But in any case the measles sickness had gone by then.'

'And Urswick has not returned?' I said. 'I have news for him. Ali has been in Flanders. While he knew nothing of the Sir John Egremont who fled there after the business at York, he heard a tale that the Duchess Margaret has found another claimant for the English throne.'

'Jesu!' Matilda's eyes widened. 'Yet more trouble?'

'Maybe. But not yet. This one is not to be put forward hastily as Lambert Simnel was. He is being carefully trained in English ways by the Duchess Margaret, especially those of the Court with which she is familiar from the days of King Edward of York, before she left to marry the Duke of Burgundy. I know nothing else yet, because Ali took no great interest, having lost touch with me since Stoke Field, and being busy with his uncle's affairs overseas. But now he will ascertain more. And if there is to be trouble again then Urswick must be told.'

'Why not King Henry himself?' Matilda asked.

'Aye,' I agreed. 'Why not? I should have thought of it.'

Joseph Anderson held himself upright by clutching his pikestaff as he leaned back against the wall. His black beard moved slowly as he breathed. I went up to him and rapped his cuirass with my knuckle.

He started. 'What did you do that for?' he grumbled.

'To wake you up.'

'I wasn't asleep. I saw you coming, creeping like a cat, hoping to surprise me.'

'Hah!' I snorted. 'And if his lordship the Archbishop of Canterbury and Chancellor of England had crept up in his soft leather shoes he wouldn't have found you asleep?'

Anderson smiled with satisfaction. 'He's in there,' he said, jerking a thumb at the doorway. 'He found me fully alert.'

'Or Richard Foxe, the King's Secretary, another silent one?'

The smile remained, and so did the thumb. 'In there too.'

'Ah, trust an old soldier to know how to appear awake.'

'Aye, and a King's agent to sneak around the place like that pair of creeping bishops. And where have you been all this time? Who else has been disposed of?' When I told him, he laughed. 'A likely story! Try something better for the King. He sent for you?'

'No. Is he closeted with his creeping bishops?'

'He might be. But Jasper Tudor is in there as well.'

'Then my presence might bring him some relief. He has little regard for those palace creepers either.'

'I cannot think your presence would be a relief to anyone, much less a duke. But I will see.' As he turned, he said, 'You might be telling the truth at that. You are thinner than you should be even after taking a few months of bawdy exercise.'

King Henry was seated at a table with a dice cup in his hand, a board in front of him, and Jasper Tudor on the other side. Beyond them, busy writing at another table, was his French-secretary, one Stephen Frion, a pale, thin fellow with wide-set eyes and flaxen hair, a shadow always at hand in case King Henry decided to dictate a letter. Kings of England have always spoken French well enough, but English secretaries were not always so well versed at transcribing, and Stephen Frion had been with him since his days of exile there. There was an Italian secretary too, but he was not often in evidence as letters to that country were rare. I nodded to Frion, and then heard Jasper Tudor laugh out loud.

'There you are, nephew!' he said. 'Blocked everywhere! Oho! The King of England frustrated by a Welsh backgammon!'

King Henry smiled back at him, then looked up to me. I breathed easier when I saw that the smile did not fade.

'Sire,' I said, going down on one knee. 'I have come to make excuses for my absence.'

'Indeed now?' Jasper Tudor said, getting up. 'If Henry Morane is about to make excuses we should all gather to listen, for his tale will be enough to soften even the sour faces of some of our company. Come over here, my friends.' He beckoned to Morton and Foxe, who were over by the window with the Lady Margaret Beaufort. I saw that she still held Caxton's volume. Then

I was hard put to it to restrain a smile at Anderson when I heard how loudly the episcopal boots clacked on the tiles.

'The lute player has been found,' King Henry said, his green eyes on me. 'You may know that. But what else have you to say?'

'Little else, my lord, except that I was struck down with the measles sickness and feared contagion to others if I returned to duty. But there is news from Europe. . .' I paused and looked at Archbishop Morton. His fleshy face was creased in a frown. He had been waiting for the King's attention, and did not relish my intrusion. Neither did the lugubrious horse-face of Richard Foxe. Then I noticed that Stephen Frion had ceased writing and his ears were cocked in my direction.

'It is a common excuse to blame one's absence upon a sickness,' Morton boomed. 'And yet you say you have news from Europe? From Flanders, perhaps? So tell us how you were able to visit there at the same time as you were struck down with sickness.'

'Let him speak, John,' King Henry said, the smile disappearing.

And then I realized that to speak of the Dowager Duchess of Burgundy would lead to further questioning. I should have to tell of Ali and how he came by his information. And while King Henry, as on a previous occasion, might overlook his illegal activities in return for information, I knew that Morton and Foxe would not. They would arraign him for smuggling, and smuggling carried the same penalties as high treason. I would not risk that for Ali.

I said, 'The news is not of great import, Sire. . .' Foxe gave a snort of derision '. . . but as you have granted me your ear, I presume. . .'

'Come to the point, Master Morane,' King Henry said, his eyes moving across to Morton and back. He had not missed my hesitation.

'It is to do with the recent voyages of exploration, Sire. While the Portuguese, Diaz, has discovered a way to the Indies round Africa there is a Genoese of my acquaintance here in London who speaks of a quicker way.'

'What quicker way?' Richard Foxe demanded. 'There

is no other, save beyond the north of Muscovy and the frozen lands of Russ.'

I turned to him. 'He swears there is, my lord bishop. He would go straight there. Straight across the Western Ocean.'

It took them a few moments to absorb it. Then Archbishop Morton said, 'A madman, eh? And when does he hope to attempt it? When the moon is full, perhaps?' I saw Stephen Frion cover his mouth to hide a smile.

'Did I hear you right, Master Morane?' It was the Lady Margaret Beaufort, speaking for the first time. 'He would sail straight out across the uncharted Western Ocean?'

'Aye, madam,' I said, bowing to her. 'He talks speciously. But the facts he relates seem to be specious enough to prove it can be done.'

Jasper Tudor started to say something, but the King, his eyes hard on me, waved him down. 'He convinces you then, Morane?' he asked.

'Aye, my lord. He would crave your attention to those facts.'

'And the contents of your purse for a hare-brained adventure, no doubt,' Richard Foxe muttered.

'But we must listen to them!' the King's mother exclaimed. 'Indeed we must! It is what we need to hear in these days of slothful opulence. It is precisely what William Caxton writes of.' She held the book in the air. 'The spirit of adventure must not be allowed to die!'

*   *   *

Yet it was to be many months before I found Bartholomew Columbus. He had journeyed to Bristol, Matthew Coombe told me, to seek news of his brother from the mariners there and, more especially, to consult with them about their earlier voyages in the Western Ocean.

CHAPTER 24

KING Henry, with no foreign ambassador to impress, was not one to waste his finery on an impoverished Italian navigator. He wore a plain brown coat edged with a fur that might once have been proud, and a soft cap with the green Tudor Dragon stitched to it which looked as if it were a gift from one of the washer-women at the palace.

It was a private audience, for King Henry's inquiring mind would first hear the arguments then, if impressed, he would put the matter to his councillors for further examination. Thus it was that only his own family were present: Uncle Jasper, his mother and his wife, both these attended by one of their ladies, as well as Matilda, whom Queen Elizabeth had especially asked to be present as I was concerned. Joseph Anderson also held his post inside the door, as a stranger was in the presence of the King.

Bartholomew Columbus bowed, then, thinking that perhaps it was not enough for this English monarch, went down on one knee, as a result losing hold of his charts so that they rolled across the floor tiles. When they had been recovered King Henry smiled and indicated that they could be unfurled on the table. 'You are welcome, sir,' he said. 'We have heard of your antecedents, of your stay in Lisbon drawing charts with your brother, whom we understand has the greater experience as a navigator. And we offer you condolences for the loss of those charts when your ship was wrecked.' He pointed at the charts. 'These have been drawn within our realm, then?' He spoke in English, but slowly, and I saw that Columbus had achieved a greater command of the language since I had last seen him.

'That is so, your Grace,' the navigator said. 'Drawn from my memory of the others, some in Bristol, and some in the Strand street where I have lodged.' He nodded towards me.

'Bristol, eh? Are you known to any of its citizens?'

'Yes.' He nodded. 'To John Jay, Richard Ameryk, and also to Thomas Croft, collector of your Customs, but now died, alas. I renewed their acquaintance made when I journeyed with my brother from Portugal to Iceland ten years ago. The Bristol mariners carry English cloth to Lisbon in exchange for wine and woad, and to Iceland in exchange for fish . . .'

King Henry held up a hand. 'Of this we are aware,' he smiled. 'And Masters Jay, Ameryk and Croft are known to us as worthy citizens.' The King had in fact spoken with them at great length on an earlier visit. 'But your brother . . . Christopher, is it not? . . . wishes to venture farther?'

I saw Anderson stiffen when Iceland was mentioned, and repressed a smile.

Bartholomew Columbus took a deep breath, struggling for words. Then he relapsed into Latin, and became more fluent. 'It is so, my lord. And for these reasons.' He looked round at the others, who were watching him keenly, not least the Lady Margaret Beaufort. 'Sixty years ago,' he said, 'the Portuguese prince sent his navigators on annual voyages to try and discover if there was a way round Africa. At first this was not so much to make trade with the Indies as to redeem the failure of the Crusades, the holy places still being occupied by the infidel Turk. And since then the situation has grown worse since those heathens captured Constantinople not long ago.'

'In 1453,' Lady Margaret Beaufort said. 'But tell us, sir, how he expected to do that by finding a way round Africa.'

Columbus gave her slight bow. 'By discovering the great Christian empire of Presbyter John, believed to be in Ethiopia, in farthest Africa, madam. Prester John's enormous army could be enjoined to attack the Turk in the rear.' He turned back to the King, smiling. 'But while a way round Africa is now known the empire of Prester John remains to be found. And what is more important today is the quest for the gold, the silks, the fine linen and spices of the Indies. The great expense of bringing these by caravan across the vast spaces of Asia, the huge

134

duties imposed on them in Constantinople by the Turk, and the cost of transporting them to Europe thereafter, not to speak of the outrageous freight charged by the rapacious Venetians in their ships. Even by wagon or pack-horse . . .'

'Yes, yes, Master Columbus,' King Henry said. 'Those facts are evident. But we would hear how your brother would reach the Indies by sailing round the world in the opposite direction across the Great Ocean.'

'The Ocean is but a great sea in which Europe, Asia and Africa float together, Sire. Therefore the uttermost coast of Asia lies on the other side of the sea out there.' He waved a hand. 'It is but a question of how far away it is. And this . . .' he drew himself up proudly, and I saw that his russet beard had been newly trimmed '. . . and this, my lords and ladies, is what my brother Christopher has calculated. It is not even as far as the nethermost cape of Africa which the Portuguese have discovered.' He paused and looked round at his audience. The ladies had pressed closer, Jasper Tudor sat at the table turning over the charts, but glancing at the speaker from time to time.

'Then tell us, sir,' King Henry said, 'of your brother's calculations.'

'First, my lord,' Bartholomew Columbus replied, 'we have evidence that land cannot be far away across the Ocean. At Porto Santo, by Madeira, floating bamboo trunks, worked timbers and tropical vegetation have been washed ashore by the westerly winds. Then, off Galway on his voyage to Iceland, he saw for himself the bodies of two men who had been driven ashore there in a strange craft. They had not been long dead, and had flat faces such as those of Asiatics. Then, sir, being a good Christian, he is versed in the writings of the prophet Esdras, who states in his second book, "Six parts hast Thou dried up", thus the continents of Europe, Asia and Africa occupy six parts of the globe, and the Ocean but the seventh.'

Jasper Tudor cleared his throat. 'Look you, Messer Columbo,' he said, 'we in this realm are also familiar with the writings of the prophet Esdras. Likewise we are aware that the world is a globe, and that the sun travels round it once each day. But what we, or anyone else, do not know is the size of the globe; how far it is to travel round, and how far across it stretches the continent of Asia. Has your brother calculated that?'

Bartholomew Columbus inclined his head to him. 'Good sir,' he said, 'there is no imputation of ignorance, especially to the English, who are renowned for their navigators, and whose King is known to have great intelligence in such matters. Thus, sir, you will know of the writings and charts of Ptolemy of Alexandria, who has ascribed to the Earth a circumference of three hundred and sixty degrees.'

'We do,' King Henry nodded. 'Printed recently in Bologna, and also ascribing to the continent of Asia an extent of one hundred and eighty degrees; half way round the world, much less than Esdras states.'

'That is so,' Columbus agreed. 'But Ptolemy's calculations were made fifteen hundred years ago. There is later evidence . . .'

'How far is a degree?' Queen Elizabeth said. They all turned to look at her, and she coloured a little, as was her wont.

'A degree, madam,' Columbus said gravely, 'has been credited with various distances according to the authority. These my brother has studied with great care. Ptolemy credits it as being fifty miles.'

'Eighteen thousand miles to girdle the earth, then,' King Henry said after a moment. 'In that case, according to Ptolemy, it is nine thousand miles across the Ocean to Cathay. Surely too far for a ship?'

Columbus shook his head. 'But there are later authorities, Sire. Of these, the Arab astronomer Al-fragan is the most respected.'

'Is he?' Jasper Tudor said.

'Aye, sir, he is well known to navigators. His length of a degree was at first thought to be even greater than that of Ptolemy, being sixty-six miles. But my brother,' Bartholomew Columbus went on proudly, 'has ascertained that he was referring to the Roman measure which, as is well known, is but forty-five miles. Thus he calculates that the circumference of the world is no more than sixteen thousand miles.'

136

'Half of that, eight thousand miles, is still too far for a ship to carry provisions and gear for itself,' Jasper Tudor said.

'That is true,' the Italian admitted, 'if Asia does in fact only stretch half way round the globe. But if its distance were calculated correctly, and found to be greater, its eastern shore would be that much closer to Europe across the Ocean.'

'William of Worcester,' the Lady Margaret said, 'writing only ten years ago, said that Asia extends across two thirds of the globe. I have also read the account of Marco Polo, who took two years to reach Cathay across Asia by caravan, and ascribes to it an even greater distance.'

'Then, madam, you will know that he states there is another island a thousand miles beyond it, the isle of Japangu. And so, my lords and ladies . . .' Bartholomew Columbus drew himself up again '. . . my brother has calculated that, with these facts taken into account, the distance from Europe to the eastern shore of Asia across the Ocean is no more than two thousand five hundred miles, less than to the cape of Africa.' He waved his hand at the table. 'And there are my charts to prove it.'

'Al-fragan,' Jasper Tudor said, 'is he the only authority for this?'

'By no means, sir. We have the workings within the last few years of the Florentine, Toscanelli, who wrote privately to the king of Portugal, sending him a map of his own design of the Western Ocean, which we have seen, and which I have reproduced from my own memory.'

They all went over to the table where Bartholomew Columbus unfurled his maps. 'This Toscanelli draws many islands in the Ocean between the Azores and Japangu,' King Henry observed. 'A ship might be victualled there.'

'There are many islands, my lord, although their exact location is not known,' Columbus replied, 'but the existence of Antillia, discovered by a Portuguese monk and called the Isle of the Seven Cities, is well known in Lisbon. And the Isle of Brasil also lies in the Western Ocean. In fact your mariners from Bristol, Sire, sent ships to search for it some ten years ago.'

'Did they find it?' Queen Elizabeth asked. She clapped her hands together. 'A fruitful island in the middle of the Great Ocean! How I could wish to visit it and see the people for myself!'

King Henry smiled and put a hand on her shoulder. 'You are more precious where you are, dear one, than embarking on wild voyages to unknown islands,' he said, and Elizabeth of York coloured again.

'Then if this Toscanelli sent this map privately to King John of Portugal,' Jasper Tudor said, 'and the island of the Seven Cities is known to the Portuguese, why did he not send his own ships to find it for himself?'

This time Bartholomew Columbus's smile was one of real triumph. 'He did, sir,' he replied, 'but he sent his ships from the Azores, where the wind blows constantly from the west, so that in due course they were driven back again without discovering it. But my brother, having visited the Canary Islands, which lie farther south, has observed that the wind prevails from the east there, and with that wind behind him he calculates that he can reach the Indies in less time than the Portuguese to the Cape of Good Hope, when they are not even half way there!'

'So he would go from the Canary Islands?' King Henry mused. 'They are a long way from our realm, though. Why not from Bristol?'

'The winds from there are mixed, my lord, and are uncertain, which its navigators well know. Whereas from Grand Canary they are constant.'

'Well then,' King Henry said, considering the Italian, 'what support does your brother ask for?'

'Five ships, my lord,' was the instant reply. 'Of which, if it were known that you supplied two, the others would follow from the mariners of Bristol, who have confidence in your judgement.'

'Two ships, eh?'

'Yes, my lord,' Bartholomew Columbus went on, 'and the right to half the gold and silver brought back, as well as the title of Admiral of the Ocean Sea and Viscount of the Indies in perpetuity for his heirs.'

'He does not want much,' Jasper Tudor observed drily.

'But he takes the risk,' Lady Margaret said. 'His

138

reputation is staked on his quality as a navigator. And for only two ships!'

'Two of *my* ships, madam,' King Henry said, his eye twinkling. 'But we will consider it. A committee of learned men shall investigate your claims, Master Columbus.' He turned to me suddenly. 'And you, Master Morane, who brought him to us, must have faith in the venture then?'

I bowed. 'I have, my lord.'

'Then,' King Henry said slowly, 'should our committee decide in favour of the project you would be willing to accompany it as our auditor?'

Matilda drew in her breath sharply, which brought them round to look at her. She bowed, confused, and retired quickly behind the Queen. I heard Jasper Tudor give a chuckle.

There was little I could do but nod, then I said, 'I should, your Grace, especially if I were to be given an escort.' I heard Joseph Anderson's pikeshaft thud against the floor. I did not need to see his face.

King Henry Tudor glanced at him, then back at me. 'Aye,' he nodded. 'But perhaps we should first wait and see how our commissioners value the project before we talk of having auditors escorted to the Indies.' I could almost hear the sigh of relief from behind the Queen.

*   *   *

While King Henry did not delay appointing those who were to examine the claims of Bartholomew Columbus, the business itself took much time. The commissioners had to be summoned by Writ, and Richard Foxe did not stir himself unduly, being aggrieved that he had not been present at the audience with the Italian navigator. Then the commission made many researches and deliberated long and carefully, which was to be expected with John Morton at their head, so that it was many months before their finding was pronounced.

In addition to the Archbishop of Canterbury those appointed were Doctor Thomas Savage, the King's Chaplain, and Sir Richard Nanfan, both of whom had returned recently after signing treaties with Spain and Portugal, and thus with knowledge of their politics. Then there was Lord Daubeney, Warden of the Mint and Constable of Bristol Castle, a man skilled in finance, and Sir Richard Guildford — my captor after Bosworth — experienced in the construction of ships. The latter had not long before been given one hundred pounds by King Henry to construct a vessel, the very size of the grant showing the King's concern for the ocean and well-built ships to sail upon it. Sir Richard, as well as being a soldier of repute, was as well versed in mathematics as John Morton to verify the figures of Columbus. Finally, there were Sir Richard Croft, Treasurer of the Household, able to compute the cost of the enterprise, and Richard Ameryk, familiar with navigation on the Great Ocean. The appointment of these men, each with great experience in his own way, showed the deep interest in which King Henry had taken in the project.

The finding of the inquiry was straightforward. The enterprise was not feasible. While Paolo Toscanelli was a reputable physician of Florence there was no more justification in accepting his theories than those of the equally reputable but more ancient geographers as Ptolemy, Strabo, or the Greek, Eratosthenes, the last two having calculated that the circumference of the earth was 25,000 miles. Neither was there any justification in assuming that the Moslem astronomer, Al-fragan, had used the shorter Roman mile when his workings were in his own language and must surely have referred to the Arab mile, which is much longer. It was true that Ptolemy had given a lesser distance than Eratosthenes and Strabo, but even if his estimation of 18,000 miles were accepted it still had to be proved how far the continent of Asia stretched out towards Europe.

Of this there had been many estimations, from the days of Alexander the Great to the more recent writings of Marco Polo, the Venetian. Both claimed farther than the limits of the land described by Ptolemy and Marinus of Tyre, but neither had any means of measuring the distance they had gone.

If, therefore, the smallest estimation of the circumference of the globe was accepted, namely that of Ptolemy, then his estimation of 9,000 miles from Europe

140

to Asia must be accepted too. This was too far even for a Portuguese caravel or nau to compass without a pause for revictualling. Islands such as Antillia might exist, but there was no evidence that they were placed correctly on the maps the commission had inspected. Islands out in the Western Ocean had been reported for thousands of years, from the works of Aristotle and Plato to the Carthaginians and the more recent Portuguese reports of the Isle of the Seven Cities. There was even reported to be an Isle of Saint Brendan, discovered by an Irish monk, but there was no justification for accepting any of these accounts.

Yet even if the arguments of Columbus were accepted, such a venture would have to pass through the sea-domains of Portugal and Spain, and their kings would not look kindly upon the appearance of a foreign expedition, thus disturbing the present amicable relations with those countries. On the other hand if it were the intention to sail westwards from Bristol the only other island offering sustenance to the voyager would be Brasil. But that isle had already been discovered ten years before by mariners from Bristol, its existence having so far been kept secret as they did not wish to disclose where they caught fish. Far beyond Brasil, known to them as the Isle of Cod, there was known to be the barren shore of Green-land, without gold, spices or fine cloth, producing only hawks and furs, and with no resemblance at all to the Japangu of Marco Polo.

That was the end of the matter, except that King Henry was somewhat put out to learn that Brasil was already known. But John Morton explained that he himself had only discovered it during the inquiry, when examination of the Customs' records had disclosed that Thomas Croft had shipped forty bushels of salt in 1481, which could only have been for preserving fish, as Brasil was suitable for nothing else, being a most inhospitable shore.

Brasil had been discovered, Morton said, because the Danes had installed a new governor of Iceland, a German called Didrick Pining, who had at once waged war on the English fishermen, so that they had been forced to look elsewhere. But relations with Iceland had since improved, he went on, a number of its people having been rescued from their homes by English mariners after the great eruption of Mount Katla, and taken to Bristol. While it was true that the city records showed that twenty-eight of them were still in menial service — even Richard Ameryk of the commission owned one — there were others who were citizens of Bristol in their own right, notably John and William Yslond, both merchants of repute.

Yet by that time King Henry had other matters to occupy him, and Bartholomew Columbus departed sorrowfully to put his brother's case to the French court. But, as is now known, his brother obtained support from Queen Isabella of Castile, and Bartholomew did not even hear of his voyage until the news of his discoveries spread like wildfire around Europe. He joined Christopher on his second voyage, but what prosperity he found is uncertain, for it is even suggested that the lands discovered by Christopher Columbus are not part of Asia at all. Neither are they the legendary isles of Japangu, for they seem to contain more disease than treasure, or, as a Spaniard has written, 'They came back with more gold on their faces than in their pockets.'

CHAPTER 25

'QUEEN Elizabeth is with child again,' Matilda told me. 'And so am I.' Her eyes had the lustre of the deep blue sea.

It took me a few moments to realize the import of what she had said, and then a great fear swept over me. I turned to her, but she regarded me confidently.

'Aye,' she nodded, 'your concern is understandable. But in spite of what I suffered that day in Leicester it has had no effect. Master Roger Leopold has assured me of it.'

Roger Leopold! That counterfeit astrologer whom I had threatened had he assured her otherwise! I cursed myself, and repressed a groan.

'And you told me that the surgeons were confident too,' she added.

That was true, and I had forgotten it. Yet the same fear still gripped me. I held out my arms. 'I am not so sure now, poppet,' I said.

'But why?'

'I cannot say. It is merely that I am afraid for you.'

She smiled. 'Is that all? Then maybe you should see Master Leopold for yourself.'

'I would rather have the surgeons again,' I told her.

'No!' she cried. 'I will not have that! Not again! Those evil-smelling old men, muttering in their beards while they make free with me . . . I could not bear it!'

'I will see to it that they do not make too free . . .'

'No!' She stamped her foot. 'I will not suffer the indignity.'

'Then all that is left,' I said morosely, 'is to pray to the Virgin.'

Her eyes suddenly filled with tears. 'And that it is a girl.'

'A girl?' I was taken aback.

'It is what I want,' she said firmly. 'She would live a life of serenity, as only a woman can. Whereas a boy . . .' she looked up at me ' . . . a boy would follow his father.

And with you as a father, Henry Morane, he would perchance become a King's agent, never far from battle, murder and sudden death. I could never bear such anxiety for two of you.'

I laughed. 'You think too far ahead, my sweet apple. Sons do not always follow their father's vocations. Ours will be able to choose for himself, because he will not be born in poverty.'

'Oh?' Her eyebrows went up. 'With my salary as the Queen's woman, and yours as her clerk, you consider we are wealthy?'

'The forest of Leicester still covers two parts of the gold that Dickon gave me on my return from Brittany, or had you forgotten?'

'I had,' she admitted after a moment. 'Then why do we not dig some of it up for ourselves now, and save the other part for our son?'

'And become rich all at once to excite suspicion? Besides . . .' I kissed her ' . . . would you give up your post to Queen Elizabeth and your affection for her, to retire to a life of ease in the countryside?'

'I would do even that,' Matilda said slowly, 'if it were to mean that you did not endanger yourself any more.'

'Ah!' I considered it. 'But there remains some of my bond to the King. And,' I added, 'should the new pretender of the Duchess Margaret appear any sudden acquisition of wealth by me would have those two bloodhounds, Morton and Foxe, bristling with suspicion.'

'It would be best to wait a while, then,' Matilda said.

'Aye,' I laughed. 'At least until our *daughter* is born.'

'Ah, Master Morane!' a voice said. The Lady Margaret Beaufort had come in, and her brow was furrowed. 'You have heard the news?'

I bowed. 'Aye, madam. God willing, it will be another son.'

Her austere face grew new lines under its wimple. 'Son? Oh, that?' She waved it aside. 'The Queen will have no difficulty, having borne two children already. As to it being a son . . .' she lost her frown 'the King himself is already at his devotions to ask it. No, Master Morane, I was referring to the sad news of William Caxton. It is to be hoped he had time to make his peace with God.'

144

'He will have done, madam,' I said sympathetically, although I did not know that Caxton had died. 'He was an old man, and death could have reached for him at any time. But who will work his presses now?'

'His assistant, one Wynkyn de Worde, who they tell me considers moving them to better quarters at Fleet Street. But that is of small moment. It is the writings of Caxton that will cease. We shall be at a great loss for them.' She waved a hand, gathered up her skirt, and walked away, leaving us staring after her.

There was another who had just died, who had once been of more import to me. Robert Stillington, former bishop of Bath and Wells, whom I had induced to betray to Dickon the falseness of King Edward's marriage to Elizabeth Woodville, thereby making that monarch's children bastards. And those children were Queen Elizabeth herself, as well as the two princes who had disappeared in the Tower. Stillington's death in prison at Windsor might raise the old question of who had prompted him. But I comforted myself with the fact that there was no one left who could point to me.

Yet the question still remained in my mind even after six years of King Henry's rule. While the bastardy of Elizabeth of York had been removed, that of her two brothers had of necessity to be removed as well, so that if either of them was still alive it could be said he had a prior right to the throne. And the matter of their fate had not been openly settled. Archbishop Morton could scarcely admit to their demise at the hands of Buckingham. The matter therefore lay unresolved in Morton's mind, and thus any pretender who called himself one or the other of the two princes would not be easy to disprove.

Such had been the pretension of Lambert Simnel, which had brought about a serious rebellion and a battle so close fought as to make the Tudor throne rock precariously for a few hours. Yet while Lambert Simnel had been dealt with, time would produce another contender for the crown. I said this to Matilda.

'Aye,' she agreed, 'and we have another already. What did King Henry think of it?'

'I did not tell him' I admitted, and explained why.

'I would have done so to Christopher Urswick had he not been away at the court of the Archduke Maximilian. And in any case the King's concern is once again for affairs in Brittany.'

'And for his wife's condition too,' she smiled.

'He has little need for that, as Lady Margaret said. She has borne two children without miscarriage, and is well formed and lusty.'

'Am I not as well formed and lusty, then?'

'The more,' I agreed, reaching for her. 'But as to children . . .'

She put a hand against my chest and pushed me away. 'Listen to me, Henry Morane, I *will* have this child. There has been no lasting injury, of that I am certain. And this time,' she added, firmly, 'there will be no one to frustrate it.'

'God forbid!' I said grimly.

* * *

King Henry's concern for Brittany had always been to to prevent it from falling into French hands, yet Morton and Foxe assured him that the danger was now passed since the marriage of the Duchess Anne to Maximilian, no matter how much Charles of France raged at being thwarted.

The marriage, however, had been made at Rennes by proxy. The ancient ceremony, whereby the fourteen-year-old duchess had been placed naked between the bedsheets while Maximilian's ambassador, Count Wolfgang von Pelham of Nassau, stripped his leg to the knee and placed it in beside her, had been described by the King of France as no more than an invention of the Breton court, and that Maximilian must be a cold wooer who would consent to be a bridegroom by deputy, and could not make the short journey to put it out of question. But Maximilian was intent upon pursuing his quarrel with the King of Hungary, and it was to entice him away from that project that Christopher Urswick's embassy had been sent, with the offer by King Henry of the Order of the Garter. But Maximilian was not seduced by any gifts from the king of England, so that matters in Brittany grew steadily worse. There were English soldiers at Redon, and some at Nantes with those sent by Ferdinand of Spain. Then these latter were withdrawn, ostensibly to assist in the reduction of Granada, but more likely after the persuasion of Charles of France, who promised to restore Ferdinand's lost provinces of Roussillon and Cerdagne once his object in Brittany had been secured. Then the Breton nobles became split among themselves, Nantes surrendered and the French armies marched on Redon. King Henry could do nothing to save his men, and that fortress was the next to fall. Encouraged, Charles of France marched northwards on the last stronghold of Rennes. The Duchess Anne closed the gates and declared a state of siege, pawning her jewellery to pay her soldiers. Meanwhile the English court moved to Greenwich, to await the birth of Queen Elizabeth's next child.

Greenwich, unlike the simple manor of Sheen, was a royal palace of great luxury. Re-built by Margaret of Anjou, the termagent wife of the idiot-king Henry the Sixth, it boasted glass in all the windows and tiles of terra-cotta on the floors. Much of the walls was of reddish brick, so that it was known as the Rosy Palace. The glass, tiles and brickwork were everywhere decorated with daisies — marguerites — the name of its royal builder. It lay on the river, close to London, and it was in the dockyard there that King Henry's great ship was being constructed.

The 'Regent', as it was to be called, would be huge, of 700 tuns, and carry no less than four masts, unheard of in the realm before. More, she was to bear 225 guns of all sizes, the heavier artillery placed on a lower deck behind port-holes, through which a deadly fire could be aimed at an enemy if she came alongside. No longer would it be necessary to rely upon a rain of arrows and serpentine shot from the raised castles at bow and stern. She would sweep the seas once she was afloat. There were some who said that King Henry had taken his wife to Greenwich so that he could more easily inspect the child of his brain than that of his loins, but I knew it to be otherwise.

147

Twenty-one oarsmen drew the Royal Barge from Sheen to Greenwich at a cost of eight pence each, with an addition of sixteen pence for shooting the rapid waters under London Bridge. The Queen's barge cost a like amount, but the expenditure was borne from her own estates, an economy of King Henry which would have been in ill accord with the citizens of London had they known of it, for they had decked the Bridge with flowers, silks and other banners to greet the passing of their beloved Queen.

The Lady Margaret Beaufort had, as expected, overseen the arrangements for the royal birth. Elizabeth of York would be delivered of her child on a pallet, afterwards being lifted to the State Bed. The pallet was covered with scarlet and ermine fur, with a canopy of crimson embroidered with gold and silver crowns. Once the Queen had been escorted to the royal chamber no other women than the midwives were admitted, and there was provided a round mantle of crimson velvet trimmed with ermine fur for her to wear about her as she lay. No such arrangements were provided for Matilda, who lay on cushions in another chamber, attended by one woman, for the midwives would be busy with the Queen.

CHAPTER 26

Q U E E N Elizabeth was delivered of a son, baptized, amid great rejoicing, by Richard Foxe in his capacity as Bishop of Exeter. There were many celebrations, with masques and disguisings and tired minstrels performing endlessly at banquets. Tournaments were held, and all those who could afford it pranced on their liveried horses in their best armour. The boy was given the name of Henry, after his father, but with a brother having already survived his first five years without mishap, there was little chance that he would ever style himself as King Henry the Eighth. The Queen had suffered more than had been expected, and there were new lines on Lady Margaret Beaufort's face to show for it. But her anxiety was as nothing compared to mine for Matilda.

Once Queen Elizabeth had recovered her health she sent for news of Mistress Morane, and forthwith commanded two of her midwives to attend her, a gesture that showed her solicitude for others, whatever their station, even at the expense of her own comfort. I made my audience and thanked her, but her fair face clouded when she saw the distress on mine. Then Lady Margaret offered surgeons, remembering, as she said, what Matilda had undergone in the convent at Leicester. I thanked her too, but was hard put to it to keep the tears from my eyes.

'Will I live?' Matilda whispered. Her face was drawn, and her body slack from loss of blood. The lustre of her dark blue eyes had faded, leaving them glazed as a stag's when pierced by the hunter's lance. I kneeled beside her and kissed her sweating brow.

'I have never lied to you, sweetheart,' I told her, 'and would not do so now. As God wills you shall live, and the surgeons think so too. They are the best that can be found, by the Lady Margaret herself, a kindness we shall never forget.'

She closed her eyes. 'At least it was the boy you desired.'

'What matters?' I said. 'He lives and already fights the nurse.'

The faintness of a smile crossed her face. 'You will cherish him?'

'I will,' I assured her. 'But you I cherish first. Come now, you must to sleep, and when you wake I shall still be here.'

Weeks passed, and I, too, grew pale and drawn, so that even Joseph Anderson made comment. 'You may kill yourself as well,' he muttered, unstrapping his harness and throwing his helmet on the floor. 'That Francis Lovell has much to answer for.'

'He has already answered as you well know,' I said grimly. 'But I should have kept him alive to witness this.'

He put a hand on my shoulder. 'No,' he said. 'What we did to him was grievous enough. He is best forgotten. Your care should be for the future, your son . . .' He stopped and eyed me roundly. 'God's Hooks! Is there to be another Morane to plague the realm? Yet perhaps it may be as well,' he added, seeing my face, 'for this palace life unmans me. I dance continuous attendance upon the Royal Body, and even for ten pence a day . . .' But I was being summoned. Matilda was asking for me.

'The Lady Margaret visited me,' she said, and there was a new brightness in her eyes. 'The Holy Virgin has answered her prayers, and I will live, although never to bear child again. She would not speak other than the truth, I know. Therefore I am already recovered,' she smiled.

'Aye,' I kissed her. 'But it is too soon to say 'already'. It will be many weeks before you can be moved to Sheen. First you must walk of your own strength.'

'But our son? I have not seen him for a moon or more.'

'He lives right well. And savages the wet-nurses abominably.'

'As his father probably did,' she smiled. 'He must also be called Henry.'

'No. The King's son has that name. We will give him yours.'

'Mine?'

'Yes. Nicholas. You were once Matilda Nicholas, remember?'

'So be it,' she said, and straightaway fall asleep again.

The new Prince Henry would later be invested as the Duke of York, which pleased the people for the sake of Queen Elizabeth. As King Henry knew he could never win their hearts entirely, he devoted his attention to his wife, hoping to gain at least their tolerance thereby. And, apart from apprehensions about Brittany, there was quiet in the realm. Until, that is, the strange disappearance of his French secretary.

A search was made in case Stephen Frion had been set upon by thieves, but no trace of him was found. Then, some weeks later, reports came from France that he was in the service of King Charles. The only explanation was that he had sought a better opportunity for advancement at the court of a more powerful monarch. But King Henry was dismayed at his abrupt departure, for Stephen Frion had been one of his more enduring servants. A month after that news came from Ireland. A new pretender had appeared at Cork, claiming that he was the younger of the two lads in the Tower, had escaped therefrom, and was styling himself King Richard the Fourth.

King Henry sat at the table, quill in hand, while his monkey chattered at the end of its silver chain. He had the accountings of the Chamber in front of him and was putting his sign manual against each item. The others stood by, waiting for him to finish. Richard Foxe and Sir Thomas Lovell, Treasurer of the Chamber and distant kinsman of the traitor lord, Francis Lovell, stood close in case of questions from the King. Beyond were Archbishop Morton and his new disciple, Thomas More. The latter, but thirteen years old, was reputed to have a brain equal to his master's behind his boyish face. It only needed Reginald Bray's hairless dome to complete the assembly, and then I saw him too, as motionless as the carpet hanging on the wall beside him, at one with it as a basilisk changes colour with its surroundings. An uneasy tightness gripped my stomach.

'Ah, Master Morane!' King Henry laid aside his pen and looked up at me. His eyes were wrinkled from reading the close print. 'What knowledge have you of this garson at Cork?'

I bowed low. 'None, Sire, beyond his assertions.'

'One of which,' Morton said, 'is that he escaped from the Tower in the time of the Usurper.'

'I have heard that, my lord,' I said to him.

'And is there any substance in it?' Morton demanded.

I spread out my hands. 'I cannot know . . .'

'But you have spoken to me of a man called Slaughter. William Slaughter, whom you said was on the wage-roll of the Tower at that time.'

So that was it! Morton had been sowing his suspicions, and King Henry was their planting bed. 'I did, my lord,' I acknowledged. 'Because I knew him for Buckingham's man, a retainer of that duke.'

Morton's white brows drew together. 'You did not tell me that.'

I had indeed told him. But if he chose to affect ignorance I was in no position to argue. 'But, sir,' I bowed humbly, 'I understood it to be well known.'

'Well known? How could the allegiance of a common jailer be well known?' He emphasised the last two words.

If Morton could lie, then I could lie too. 'I understood it to be known to you at least, my lord, because before that he had been on the wage-roll at Brecon castle at the time you were held there by the duke of Buckingham. I did not think he was a common turnkey, because the records showed that he was in attendance upon you.'

It was all Morton could do to restrain a gasp. It also gave me time to pray silently that the records of Brecon had been destroyed after its occupation by Jasper Tudor.

King Henry, who had been eyeing each of us, said, 'What is this about a common jailer? Buckingham was Constable of the Tower at that time. He would have had every right to place a servant there.'

Archbishop John Morton, now recovered, turned to him. 'There is more, Your Grace. Morane also told me that the fellow Slaughter had changed his allegiance.'

The green Tudor eyes swung to me. 'That is true, Sire. Slaughter spoke of it as he died.'

'Then nothing can be proved; we have only your word for it?'

I bowed. 'That is so, Sire. But I would swear to what he said.'

'Yes, yes, Morane. We would not question it.' He turned back to Morton. 'Then what is it you wish to assert, John?' he asked him.

'A moment, my lords,' Reginald Bray said, stepping out of the shade. 'He changed his allegiance from the duke of Buckingham, you say, Morane? Then to whom did he change it?'

'He died before he could tell me,' I replied shortly.

'Then,' Reginald Bray said to the King, 'it seems to me that the assertion John Morton makes is that this fellow Slaughter could well have assisted in an escape from the Tower.'

'Precisely!' Thomas More spoke suddenly, then retired behind his master in some confusion.

Morton smiled at him. 'It also seems,' he said, glancing at me, 'that Morane will have to guard his tongue, or . . .' He left the rest unsaid, but his meaning was clear. A tongue torn out needs no guarding.

I took a risk and affected great affront. 'I have not spoken of this before, my lord,' I said to him, 'except to you when questioned. And I would not have spoken of it again but for you.' I went down on one knee before the King. 'Sire,' I said, 'I have taken a solemn oath of loyalty to you, and beg leave to resent the imputation. Besides,' I added, taking a further risk, 'my own conscience before God forbids me breaking an oath, and that is of even more importance to me.'

'A pretty speech!' Richard Foxe observed, taking a paper from those on the table. 'And a bold one too,' he added, affecting to study it.

'To your feet, Master Morane,' the King said. 'We are aware of your allegiance, and have not forgotton your conduct at Stoke Field, and more recently at . . . on our business. Yet we would know if you have any information about this garson's claim to have escaped from the Tower.'

I looked at him straightly. 'I have none, Your Grace. Yet I would presume to add that, if the claim be true, Will Slaughter's part in the matter is no longer of any importance, for there must have been some other person who has sheltered him these eight or nine years.'

'That has also occurred to us,' King Henry said. 'And we require to know if it has been in our realm or over the sea.' He put his hands on the table and pushed himself upwards, leaving the ape gibbering on its chain. 'See here, then, Master Morane,' he went on, 'we repeat that we do not doubt your allegiance, but you were familiar with Richard of Gloucester's court . . .' I was pleased that, unlike Morton, he did not refer to him as the Usurper ' . . . and therefore command you to ascertain the facts and, in particular, the origins of this garson.' He turned to Morton, who nodded, then back to me. 'You will therefore journey to Cork and obtain those facts.'

'Aye, my lord,' I said, my heart sinking.

'And,' the King went on, 'you will also discover who is behind him, who supports him in his enterprise, for by himself the garson is nothing. You understand, Master Morane?' He pointed a long finger at me. 'This garson may not be one of our subjects, but denizen of another land, and therefore no harm must come to him.' A thin smile crossed his face. 'Not yet, at least.'

CHAPTER 27

J O S E P H Anderson turned and spat towards the side of the road. The wind blew it straight back on to his horse's neck, but the animal, head lowered against the weather, plodded on unnoticing. 'How many more days of this?' he complained, the raindrops glistening in his black beard like jewels on a bishop's cope. 'The west country is supposed to be a place of warm, balmy airs.'

When I affected not to hear he repeated his question, adding, 'It will be night soon. How far to this inn at Keynsham you spoke of?'

I told him, and he grunted. 'Ah well,' he observed, 'at least there will be no ships putting out from Bristol this weather. There will be time to inspect the city and its women.'

'Whores are the same anywhere, as you well know,' I told him. 'Besides, Bristol mariners are not afraid of the weather. It will take more than this to keep them in port.' He scowled at that and pulled his cloak tighter about him.

The next morning the wind was even stronger, and the road hard with frozen mud. Our mounts slithered down the hill to the Temple Gate in the Port Wall, the latter stretching all the way along the edge of the old channel dug across the loop of the Avon. It had been a great feat of engineering for its time, more than two hundred years before. The whole river had been diverted, leaving the main stream round the loop dry enough for a stone bridge to be built. Bristol Bridge, it was called, and of as much pride to its citizens as London Bridge is to us, even though it crosses a river miserable in size compared to the Thames, and cannot even allow ships to pass through.

'So,' Joseph Anderson remarked as we passed unchallenged through the gate. 'We have come here without being waylaid by Sir William Stanley. Or this time have you told him we were bound for York?' he grinned.

'I told him nothing. And even if he knows our destination he can do nothing since King Henry has summoned parliament again for money to make war on France, and Stanley is in North Wales as his commissioner for array.

'Aye, the war. Maybe we can be back in time for me to take a part, and draw a proper arrow again.'

There would be war this time without a doubt, since Anne of Brittany, impoverished and without hope, had surrendered Rennes to the French, and all of Brittany had been overrun. King Henry had little choice, although I could not see what he could achieve against the most powerful monarch in Europe. Perhaps he could draw Maximilian to his side, for that duke too had suffered humiliation when Anne had been persuaded by the Pope to repudiate her proxy marriage and wed the French king. And so Anne was now Queen of France, and Charles the Eighth the Duke of Brittany. It was a situation that threatened the rest of Europe.

'We must deal with this garson quickly,' Anderson went on. 'A fire lit on his stomach will soon persuade him to speak.'

'You would break into the Mayor of Cork's house and drag him out, then?' I inquired.

Information from Ireland said that the garson was of Flemish origin, and up to now had gone by the name of Warbeque, Pierrequin Warbeque, although the English in their forthright way with foreign tongues would soon refer to him as Perkin Warbeck. He had arrived at Cork as apprentice to a Breton ship-master, one Pregent Meno, and had gone ashore to display his master's wares of silks and jewelled cloths, parading the streets in that finery. Having attracted a crowd he then declared himself as being of Yorkist line, the son of King Edward of York himself, the younger of the two brothers who had disappeared in the Tower. The citizens had promptly acclaimed him as such, for while none had seen that monarch they remembered his brother, George of Clarence — long dead in the celebrated Malmsey butt — who had been their Lieutenant, and the resemblance was said to be striking. Even the Mayor of Cork had been convinced, and lodged the fellow in great style.

Yet the nearby port of Waterford had not been convinced. It was part of the domains of the Butlers, earls of Ormonde, while Cork was of the Fitzgerald earls of Desmond, and between those families there was no amity at all. What was more important was the attitude of the other, more influential Fitzgeralds of Kildare. Its eighth earl, Gerald, the most powerful man in Ireland, was still nursing his bruises after his support of the earlier pretender, Lambert Simnel, and, while he had been pardoned, the bruises were more to his pride than to this body. Perkin Warbeck would have to be dealt with by King Henry before the earl of Kildare made up his mind.

We rode slowly along Temple Street towards the market at Stallage Cross, but snow was falling and few people were about. 'Where do we find this nephew of yours with the hand-gun?' Anderson wanted to know.

'He lodges by the Redcliffe Beck. We will ask.'

'Aye, if he is still there and hasn't gone to sea again.'

Matthew Coombe, in spite of being dismayed by the rejection of Bartholomew Columbus, had maintained his ambition and gone to Bristol as soon as his masterpiece had been proved. It had caused his father much grief, but I had gone to Kingstone and explained the boy's desires. Edward Coombe, understanding as ever, had given me a letter to his son which forgave him and wished him well. Not so his mother, Matilda's sister, who had nearly split the roof with her lamentations, but as they always came to her mouth readily I gave her little of my ear.

We found Matthew in a dockside tavern, in sailor's gear of woollen shirt, breeches and cap striped in different colours as is their way. But he was no lad any more. The tang of salt was all over him, from his flourishing beard to his leathern boots, and already there was in his eyes the far-seeing look that mariners acquire. They lit up at first when he saw me, then his jaw set obstinately.

'It is good to see you, uncle Henry,' he greeted me, 'although I know you bring reproaches from my father.'

I gave him the letter without saying anything. He glanced at me curiously as he took it. Then he read it

157

and a tear came to his eye. 'Praise God for an under-standing father,' he said devoutly. He smiled as if ashamed. 'But perhaps you had something to do with it?' He stood up and shouted at the serving-wench for ale. I saw the smile she gave him, and knew that my nephew had more than just experience of the sea.

'But we did not come to Bristol merely to deliver that letter,' I said when our mugs were full. 'There is more important business.'

'Maybe, but without that letter I could never have faced my father again. And your other business?'

I told him, while Joseph Anderson's attention wandered to the dockside morts.

'Yes, uncle, we have heard much of this fellow who claims old King Edward as his father, but we do not believe him in Bristol. In any case the city is for King Henry, for he has shewn that his sympathies lie with the merchants and sea-venturers. And...' he looked round the room '... the Breton mariner who brought him to Cork does not believe it either.'

'You have heard that?'

'Oh, aye. He told me so himself.'

'He told you so himself? You have been to Cork, then?'

'No no, uncle. He is here in Bristol, and comes to this tavern. But his ship still lies at the dockside out there.' He waved a hand.

'Aha!' Anderson said, swinging round. 'Then we can light a fire on his belly instead.'

Matthew Coombe laughed. 'If you have a mind to do whatever you did at York,' he said, 'you cannot do it here, Captain Anderson. Pregent Meno is a respected sea-merchant and is well known in Bristol. He is still downcast because the citizens of Cork took more notice of his apprentice than of his merchandize. He lay there for a whole month, then in the end came to Bristol, where he has had more success.'

'Then why is he downcast?'

'Because he cannot return until the gale blows itself out.' I saw the smile on Anderson's face, but affected not to notice it. 'Listen, uncle,' Matthew Coombe went on, 'no doubt you bode ill for this Perkin Warbeck

158

but do not take it out on Pregent Meno.'

'I bode no ill for anyone,' I began, and Anderson snorted. 'But I seek information about this Warbeck.' I got up. 'Let us talk with this Breton mariner first.'

A long line of vessels lay tethered fore and aft to the wooden posts along the edge of Redcliffe Back. Behind, the mansion of William Cannings looked across at the wharf where he had made his fortune and that of the city which had borne him. On the other side of the river reeds stood up stiffly through the ice of the frozen marsh. All the ships seemed deserted, the crews ashore in the taverns enjoying their idleness. Not even a sea bird mewed at our approach. Matthew Coombe found the Breton cob, and we thumped down on to the snow-filmed deck. The noise brought the narrow door of the after-house creaking open and a squat figure, solid as a castle turret, came out. Grey eyes inspected the sky and then came down to us. A bleak voice demanded our business.

'My friends from London, Messieur,' Matthew Coombe said, and the shorn head nodded.

'Ah! The silver lad, hunh? What do they want?' He spoke English well enough, as most Breton seafarers do.

'We have come for information,' I said, 'about the Flemish lad who sailed with you to Cork.'

'Him hunh? I want no more of him. But you are from the English king? And come to buy the letter?'

I did not let any bewilderment show on my face. 'I merely ask for information about him, where he joined you, and if you know where he was born.'

'How much?' he asked. A rose-noble, after he had tested it with his teeth, bought the information that Warbeck had come aboard at Lisbon, and that his birthplace was unknown. 'But he has gone from Cork now,' the Breton added, 'and I have the letter.'

Gone from Cork? I kept my face expressionless as I gave him another noble. 'He sailed for France soon after the Frenchman who brought the letter. I will sell it to the English king for a thousand crowns.'

Anderson whistled at the enormous sum, but I waved him to silence. 'How did you come by it?' I asked the Breton.

A slow smile spread itself across the weather-carved face. 'He is but a boy and was overcome by the prospect it offered. He threw it down in his excitement, and later could not find it.' The smile grew broader. 'The English king will pay a thousand crowns for it, I know.'

'I am empowered to pay no more than twenty crowns,' I told him.

Pregent Meno shrugged and turned away towards his cabin. Anderson whispered in my ear, 'Why don't we take it off him?' But I waved him down again. Then, as the Breton opened the door, he said over his shoulder, 'The King of France will pay more than that to have it back.'

'Not he!' I said confidently. 'He will have you seized and the letter taken from you, or put you to the torture to say where it is.'

'Not he!' Pregent Meno mimicked. 'I will send news of it to him from a Breton port, where he cannot touch me, except to send his man with the money, like you.'

'You think to find safety in Brittany,' I said, 'when there will be a French Customs officer in every port?' That held him, and I added, 'Brittany has surrendered to the French king. It is now part of France.'

The grey, stubbly jaw dropped, then clenched again. 'I do not believe it,' he said obstinately.

'Then take your letter back to Brittany and see how you fare, my friend,' I said, turning away and beckoning to the others.

'Wait!' Pregent Meno said. 'Is this true?' he demanded of Matthew Coombe.

Matthew shrugged. 'The news has not reached Bristol yet, Messieur,' he replied, 'but if my uncle says so then it must be true.'

We left the Breton ship-master with a despondent look on his face, even if his pocket was heavier by twenty crowns. It was money well spent. The document was signed by Stephen Frion, as Secretary to King Charles the Eighth of France. It invited his highness King Richard the Fourth of England to take up residence at the French court, whence the king himself would further the Yorkist cause. It seemed to me that King Henry Tudor would not be averse to repaying me my twenty crowns.

CHAPTER 28

T H E King himself addressed the lords in parliament. He told them that the occupation of Brittany was an insult to the realm, that the treaty with that duchy must be honoured and, above all, that English blood had been shed and must be avenged. The speech stirred them, especially the reference to English blood, and brought acclamation. The taxes which the King asked for were granted without demur.

All that spring preparations were made. Musters were held in each county, and men came with enthusiasm. There had not been a foreign war since King Edward's time, and the prospect of booty in France was alluring.

There was also much activity at Sheen Manor. A new nursery and chapel were being built for the infant Prince Henry. That child already had a washerwoman of his own, as well as two trumpeters. Then there was the normal establishment of chief nurses, wet-nurses, cradle rockers and seamstresses, all of which infuriated the five-year-old Prince Arthur, who tormented his young brother beyond reason. Perhaps it was because he suspected a rival for the affections of his baby sister, Princess Margaret, whom he adored. Whatever the reason, Queen Elizabeth was heard to sigh with relief when the nursery was finished and the child could be housed separately. At Eastertide the Prince of Wales was further pacified by being given his bath in six gallons of sweet wine, and a painted cart with wheels that actually turned, costing nine pence, and against which King Henry had put his personal sign-manual.

Another infant contributed his part to the din, but this was one of a lower station, and already known to the Household Guards as Nick. He had no retinue of servants, but the Lady Margaret Beaufort took almost as much interest in him as the royal children, and Matilda was content.

'I will have him apprenticed to a silver-smith like my nephew, she announced one day, 'then, unlike his father, he will live in peace.'

'Or like Matthew, he will have a mind of his own.'

'Jesu!' she shuddered, 'And go to sea? And be away for longer periods than even you?' She put her arms round me. 'When all I can do is to pray to the Holy Virgin that you will come back safe.'

'She has kept me alive so far,' I said.

'Aye, with scars on your face, a limp in your foot, and great holes in your chest and back. What could happen next time?'

At the mention of those holes my face set hard. She saw my expression, and cried, 'And all you think of is to repay Sir William Stanley! Cannot you see, Henry Morane, that it is no longer possible? He is too close to the King these days, too powerful for someone like you to harm.'

'His pride must unseat him in the end. And his rancour at Prince Arthur being created earl of Chester is barely concealed. King Henry must have noticed it.'

'Yet the King treats him as a friend, listens to his counsel. . .'

'King Henry is no fool. Stanley has already raised five thousand men for the war, and his fat brother more than that. Is this a time for him to exhibit suspicion?'

She sighed, then smiled a little. 'Well, at least you should not refer to the Earl of Derby as his 'fat brother'. If the Lady Margaret were to hear you refer to her husband as such. . .' She did not finish, but kissed me instead.

The enthusiasm for the war was greater than the money available to pay for it. The taxes granted by parliament would not be enough and were, as always, difficult to collect. Archbishop John Morton revived King Edward's system of Benevolences, loans made out of goodwill towards the King, and which would never be repaid. It was a practice Dickon had refused to continue, but Morton was not above using Yorkist methods if they served. And he had another, more direct way of assessing tax, suggested by Richard Foxe. Those who flaunted their opulence clearly had enough to pay more, and those of the nobility who lived frugally were deemed to have saved their wealth, and could do the same.

It was a dilemma none could escape, and soon became known as Morton's Fork. I told Matilda that, noble or not, it was as well I had not dug up anything from Leicester forest.

It was then that the Duke of Suffolk died, he who had married one of Dickon's sisters and fathered the rebel earl, John of Lincoln. The new heir, Edmund, said flatly that he could not afford King Henry's price for the dukedom, and settled for five thousand pounds to remain an earl. By this and other like methods the King was able to finance the war.

The adventure was to be launched from Portsmouth, and an army of carpenters and masons was the first to arrive there to build three great breweries for the soldiers. I heard afterwards that King Henry's plan was to assist Brittany by seizing the sea-port of Brest, but I did not see how he could re-establish its independence now that its duchess was Queen of France. In the event, the news of the activity at Portsmouth reached King Charles, and he sent an envoy threatening to seize the Isle of Wight if it continued. The threat could not be ignored, because Charles had ships of his own, while King Henry would have to rely mainly on galleys hired from Venice. After that the soldiers were re-assembled at Sandwich and Dover, ostensibly as a reinforcement for Calais, to which Charles could not object.

At that time, too, Elizabeth Woodville died at Bermondsey, in the convent to which she had been banished before the Simnel rebellion. Consort of King Edward the Fourth, mother of Queen Elizabeth and the lads in the Tower, and a trouble maker all her life, she died in obscurity, her body being carried up the river to Windsor to be buried in her husband's tomb. No bells were rung, no dirges chanted, and the only follower of the coffin was her youngest daughter, Bridget, herself a nun at Dartford Priory. Matilda and I watched the barge as it was rowed past Sheen, but the Queen kept to her chamber, and her grief to herself. Then, in May, a summons for me came from West Minster. Christopher Urswick had returned from the court of Archduke Maximilian.

CHAPTER 29

T O go by road from Sheen to London takes longer than by boat to West Minster, but the weather was fair, the countryside wild with spring flowers, lunatic hares and other small animals, and young birds hopping with curiosity in their bright new surroundings. Even the sheep seemed to move out of my way more quickly, their new-born lambs stopping to peer at me, then leaping into the air as if propelled by a sudden jet from the warm grass below. After all this time, I told myself, Master Urswick could wait a few more hours, and, besides, I had a debt to pay in London first. The crossing of the Bridge was as slow as I had expected, for a horseman is at a disadvantage in that narrow street between the houses unless he has retainers to clear the way, but I reached Mehmet's stables in the end, and then found that he would take no payment for the horse that had been stolen from me.

His nephew regarded me as an uncle, he said, and therefore, as an honorary brother he could take no recompense. Perhaps though, he added with a bland look on his face, if ever I were to travel across the sea I might deliver some jewels and gold coin for him, as the exportation of these had recently been forbidden by the English king. As to Ali, he went on quickly, that feckless spawn had gone back to Europe and was no doubt wasting his uncle's substance in some thieves' market place. But he had left messages, as well as a jug of diabolical spirit which Mehmet had kept for me even though it was against all principle to house such evil stuff in the home of a True Believer.

The jug of diabolical spirit was produced, followed by much sad head shaking when its guardian inspected the contents. It was remarkable, he said, his Saracen eyes limpid with innocence, how quickly the spirit evaporated in this English clime. I nodded in sympathy, suggesting that he assist me to outpace the weather and empty the jug. After a proper show of reluctance,

164

followed by an expression of distaste after each mouthful, he finally agreed that it would have been a pity to waste Ali's gift to the London air. Then he went to the stable and came back with a wooden box, and pulled out a roll of paper. It was covered with designs that might have been made by a demented astrologer, but which he said was written by Ali in the language of the Turk. He would read me its message, which I must commit to memory, as the paper must be destroyed forthwith. He, a Saracen in London, could not risk keeping messages from overseas in these troubled times. It seemed to me that if the paper were found he would as likely be burned at Smithfield as a warlock than hanged as a spy, but, as the end would be the same, I gave him the assurance he required.

At West Minster the Painted Chamber was almost as thick with people as London Bridge. But they were no ordinary citizens; earls, barons, knights and captains were turned towards the dais at the other end where King Henry was holding his Council, fenced in by the pikes of Joseph Anderson and other Yeomen of the Guard. I worked my way through the crowd until I came to the black beard, and saw that with the King were the most important men in the realm. Apart from the priests, led by Morton, there was Uncle Jasper duke of Bedford, the earls of Oxford, Devon and Arundel as well as the 'fat brother' Thomas Stanley earl of Derby, and the Lord Chamberlain. Thomas Howard of Surrey was there, too, and I knew that the meeting must be important to have brought him all the way from York.

'They're planning the war,' Anderson murmured complacently. 'And they've been at it for several hours without refreshment, or even time to relieve the weak bladders that priests are supposed to have, especially an old man like Morton.' He grinned. 'I can't see behind me, but has he started shifting from one foot to the other yet? For when the Archbishop of Canterbury wants to piss. . .'

'We can collect it and sell it for Holy Water like they do with the Pope's in Rome,' I laughed. 'Ah! It will not be long now. He has begun to fiddle with his privies.'

When the interval came King Henry looked up. The

royal forefinger, long and bony, beckoned to me and I went forward to make my obeisance. Thomas Howard nodded a greeting, and then I saw the slight figure of Christopher Urswick. He gave me a thin smile, but the others ignored me.

'Master Morane!' the King said, waving me up. 'We commend you on your recent journey. We have at least learned of those who are supposed to be our friends.' Some of the others looked blank. They had not been told of the French Secretary, it seemed. 'Yet,' King Henry went on, 'as the Garson eluded you we have yet to discover his origins.'

'I have further information now, Your Grace,' I said.

'You have? Then we will all hear it.'

'He is registered in the civic rolls of Tournai in Flanders as the son of Jehan Warbeque, a customs' collector and boatman of that town,' I said, repeating carefully what I had learned from Ali's message. 'He was brought up by his father's sister and apprenticed to Berlo, a merchant. He tired of that and went to Portugal in the service of a one-eyed knight called Vacz da Cogna.' I did not include the time he had spent at the court of the Dowager Duchess Margaret. That could come when fewer ears were present.

'Ah!' The green eyes narrowed. 'Then he is not of Yorkist blood?'

'Unless the records have been falsified,' Archbishop Morton said, coming back and still fiddling with his gown.

'Or,' Sir William Stanley said airily, 'the information itself is false.'

'Then we will hear how Morane learned it,' the King said, with a quick glance at him.

I bowed, drawing in my breath, 'Sire.' I said, 'I would humbly ask your forebearance in the answer to that.'

The earls of Derby and Oxford drew in their breaths, and John Morton made a noise of exasperation. But Jasper Tudor gave a loud guffaw. 'There you have it! he said. 'We know Morane for a bold fellow. Now it seems he is unwilling to risk his informant. We can conclude, look you, that it must have been a woman.'

166

'My lord!' I protested with as much dignity as I could muster.

'All right, all right, man,' he grinned. 'I am sure His Grace will respect your friend if the information is for the good of the realm.'

King Henry smiled a little. 'So long as it is accurate,' he said.

'I would swear to it, Sire,' I said quickly.

'One spy swearing to another,' Sir William Stanley observed, looking out of the window. Then he swung round at me. 'Or have you been to Flanders yourself to gain this information?'

He would have liked the answer to that, I knew. I gave him a benign smile that brought fury to his face. 'With respect, my lord,' I said, 'I should prefer not to be called a spy. As I dig deeply to gather the King's intelligence, a mole would be a better description.'

'A mole!' Jasper Tudor laughed out loud. 'Aye, Master Morane, the King's Mole, it is!'

They all laughed, except for Stanley and the priests. Then King Henry brought them to order. 'My lords,' he said, 'we have heard from Master Urswick that the Archduke Maximilian cannot move against France as he has what is called 'a sore flux of the purse'.' He smiled. 'But that will be remedied when he succeeds his father as Holy Roman Emperor, which may not be long delayed as his father ails badly. But we cannot depend upon it yet.'

'And even when his purse is filled again,' Morton said, 'he will likely empty it again on musicians, painters and such fellows. Indeed we cannot depend upon it. But. . .' he turned to Urswick '. . .we have it from France that King Charles is more than ever enthused with designs upon Italy, and Naples in particular. In this the Holy Father encourages him, hoping to ensnare him in another crusade against the Turk.' I had heard that before, but Morton went on, 'Therefore, Sire,' he said to the King, 'this cozening of the Flemish garson is no more than a counterweight. As soon as he is assured that yours is no empty threat he will make haste to bargain for the fellow.'

There was a silence while they considered this. I

saw Christopher Urswick eyeing me, and shook my head slightly.

King Henry noticed the gesture. 'Yes, Master Morane? Have you further to say before you take your leave?'

'Your Grace,' I bowed, 'it is said that the Holy Father ails too, even more grievously than the Holy Roman Emperor. The cardinals are already busy considering the next election.'

This time it was Morton's breath that was sucked in. If the Pope were to die what would happen to the Cardinal's Hat he had been promised? 'I have heard nothing of this,' he said, but his voice was unsure.

'Indeed, there was talk of it at Maximilian's court,' Christopher Urswick put in. 'But it was thought to be no more than a passing ailment. How certain is this?' he said to me.

'I could not swear to hearsay,' I replied, with a glance at Jasper Tudor. 'But it is being wagered in Rome that a certain cardinal will succeed, as he is already spending vast sums on the others to ensure his own selection.'

'Great God in Heaven!' Lord Stanley exploded. 'The imputation is slanderous!'

'Look at who it comes from,' his brother added silkily.

Archbishop John Morton looked me up and down, and swung round to the King. 'By your leave, Sire, the slander must be punished.'

'My lord,' I said to him, 'I only repeat for His Grace's own information what I have learned.'

'Then perhaps you will oblige us with the name of this cardinal.'

'Certainly, sir. He is of Spanish descent, a Borgia. Cardinal Alexander Borgia, father of the better known soldier, Cesare Borgia.'

'That one, eh?' Jasper Tudor said. 'Well then, if the Cardinal's his father I wouldn't put it past him.'

King Henry wrote in his little book, then looked up. 'My lords,' he said, 'we shall delay our attack until the autumn.' Oxford moved forward in protest, but the King went on. 'By then the question of these two ailing men may be resolved and King Charles will be further immersed in his preparations for Italy. Besides,' he smiled, 'as he thinks he is such a master of strategy he will not be expecting us at that season.'

Afterwards, Thomas Howard put a hand on my shoulder. 'I trust, for your sake, Morane, that your information is correct.'

'I have no reason to doubt it, my lord,' Christopher Urswick said, 'knowing its source. . .' his dull eyes turned on me '. . . a certain Saracen with a golden tooth who travels Europe frequently, and whose activities include smuggling in and out of the realm, which could be called treason if he were caught, eh, Morane?'

'Then let us hope he is not caught, hey?' Surrey laughed.

'Aye,' Urswick said gravely. 'It would be a pity.'

*   *   *

On the second of October in that year of 1492 twenty-five thousand English soldiers began crossing from Sandwich to Calais. On the eighteenth of that month they marched down the coast and laid siege to Boulogne. Nine days later Archbishop Morton was proved right, for an offer of terms was received from King Charles, and on the third of November a treaty of peace was signed at Etaples. The war was over. The French army had not even put in an appearance.

King Henry did very well out of the treaty of Etaples. He recovered all his expenditure in Brittany — no less than 620,000 gold crowns — as well as the arrears under the treaty King Edward of York had imposed seventeen years before. That was a further 125,000 gold crowns, and the whole was to be paid in annual instalments of five thousand pounds until the year 1511. All mention of Brittany had been carefully excluded from the treaty, for King Henry had known from the start that its restoration was beyond his strength. And now, with so much greater wealth, he was in a position of unchallenged security at home, and he had shown the rest of Europe that England had a power of its own.

There was one further clause in the treaty. King Charles agreed not to support any enemies of the English crown. That took the fire out of any ambition the Scots might have nourished, and it also meant that Perkin Warbeck would be expelled from the French court. No one could deny the astuteness of King Henry, even though many of his nobles were indignant. While they had been repaid to the penny for their expenditure, they complained that they had been put to inconvenience in mustering their men and, worse, had been deprived of the opportunity for glory and the loot that went with it. It was exactly the same situation that had faced King Edward of York after the earlier treaty, but then the only dissenter had been his brother Dickon, always athirst for a fight.

The City of London gave the King a great reception on his return. The streets were decked with banners, wine flowed from the conduits, and there was music everywhere. The aldermen and merchants had not wanted war, and if the nobles retained their resentment they kept it concealed.

The citizens of Calais gave a sigh of relief too. All the soldiers had gone home, and they could go about their business peacefully again. One important soldier, however, had not. Sir John Savage had been killed by a sortie from Boulogne while riding close to its wall to inspect the damage done by English guns. He was the brother of Thomas Savage, bishop of Rochester, one of those sent to negotiate the marriage of Catherine of Aragon. He was also a nephew of Lord Stanley, which was no recommendation, and neither was his defection from Dickon a few days before Bosworth, of which we should not have been warned had not I heard Lord Stanley's son gasp it out when stretched upon the rack. It had been Sir John Savage's white-hooded men who had killed the Duke of Norfolk at that battle, and taken prisoner his son, the earl of Surrey. I knew that when Thomas Howard heard the news he would not shed any tears. Thus perished another traitor of Bosworth field, although I had no hand in the matter. But it served to reinforce my faith that the greatest traitor of them all would not escape his deserts, in spite of what Matilda believed.

CHAPTER 30

P E R K I N Warbeck did not go to the court of his sponsor, the Dowager Duchess Margaret, at Malines as expected, but was invited by the Archduke Maximilian to Antwerp instead. The invitation was not only a surprise to King Henry, it was a direct affront. And when Maximilian's father, the Holy Roman Emperor, died a few months later, Warbeck went to the funeral at Vienna as an honoured guest. Once in Antwerp again Maximilian announced that the Garson was the true king of England, and granted him the arms of King Richard the Fourth as well as those of the White Rose of York. Thereupon Perkin Warbeck set up his own court in Antwerp, much to the disgust of the English residents there, who bombarded his 'palace' with stones, garbage and rotten eggs.

King Henry thereupon sent Sir Edward Poynings, a knight of long and loyal service, and William Warham, a formidable advocate, to protest to Maximilian. The latter gave evasive answers, saying that he could not be responsible for the acts of his mother-in-law, the Duchess Margaret, who had her own domains, and even though he was Regent of the Netherlands for his son, the young Duke Philip, it was only nominal, as the regency council refused to accept him as such, and he could do nothing without Philip's consent. It was a quibbling reply, as might be expected from that fickle Archduke, now Holy Roman Emperor, and King Henry's retaliation was sharp. All trade between Flanders and England was forbidden, and the Wool Market, the Great Staple, was moved from Antwerp to Calais, thus ruining the Flemish weavers who depended on English wool, the best in the world. It was a drastic measure, and there was much discontent among English Merchants, to whom Calais was no more than a provincial town, and no market place for the rest of Europe.

In the meantime Christopher Urswick had been in

Scotland, arranging a new treaty. Soon after his return he sent for me.

'You are for Flanders,' he said without preamble.

My heart sank. Life was peaceful at Sheen with Matilda and young Nicholas, who was now wrestling companion to the new Prince Henry. 'Who am I to kidnap now?' I inquired. 'The Emperor Maximilian?'

Christopher Urswick clicked his tongue. 'This is no time for facetiousness, Henry Morane. The King desires information about this Garson Warbeck. While he is no danger to us of himself there are others who would use him to stir up trouble in the realm.'

'No?' I said. 'Surely not the Emperor and the Duchess Margaret?'

He waved the irony aside. 'There are others more closely concerned,' he went on impatiently. 'As with Lambert Simnel. But with him his associates were known, whereas now we have only the names of less important people, knights and others of lower rank who have fled abroad to the Garson. But we have cause to believe that he may be in secret communication with others of more exalted station in this country, perhaps even close to the throne, and your open departure from here would arouse suspicion.'

Close to the throne? Open departure? I stared at him.

'Aye, Henry Morane. I will come to the point.' He saw my face and frowned. 'If the Garson is sending messages here we have not been able to intercept any from Antwerp for a year and more. Neither have any of those whose names we know dared to return bringing them by word of mouth. Therefore we are sure that the Duchess is sending them for him from Malines.'

'But hers is a court where Englishmen are unwelcome,' I objected.

'Except those disaffected with the present regime.'

I saw what he meant. 'I am to go to Malines?' I said hollowly.

'That is not the intention,' he replied, and I let my breath out slowly. 'For, even though the Duchess acts as agent for the Garson, and sends messages for him, there must come a point when she has to meet the person she is in communication with — or his accredited

172

representative — and that person must be able to visit her and return to this country without exciting suspicion. Such a person could not risk being seen at Malines, where they must know we have resident spies.'

'Where then?' I asked him.

'Why,' he smiled, 'at some town on her Progress. Like all other rulers she must make a Progress round her domains from time to time to show herself to her subjects, and we have just heard that she is to make another. If she is to meet anyone privily from this country it will be at one of her towns. And that, Morane, is the reason for your immediate departure.'

'If she meets anyone at all,' I objected.

'Maybe not. But it is more likely on this Progress than the last, two years ago. Matters are nearer the boil now, since Maximilian has recently promised the Garson aid in ships if the Duchess will furnish the soldiers.' He smiled thinly. 'It seems he still needs soldiers for Hungary. And that, Morane, is the reason for your secret departure.'

'But I would be suspected of disaffection, even of treachery.'

He eyed me and nodded slowly, then went on to explain.

'No!' I said. 'It is too dangerous. I will not do it.'

He went on eyeing me. Then he said, 'You are aware of the recent ban on all trade with Flanders?' Without waiting for a reply, he went on. 'Yet, in spite of it, there are many who defy the ban. If they are caught they will suffer the penalty, the penalty of treason.'

'What is that to do with it?'

'I was merely wondering,' he said as if to himself, 'whether a certain golden-toothed Saracen might be engaged in such activities. . .'

'Body of God!' I said with disgust. 'You would stoop to intriguing against my friends?'

'I have no intention of intriguing against your friends,' he said coldly. 'What I am saying is that, should he be caught at it, he would be given all assistance by me. . . by us. Provided you are still in the King's service,' he added after a moment. He got up and put a hand on my arm. 'See here, Morane, there is more to this than I can explain. If I were to mention those in this country whom I suspect, without proof, it would be the end of me, for King Henry could give me no support. It is that proof which I need.'

'Aaaah!' I growled. 'And when must I go?'

'A ship at Greenwich already waits for two passengers for Dixmude.'

'Two?'

'Two. You may need assistance. Who else but Captain Anderson?'

I nodded. 'He will not be pleased. He enjoys his present life of idleness, even though he would never admit it.'

'Then he will be given the means to enjoy it the more when he returns,' was the reply, 'if you are successful.' A finger waved at me. 'But remember, Morane, no harm must come to any foreign citizen of importance. The Emperor Maximilian must be given no opportunity for recrimination. It is only the information that we need.' He began to smile. 'And you, as a mole, will dig it up. And . . .' the smile broadened '. . . as a carrier-pigeon, will bring it back.'

'A carrier-pigeon?' I said bitterly. 'More like a target-crow.'

CHAPTER 31

T H E royal fingernail scraped gently through the sparse hairs on my chest, met the hard ring of flesh and stopped short. Then it began slowly to explore the edges of the scar.

'A wound, Master Morane?' she inquired. 'A sword-blade? Or perhaps the thrust of a spear?'

'A sword, madam. Its fellow adorns my back.'

Another hand went round me and found the place. 'So it does,' she smiled. 'It went right through you, then? Only the Holy Virgin could have helped you survive such a thrust.'

'I would believe it so,' I agreed. 'Although . . .' I smiled at her '. . . it is also said that the Devil looks after his own.'

At that Margaret, Duchess of Burgundy, sat up suddenly, taking her arms away from me. She crossed herself, making a grand sweep of it, touching each naked breast in turn, and then the jewelled crucifix that hung between them. The pale blue eyes hardened.

'May the Mother of God forgive you for that, Henry Morane!'

Then she smiled again and, in spite of her forty and more years, she was beautiful again. 'But *I* would forgive you if it was in the service of my brother Dickon.'

I met her gaze and nodded. It could have been argued that I had received the wound in the service of King Richard the Third, but no doubt Sir William Stanley, the owner of the sword, would have had it otherwise. Yet Sir William was far away in England, and Margaret was very much at hand. It was no time for equivocation. I nodded again, more firmly.

She sighed, and for a while was quiet. I could hear the whisperings and muted giggles of her servants as they waited beyond the curtains of the ducal lying place. Some of the afternoon sunshine fought its way through the coloured glasses of the windows, designed with mysterious creatures. There were griffins, chimeras,

and dragons such as the amphisbena with a head at each
end, the manticora, as big as a lion with a man's head,
and winged salamanders with ice dripping from their
scales, armoured rhinoceroses and sparrow-camels as
described by Marco Polo, and all entwined with magic
trees bearing young geese for fruit. This castle at Hesdin
had been re-built by an earlier Duke Philip and contained many devices to entrap the unwary. Bridges
stood over streams in the park which collapsed under a
stranger, holes in the floors which blew soot up the
skirts of women, and strange voices that spoke from
suits of armour.

The yellow light made a chequered pattern on the
silks around us, giving lustre to her flaxen hair, and
making her resemblance to her Yorkist kin more pronounced. But that resemblance was to her older
brothers, King Edward the Fourth and George of
Clarence, rather than to the younger Richard, for Dickon had been short and stocky, and dark of mane; yet
he, perhaps because they had been brought up close, had
been her favourite.

'I would hear more of it, Master Morane,' she said at
length. 'Was it on that dreadful day at Bosworth Field?'

I sat up, more confident now. I told her of the battle,
although she had heard many accounts of it, and said
that I had been wounded early, and thus did not know
many details. It was a lie that saved me having to
explain Sir William Stanley's part in it, for there was
something that forbade me from mentioning his name
at that juncture. There was some vagueness, some un-
certainty which I could feel, as one senses a viol string
that has not been quite fully stretched.

'And then the battle at Stoke?' she asked, 'where my
nephew John of Lincoln so nearly unseated the Tudor
upstart?'

That was more difficult, for she had her sources of
information, and was no fool. Then she said, 'And
how did Sir William Stanley fight?'

Concealing my astonishment, I said, 'He brought his
men too late to enter the battle.'

'Then he did not fight on the side of the Tudor?'

I shook my head and wondered, for she had given a

small sigh. I thought quickly. Here I was at the court of Margaret of Burgundy, who only welcomed disaffected Englishmen, and whose reputation for comparing their prowess today with those of her own time was common gossip. I turned suddenly and held out my arms to her.

'What, Master Morane?' she inquired, affecting surprise. 'You would have your pleasure of me thrice?'

'Thrice, madam? Oh, no!' I smiled at her. 'Twice only. The first time was but the privilege. It was the next that was the pleasure.'

At that she laughed and put her arms round me again. I hoped it would serve to divert her attention from other, more complicated matters.

*   *   *

'Whatever else,' she murmured, some time after. 'You are my man, Henry Morane?'

'I was Dickon's man,' I replied gravely.

'For I have it that your name is on the Bead-roll of the Welsh usurper's enemies preached every Sunday at Saint Paul's.'

'It is no more than could be expected,' I said with as much nonchalance as I might. Yet, even if expected, to be publicly denounced as a traitor still comes as a shock to the ears. It was also a shock to hear that she knew of it so quickly. 'Although,' I went on, 'I did not hear it when I was at Paul's yard two weeks ago.'

She smiled. 'Such news travels fast, Master Morane, the more so when new names are added to the Bead-roll.'

'Mine cannot be of such import as to warrant special intelligence.'

'The names of all Englishmen are important if my nephew is affected.'

I made a noise of assent, wondering for a moment to which nephew she referred, but quickly realised that it must be to the Garson Warbeck.

'Come,' she said, 'we will move from here tomorrow. This castle of Hesdin is too close to the smell of Tudor soldiers in Calais for my comfort. You will accompany me to Malines to pay your respects to my nephew, son of King Edward of York and rightful heir to the throne

177

of England.' She clapped her hands, the drapes were drawn aside, and two of her women stood there with a silver-braided cloak for her, and a linen one for me. It was as if they had been waiting for her command, well rehearsed in their duties.

The woman who held out her gown was a crone of uncertain age with a face of parchment, and the bleak and resentful eyes of one who had supervised much sin without being able to take part in it. I gave her a huge wink, which froze the parchment and narrowed the eyes, which then looked me up and down as if I were one of the toads that were said to inhabit the dungeons of Hesdin castle. As she covered her mistress, she said, 'Your secretary waits in the Presence Room, your highness. He has been there this past hour.'

'That is part of a secretary's duties,' the Duchess snapped. 'See to it that Master Morane joins me soon after.' With that she turned and stalked off towards the arras, her brocades swirling behind her. The other women rushed after her, leaving me with the crone.

'What is your name, mistress?' I asked her.

'It is not your affair. I am the duchess's lady. That is enough.' She spoke in French.

I shook my head and essayed a smile. 'I ask, madam, because you are from England, not France or Flanders. And when you addressed your mistress it was in the speech of London. And I am from London too.'

She hesitated while the bleak eyes inspected me. 'Where in London?' This time the words were in English.

'By the Wall Brook.'

'The Wall Brook!' She clapped her hands together. 'Good sir, it is a dozen years since I saw that clear, running water. Does it still run smooth?'

'It does,' I laughed. 'But not so clear. The fishmongers cast their offals in it now.'

'But there are city ordinances . . .!' She stopped, remembering where she was.

But I would have her forget for a while. 'Twelve years?' I said. 'It must have been when the Duchess Margaret visited England to see her brothers, and Edward was king.'

'Aye, good sir.' The eyes were no longer bleak. 'The greatest king of all.'

178

The women of England had loved King Edward, a giant of a man who had charmed them all. I smiled. 'I was clerk to him,' I told her. 'And to Dickon who followed. I look for revenge on those who killed him.'

'On the Tudor?'

I took a risk. I shook my head. 'Not so much on him. He was only a tool, a knife in the hands of the butchers who used it.'

She stood back and eyed me carefully. 'You would help to unseat him, though?'

'I would first have the blood of those who killed Dickon.' At that she sighed, and I went on, 'Yet would this Perkin Warbeck measure up to such a one as Dickon?'

'Warbeck? Perkin?' She made as if to spit. 'A lovely boy. A fitting mate for other beautiful boys, no more. I would . . .' There had been a movement by the arras. She swung round quickly, pointing a finger at it. 'Come out, you little wretch!'

The drape was moved aside and the 'wretch' came out. He was no taller than my waist, a sad-eyed little dwarf. 'I crave your pardon, Madame de Beaugrant,' he said, 'but I would hear more of King Dickon, who they say was under-sized too.'

'Alas,' I said to him, 'I cannot comfort you in that, my friend. He was nearly of my own height, yet stronger of arm and broader of back. And a man with even more troubles on it than you.'

The dwarf regarded me morosely, then nodded as if to himself, and walked away with dragging steps.

'One of the dwarfs of the Duchess Margaret, for which she is well known?' I asked Madame de Beaugrant.

'Aye, sir. But now the only one. The . . .' She stopped suddenly for I had pulled her towards me and given her a kiss. It was no more than a salute to a fellow-countryman, but she clung to me for a moment before disengaging herself. 'Jesu!' she said. 'You must not do that, sir!' But her eyes were very bright. 'Come,' she went on, 'my lady will wonder where you are.' As she led me out of the chamber she whispered in my ear. 'Take care, good sir. My mistress could lose her enchantment with you as quickly as a storm cloud hides the summer sun.'

And in that it looked as if she might be correct, for I almost halted in my stride as I saw the secretary. It was Stephen Frion.

CHAPTER 32

H E stood on one leg, the other foot resting on its fellow. But Stephen Frion was no longer the pale shadow that flittered at the edges of the Tudor court. Now he was geared like a duke, in soft linen and a blue gown edged with fur, a feather in his cap, and perfumed like a tilting horse. His wide-set eyes looked me up and down. I gave him a bow, and a deeper one to the Duchess Margaret. There was an unrolled parchment in her hand.

'Ha, Master Morane,' she said, 'there is news from Spain.'

I waited, wondering how news from Spain could concern me.

'It seems that Messer Colombo, or, as he would have it,' she added contemptuously, 'Admiral Colombus of the Ocean Sea, has returned from Cathay and makes provision for a second voyage to plant a colony.'

'Indeed, madam?' I could not help but stare at her.

'Indeed, Master Morane,' she repeated, the pale Yorkist eyes inspecting me as if I were a stranger. 'He seeks recruits. It will be to your advantage to be one of them.'

'But madam, I have no acquaintance of him. And Spain is far. . .'

'You have acquaintance of his brother. And with my recommendation it can be arranged.'

I remembered that Bartholomew Colombus had gone from England to the French court, and Stephen Frion had been there. I turned to look at him. He stared back at me without expression.

'It will be to your advantage, Master Morane,' Duchess Margaret repeated. 'For I am a woman of mercy. And my secretary informs me that, in spite of your name being on the Bead-roll at Paul's Yard, you are still in the service of the Tudor upstart.'

I held in the bee that murmured in my stomach and nodded casually.

'I have been, madam,' I admitted. 'But through

181

necessity.' I pointed a finger at Stephen Frion. 'But was he not also? And is his name not being preached against?'

She smiled. Straightaway I saw her brother Edward, gory from the field at Tewkesbury, as he prepared to break into the abbey sanctuary and drag out Lord Somerset for execution. The cold smile had been the same.

'I will be the judge of that, Master Morane. My secretary has been directing intelligence for me these several years now.'

So that was it! Here was one of the traitors of the Tudor court in his true colours. His visit to Charles of France had been no more than to try and persuade that monarch to support the Garson with men and arms against England. He might have succeeded but for the cupidity of the French king for the greater glory to be gained in Italy. King Charles' ambition was such that he had even sent French mountaineers to scale L'Aiguille, an alpine peak hitherto considered inaccessible.

'You are too merciful, madame.' Stephen Frion spoke for the first time. 'To hang him now would show the Welshman that his spies can attain nothing here.' His hands began to caress each other.

Margaret, Dowager Duches of Burgundy, contemplated me. 'Perhaps you are right, Master Frion,' she said after a moment. 'Then have him locked away while I consider that question . . .' King Edward's smile appeared again '. . . or whether the executioner's instruments might bring us the truth of the matter.' She clapped her hands together, summoning the guards.

*   *   *

If one has the choice of where to be incarcerated — when such a penance can not be avoided — I should prefer a cell in my own land. English rats are better fed and, after a preliminary examination of a newcomer, oft times leave him to his own devices. This is not so in the case of foreign rodents, or at least of those in Flanders. My arrival was greeted with shrill squeals of anticipation, and the gloom around me was flecked with the red points of eager little eyes. They held back at first, which allowed me to recover a little from the shock of being dropped through the grating on to the stone floor below, and then they moved in. Scores of vicious, hairy bodies swarmed over me, making tentative bites through my clothing as if to test whether my flesh tasted better than the local sort, but soon the bites grew sharper.

I had no weapon, not even boots, for the jailer had taken them, and was hard put to beat them off. And then I found by chance that, by strangling one of them, they favoured the meat of their own kind over that of any other, and even preferred that it should not be quite dead. I seized one wriggling body after another, breaking it between my hands and throwing it aside quickly, so that in the end, sated like the Cannibals of Africa, they drew away. But I knew it would not be long before others heard of their discovery, or the smell of my blood brought the toads from their crevices in the walls.

The grating was in the floor of the passage above, at the end of which I had seen a cresset on the wall, so that some light filtered down to me. But of air there was less. The smell of countless prisoners who had been in there before hung thick in the shadows. The terror, and the ordure it brings, permeated the very stones, so that I leaned against the wall, fighting against my nausea. For in a dungeon there is no sewer to lead away the filth.

Yet the grating was not too high to reach, and the stink up there might be less. I jumped upwards and hooked my fingers round the iron squares, but before I could draw myself higher a heavy boot ground on my knuckles, and I fell back to lean against the wall again, trying to stem the blood with pieces from my tattered shirt.

I had no means of knowing how much time passed before the cresset in the passage above flickered, guttered and grew dim. It would have to be replaced, and then at least I might hear human voices. But it was not replaced, and after some time a single mutton-candle was held above me.

'Hist!' a voice said quietly. 'Do you live?'

'Aye,' I grunted. 'What of it to you?'

'Then help me raise this grille.'

I climbed up to it quickly, and saw, in the candle-flame, the tiny face of the dwarf. 'What . . .?' I began.

'Quiet!' he hissed. 'I am too small to have the strength. You must push from below.'

'Ah!' I groaned. 'I cannot, for my feet will not touch the floor.' The iron-work was heavy, and lay squarely in its recess by its own weight. They had lifted it to throw me in by hauling at a chain which ran over a wheel in the ceiling. Then the thought came to me. 'Where is the other end of the chain?' I asked him.

'The chain? Ah!' There was a pause while he put the candle down, and then a clank. 'Here it is,' he said. 'It was on its hook in the wall. I'll drop it through and you can pull your weight on it.'

'Alas,' I told him, 'even if I had the strength it would be of little use. For I'd have to let it go before I can climb out, and then it would crush me as it fell.'

'Ah, yes!' This time there was a longer interval. Then I heard something heavy being dragged across the floor, and much hard breathing from the dwarf. When he sat down, gasping, I saw what he had been struggling with. It was the body of the jailer. 'Now!' he said, 'when you pull at the chain I will try and shove him under the grating to prop it up. Can you do your part?'

I made no reply, but seized the iron links. I did not think I would have the strength, but fear and desperation gave it to me. The grating creaked, rose slowly for a few inches, and then I fell back, rubbing my wrists in their pain. The ironwork should have fallen back with a clang, but it did not. The dwarf had pushed the jailer's leg across the gap. I heard him chuckle. 'Once more,' he called down, 'and the rest of him goes through.'

But it was not once more, nor twice. I do not remember how many times it was before I climbed through the gap and threw myself on the floor beside the dwarf, my lungs screaming silently for breath. The body of the jailer lay there too, caught as a coney in a trap.

'Come,' he said. 'Here are your boots. Do not delay. Another guard takes his place soon.'

'Then we'll wait and kill him too.'

'No, no!' he said quickly. 'This one is not dead. I only put a potion in his wine.'

I stopped and stared down at him. 'You only put a potion in his wine?' I began to laugh quietly. 'Then look at him, my friend. One edge of the grille lies straight across his neck.'

My prison had been the nearest to the oaken door that sealed the end of the passage. Other gratings lay in the floor. I heard a moan, and hesitated, but the dwarf plucked at my sleeve. 'We have no time to waste,' he insisted. 'Leave him. It is not your friend in there.'

'Show me where he is, then. And I need a weapon. The guard will have a dagger . . .'

'His belt only holds a sword, and it lies twisted beneath him.' He held up a big iron key. Putting it into the lock he signed at me to pull open the heavy door. 'You must be away before the hue-and-cry,' he warned, 'and that is not as easy as it might seem, for it rains hard, and the castle and its ground have many traps. Follow me.'

We reached a postern without being encountered, and then the little fellow set off running through the rain-filled darkness at a pace that I was hard put to keep up with. In the end he stopped, panting, his breath coming in gouts of steam into the damp air. 'There!' he pointed. 'Up there, behind those tall bushes. The wall is crumbled, and is for repair. Go, my friend, and God be with you.'

'A moment,' I said. 'You haven't told me where my friend is. He wears a black beard. . .'

'Him? Oh, yes! He was taken soon after you were. He will suffer the cage in the market place tomorrow, after the esbatement.'

'The esbatement?'

'Do you not know of it?' He looked round us, but there was no one to be seen. 'It is a spectacle much enjoyed in Paris, and brought here by the Duchess for her own sport. The market place is fenced into a circle, and four blind beggars are driven in, each armed with a stave. Then a pig follows, and they set about to kill it, each one for himself, fending away the others.

185

It causes great mirth, especially when the game palls and I am sent in with a sword to prod them.'

'But what of Ander . . . the black beard?'

'He will be in the iron cage, which sits on a trunnion surrounded by brushwood and faggots. After the esbatement it will be wheeled in with a great fanfare of trumpets and set afire. Yet it is not so great a sight,' he added with some disappointment in his voice, 'for while they will cut out his tongue so that he cannot scream, if there is a lack of wind the pall of smoke will hide his suffering.'

'Jesu!' I muttered. He turned to go, 'Wait,' I said. 'I owe you some reward, some gratitude.'

'None!' he said firmly. 'If there be gratitude then it must be on my part.' He slapped me on the knee. 'Because you, my friend, when we first met, addressed me as a fellow man, not as an object of derision.'

'Is that all?' I said wonderingly.

'No. Not all.' He wiped the rain off his small face. 'My mother commanded me to see to your release.'

'Your mother?'

'Aye. My mother. Madame de Beaugrand.' He chuckled. 'She has not been kissed these twenty years.'

CHAPTER 33

I was hungry, wet and cold. I had no money, nor any weapon. I saw a fellow staggering drunkenly from a wine-shop in the market place. A man who would be cheering on the blind beggars tomorrow, and yelling himself hoarse at the antics of the English prisoner slowly burning to death. He would have money, and perhaps a dagger. Yet I held my hand. I had no cause for resentment against the citizens of Hesdin. Neither should I have one against the Duchess Margaret. For she had only done what Dickon would have done in the same circumstances, held me until the allegations against me could be investigated. But Dickon would never have condemned Joseph Anderson to be burned alive without further inquiry. And there lay the difference. Margaret was like her other brother, Clarence, who had no regard for ordinary people. They were a constant irritation, and had to be kept quiet by work, by church-going, and by the occasional public spectacle such as this esbatement and the immolation of a prisoner. No, I told myself, it was not the citizens, but Margaret and her soldiers who were the enemies now.

The rain came down in a torrent. No trunnion with brushwood would be left outside on a night like this. There would be a town hall, where the mayor held his court when the Duchess was not in residence at the castle. It was not difficult to find, being the largest building in the place, wood-built, and only one storey high, but covering a vast area on the other side of the market place. Three sides had walls, the other, facing outwards, was open with thick wooden columns supporting a heavy, overhanging roof of thatch.

Beside one of the columns I could see the outline of a sentry. His helmet was tipped forward against the rain drops from the thatch, and the butt of his halberd was thrust deep into the mud beside him. Every now and then he turned round to peer into the recesses of the hall. It was dark in there, the only light coming from a

187

cresset, smouldering damply at the far end, where three shadows sat huddled by a brazier.

The heavy rain deadened the sound of my approach. Each time the sentry turned I moved closer, until I was behind the column next to his. Then, as he looked round once more, I reached across and pulled the dagger quickly from his belt. That brought him swinging back, straight on to the point of the blade which I had brought up level with his beard. The shout that started from his lungs ended abruptly in a gurgle from his severed windpipe. I held him while he sagged against the post, sliding him down into a sitting position with his head on his knees, as if asleep. Then I went inside, creeping along the edge of the wall.

All at once it was very quiet. The battering of the rain was absorbed by the close-packed reeds above me. I could hear the three soldiers muttering as they threw their dice on the hard earthen floor. I moved on, as far away from them as possible, and came to the edges of a tall cage. It was of iron, much pitted by fire, and circular, built to close round a prisoner so that he could only stand erect. And there was no mistaking the prisoner inside it now, for there was a faint gleam on his head from the distant cresset. I put my hand through the bars and patted him reassuringly, whispering at him to try to keep from retching as I cut away the gag over his face. It was as well I did, for one end of an iron horse-shoe had been thrust deep into his mouth. I took it out carefully, cursing the man who had put it there.

'God's Hooks, Morane!' Anderson gasped. 'Where have *you* been?'

'I cannot find your hands. Are they tied as well?'

'Tied? No. I am fenced in like a cat, that is all.'

At that moment I saw a movement by the brazier. One of the guards was looking towards the entrance. 'Where's that poxy Switzer?' he said. 'If he's gone to sleep out there the sergeant'll have his gonads when he gets back.' His voice carried clearly across the space of the hall.

'So long as he comes back from the castle with our money he can have the Switzer,' another, deeper voice replied.

'You think the Duchess'll give it to him?' a third voice asked anxiously.

'She had better. I told him we want double for having to spend the night in this rat-infested barn. And if she does not, then it's me for Italy with the King of France's army. They say he's paying twice as much as we get with this Burgundian rabble. . .'

'Aaaah, stop your prattling and make your throws.' The deep voice laughed. 'If you want to win back the money the sergeant's fetching for you.'

They sat down again, and I turned back to the cage. It was in two parts, massive hinges on one side, built to withstand fire, and an even more massive lock on the other. 'The key?' I whispered to Anderson.

'The sergeant has it. But there are more prisoners about the place somewhere. Although they keep strangely quiet.'

'Wait then,' I said, and moved away into the darkness. I had not gone far when I tripped over a body, bringing a grunt from it. It, too, was gagged, but without an iron restraint, and the hands were tied behind.

'Who're you?' a voice demanded when it was released. Fingers came up to probe my face.

'A friend. I need your help, and that of your companions, to free the man in the cage. Unless you want to wait to kill the pig tomorrow.'

'I can find myself a fat pig any time I wish,' he chuckled. 'But leave the others. They are too old and crippled to help. But the key is with the sergeant, and there are four guards. Didn't you see them?'

'Only three now,' I said, and the fingers felt my grin.

'Ah! But there are lights of some kind over there. One gave out heat as I was led past. It will be a brazier. Douse them, and we'll kill the three of them before the sergeant returns. They'll be helpless against me in the dark. Give me a poniard.'

'I cannot until another of them is dealt with.'

Another quiet chuckle came. A hand felt my shoulder. 'Yes. You are a hard man such as I,' he said. The hand took mine. 'Man, that's my name. John Man, soldier of Brabant, blinded by a sword-thrust. But still able to fight when I can find my enemy with these

189

hands. . .' He stopped. 'Hist! They are searching for their friend. Will they find him?'

'Soon enough.'

'Good. Then after that they will come this way hunting for you. How many can you deal with?'

'No more than one at a time.'

'At least you do not boast,' he said quietly. 'Then let the first stumble over me while you see to the next. The chance for the third will be in the hands of God.'

I hid in the shadow while they rattled at the cage. 'He's still in there, at least,' the first man said, turning towards us. Then he tripped over John Man's outstretched leg. At that I leapt forward and dug my blade into the man behind him. But my aim was not as true as it had been with the sentry, for I had seen the gleam of a sword in his hand. He fell aside gasping and holding his hand against his belly, below where the breastplate ended. But there was no time to see him off. The last man had a sword too. Yet as I turned I saw him standing wide-eyed at the sudden loss of his companions. He was young and beardless and unused to this kind of battle. He never saw another.

'Hah!' John Man said, getting up with his victim's sword in his hand. He stood for a moment, listening, then went over to where my first quarry lay gasping, and the noise ceased.

'You know how to fight, my friend,' he said with satisfaction, running his fingers over my face, 'and have the scars to show it. Now we will wait for the sergeant. Douse the lights. I do better in the dark.'

'You do well enough without it,' I laughed. 'And I need the light. . .' There was a metallic clank outside. It was a horse's gear. John Man heard it too. 'Leave him to me,' he whispered. 'I owe him much.'

A great crag of a man stood outlined against the entrance, peering in towards the distant brazier. 'Where's that Switzer sentry?' he yelled. When no reply came he went on, 'You'd better find him quickly if you don't want horse-shoes stuffed down your throats instead of money.' He moved inside. The shadow of the blind man rose behind him and iron fingers closed round his throat. But the sergeant was made of sterner stuff than his men. He swung round as if John Man were no more than a sack of oats on his back. I saw his hand going to his belt. But it never reached his weapon. The point of my dagger went right through his palm and screeched against the armour he wore. He gave a bellow of pain and grasped for me with his other hand. I dodged it and brought him down with a boot in the groin. John Man went down with him, the fingers still hooked in place.

'Don't kill him,' I said. 'I have another use for him.'

We helped Joseph Anderson out of the cage. He stood stiffly, cursing at the pain. 'What detained you?' he grumbled.

'That fellow,' I said, pointing at the inert sergeant. 'He's the one who gave you the horse-shoe. Now help me with him into the cage. Then we'll push it on to the brazier.'

John Man laughed. 'A fitting end to him,' he said, and sniffed. 'Aye, and they've sprinkled gun-powder on to the faggots to make them burn the better. Come on then.'

'Not you, old soldier,' I said to him. 'Go and free your friends and then make yourselves scarce. And to-morrow, when they find the charred bodies they may think them yours, and not molest you again.' I inspected the disfigured face. 'But you deserve a reward. . .'

'What better reward than smelling this place burn down?'

'True, but there is money at the sergeant's saddle. Take what you want.'

'You have more need of it than I, my friends. Besides, what use has a blind man for money? Except to be cheated of it?'

I took his arm. 'Then where will you go, my fighting Brabanter?'

He put his hand over mine and gave a loud chuckle. 'Go? Why, my scarry-faced Englishman, where better can I go than to find a fat pig to roast all for myself?'

191

CHAPTER 34

W H E N we reached the trees I reined up my horse and looked back. The low clouds over Hesdin were aglow with the flames from the town's hall. Joseph Anderson watched it for a moment, then said, 'What now?'

'I need rest,' I told him. 'There will be no pursuit till dawn. And they will expect us to have fled as far as possible by then, so they will keep to the roads close to the town, and search more widely later when inquiries at villages and taverns grow fruitless. The Duchess said she would leave tomorrow in any case, but it will be in the afternoon, after the esbatement.'

Anderson nodded. 'Well, that won't take place now, but if the whole court is geared to move in the afternoon it would be too complicated to alter. It is only the morning pursuit we have to consider, then.' He wiped the rain drops from his beard. 'Aye, I could sleep too. It is not too wet under these trees.' He dismounted slowly and stiffly.

'There is one thing first,' I said. 'They will be searching for a man with a black beard.' I drew my dagger, grinning mischievously. 'It will have to be removed, Captain Anderson, and forthwith.'

He stopped, turned round, and stared at me. 'God's Hooks, Morane! Must it come to that?'

Afterwards, I wrapped myself in the saddle blanket and was asleep before he lay down beside me.

My sleep was troubled by fearful dreams: of dwarfs and sightless men peering at me from cages; of naked duchesses and dead soldiers fighting each other in the dark, and of a huge toad on Anderson's beardless chin. And when I woke it was still dark, so that I was about to turn my aching bones over when I heard him speak.

'Mother of God, the fellow wants to make another day of it!'

'All day?' I said, sitting up quickly. 'I slept all day?'

'Aye. Even through the trumpets sounding down there in the valley while the pursuit set out. Here,' he added, holding out a leathern jug, 'here is wine. And some ancient Flemish beef.'

I asked him where he had got it and he waved a nonchalant hand. 'At the inn down there. The landlord is French, and cares little for Burgundians. Besides, I had money, even if I was an Englishman.'

'But he will report your visit to the horsemen when they return.'

His face fell. Then he smiled. 'They may not come back that way. And the other Englishmen may confuse them.'

I got to my feet, grunting at the pains in my damp muscles. 'Other Englishmen, you say?'

'Aye. Three of them. A knight and two servants. They came in demanding food and wine. I made myself scarce when I heard English talk outside, but I watched them through a broken shutter. It seems they also came from Hesdin, and make for Calais, but go to Guisnes first for some reason I did not learn.'

'A knight, eh? Did you hear his name?'

He shook his head. 'His men called him Sir Robert, that is all.'

'Sir Robert?' I thought for a moment. 'No, I cannot think who it might be, leaving Hesdin at this moment, and so soon.'

'Yes, he came from Hesdin. Didn't you see him at the court?'

'I saw no one except the Duchess, and that treasonous secretary. We were questioned immediately on our arrival, you remember, and I was taken to her at once.'

He grinned. 'How many times did you have to swive her?'

'Not enough,' I said sourly, spitting out the beef. 'Come on, then. We have good horses. Let's catch this Sir Robert at Calais.'

'That was yesterday,' he pointed out. 'And we have to avoid the Duchess's court on the way.'

'It will take the road to Malines. Have you seen it pass?'

'Why no!' he frowned, as he climbed into the saddle.

'Then she has been delayed by having to call the citizens together and promise them a new hall for their town,' I said, and we both laughed.

*   *   *

Calais seemed to be much smaller than when I had
last seen it. Now there was no great army camped
around it. All the tents had gone, and the town had
withdrawn into its walls. In fact, but for the crowd of
merchants who travelled there to buy English wool, it
would have been a very small town indeed, its importance being that of the only English outpost in
Europe. Calais, with its outlying forts of Guisnes and
Hammes, was thus strongly held, the guards on its walls
being doubled when the gates were closed. They were
closed not only during the hours of darkness, but also
after noon while the citizens were at dinner, and on
holidays when Mass was being held in the churches.

Once inside we made our way through the slimy,
cobbled streets to an inn by the harbour, where we inquired about ships to Dover. The landlord, once a
mariner himself, to judge by his matted beard and
striped woollen shirt, waved a scornful hand at the
multitude of vessels lying in the mud. He told us that
the tides rose and fell as much as thirty feet every
twelve hours, and we should have to wait. He was about
to ask us if we had the money to pay for our passages,
when his eyes fell on our horses, and a look of cupidity
crossed his features. The scorn left them and his ob-
sequiousness became patent. I asked him if there had
been any other passengers that day, and when he said
that more than one ship had left that morning and he
could not remember all of them I remarked casually
that perhaps Sir Robert had not yet arrived in Calais.

'Sir Robert? Is Sir Robert returning to England?'

Further indirect questioning disclosed that he was referring to Sir Robert Curzon, captain of Hammes castle,
and not likely to be the Sir Robert in whom I was interested. I waved it aside, then he said, 'Ah! You mean
Sir Robert Clifford, of course!'

When I nodded agreement, he went on, 'I did not
know he was returning today, sir. But, if so, I have
not seen him yet.' He sniffed, then spat at a bollard

194

on the wharf. 'He only passed through here a week ago. I heard it said he was to inspect the defences of Hammes and Guisnes, but. . .'

I glanced at Anderson, and saw him nod. It was just such a story as someone about to visit the Duchess Margaret would put out. With peace recently restored with France the defences of the outlying castles were not of great moment. It was clear that this Clifford would not visit either, but would make a detour to come in to Calais on the road from Guisnes.

'Shall I have messages sent to have Sir Robert Clifford seek you when he arrives?' the inkeeper asked anxiously. 'If I had your name . . .'

'No, no,' I said, 'it is not necessary. We make for Dover before him, and will meet him there.' I turned to Anderson. 'See to it,' I told him. 'On the first vessel that leaves, and our horses as well.'

Anderson saw my wink, grunted something and led the animals away. The inkeeper eyed him curiously, not until then deciding whether he was my man or my equal. But now I must be someone of importance with horses like those and the Flemish breastplate I wore. He bowed. 'Meanwhile, good sir, I will bring you hot meats and well-spiced ale.'

'Ale?' I raised my eyebrows. 'Oh, aye, ale for him. But I will have some of your Burgundian wine, if there is any of good quality.'

'Indeed there is, sir,' he said, bowing again, and made haste to his barrels in the vault.

'You should have been more circumspect,' Anderson said when he came back. 'Now the whole of Calais will know that we seek out Sir Robert Clifford.'

'Maybe,' I agreed, 'but until we came here we did not know his name. And even now we are not sure he makes for England.'

'We?' Anderson growled. 'I, for one, am not sure of anything. But why else would one come to this cess-pit of a town?'

'Maybe to buy wool,' I suggested, causing him to spit down at the thick layer of sea weed heaving gently in the rising tide. 'He might take ship to Antwerp to see the Garson. It is quicker than all the way by road.'

The first vessel to depart was a galley from Venice, bound for Bruges and thence for Antwerp, but Sir Robert Clifford had not put in an appearance. That pleased me somewhat, for I had little stomach for being rowed by sad-eyed Turkish prisoners shackled to their benches, even if they were heretics.

It was when a stout two-masted cog showed signs of activity that three men appeared from the narrow streets of the town and rode down to the wharf. 'That's them,' Anderson said as we stared out through the tavern window. The innkeeper came up at the same time and confirmed it.

'Shall I send a message to him now, sir?' he inquired.

I turned and looked him up and down. 'Sir Robert,' I said to him, 'has been warned not to recognize us.' I beckoned to Anderson. 'This man,' I said, jerking a thumb at the innkeeper, 'seems to me to be much too curious with his tongue. Perhaps . . .'

I did not need to add any more. Joseph Anderson's leer seemed all the more savage with only a black stubble wreathing it. He fingered the dagger at his belt. The innkeeper bent almost double and backed away. 'I meant nothing, sir,' he said, his voice no more than a whisper. 'And my tongue knows its master.'

'See that it continues to do so,' I told him. 'For we shall be returning to Calais soon, and will call you to account if it does not.'

'Aha!' Joseph Anderson laughed as we went down to the dock. 'What better omen, Henry Morane? See the name on the stern? 'The Gracious Henry of Pembroke Castle','

'Except that I am not from Pembroke,' I grinned at him. 'And an omen means nothing, as you should know by now. An omen is for the weak who seek solace by signs.'

He went on laughing. 'No,' he agreed. 'It should have been 'The Murderous Morane of Wall Brook Gut'.' That made him laugh all the louder, so that he could hardly collect himself to bargain with the ship-master for our passages.

CHAPTER 35

T H E waist of the ship carried some twenty horses and a dozen travellers making for England; tinkers, chapmen and vendors of silks and spices. One enterprising fellow had two pack horses laden with Italian weapons of the smaller kind; axes, daggers, mace- and arrow-heads, for Italian steel is still considered the best by those who can afford it. Seeing that Sir Robert Clifford and his two men had taken their position near the bows of the vessel, I found places for Anderson and myself at the other end, with the horses between us. We sat on the planking beside the short ladder up to the poop deck, where the steersman leaned on the great oar that hung down from the right-hand side, the steer-board side. The master stood on the other, leaning over the rail, eyeing the passengers morosely. I gave him a nod, and he nodded back, returning to the others. I did not look as if I might make trouble for him.

Calais was no more than half an hour behind us when there was a movement among the passengers in the bows. Sir Robert Clifford and his men were pushing their way between the horses towards us. He was a tall, angular fellow with greying hair, a hooked nose and a mouth circumscribed by creases that ran down from each nostril. The tiny mouth would have been better covered by a moustache, especially as the two teeth I could see inside it were nearly green.

He stood with his hands on hips and looked at me with sallow eyes, his men behind him fingering their belts. 'What is your name?' he demanded.

I shifted my buttocks on the planking, and said, 'What is that to you, sir?' I spoke as if surprised by such a question from a stranger.

The shorter of the two men stepped out fingering a long poniard. 'You heard the question,' he said truculently.

I was about to reply peaceably and give him some name other than my own, when the ship-master came thumping down the ladder with an iron bar in his fist. Before the man with the poniard could turn the heavy weapon came down on his shoulder with a crack like the splintering of a glass bottle. The poniard clattered to the deck and its owner gave a squeal of pain, to fall writhing beside me, clutching his broken shoulder with his left hand. The ship-master gave him a quick, contemptuous glance, then eyed the others.

'There will be no weapons drawn on my ship,' he said throatily, swinging the bar in front of him, and I saw that two of the crew had appeared behind Sir Robert Clifford and his other man with pike-points at their backs. It was a procedure too smooth not to have been practised many times before. 'Take their weapons,' the captain said. After a sword and two daggers had been thrown over the side, he added, 'Now take them back to where they came from.'

'Do you know who I am?' Sir Robert Clifford said haughtily.

'Oh, aye!' The sailor gave a mocking bow. 'You are at least cousin to both the Kings of England and of France, and second son of the Holy Father himself. But . . .' and his smile became grim '. . . I am the captain of this ship, and while you are on it you will behave.'

'But that man,' Clifford said, pointing at me, 'is on the Bead-roll of the King's enemies, and must be arrested.'

'Is he now?' The narrowed eyes remained on Clifford. 'Then you knew his name? Have the sheriff arrest him at Dover if you wish, but . . .' the weapon swung in my direction '. . . it seems to me he will ask why the fellow is escaping from justice by going to England instead of fleeing in the other direction. Now go back to your place.'

'Listen you . . .' Sir Robert began.

'If you have any more to say you can say it from up there.' The iron bar pointed at the mast-head. 'Disobey my orders and I'll hang you for mutiny. Even you, my lord.' He bowed deeply, bringing laughter from the crew.

Sir Robert Clifford muttered something about him hearing more of it, and pushed his way back to the bows,

198

followed by his man. The ship-master eyed me, nodded, then climbed back to his post. 'Throw some water over that fellow,' he called down to me, 'and keep him quiet until Dover.'

It was no surprise that Clifford knew who I was, but he should have known ships better than to have made trouble on one. I looked at his servant, who lay groaning beside me. He was in a sorry state. It had been a terrible blow, and the whole of his right shoulder was stove in. A froth of blood came from his mouth. 'I am like to die,' he said.

'You are,' I agreed. 'But that is what comes of waving weapons on ship-board. Yet, if you last until Dover, I will see to it that a priest comes to shrive you.'

'Aaah, God, that would be a comfort!' he whispered.

'Provided you answer some questions,' I added.

The weather held fair, with a good breeze, so that by dark the great lantern above Dover Castle gleamed its welcome back to England. I got up and called to the ship-master that the man had died.

'He has, has he? Then throw him over the side. And you,' he added, 'can go ashore first at Dover if you wish to avoid the sheriff.' I began to thank him, but he brushed it aside. 'It is no concern of mine whether you are a traitor or not,' he said, 'to this king or any other. They are all the same to me.'

I saw his face in the darkness, and knew him for a smuggler when passengers were scarce.

CHAPTER 36

AUTUMN twilight was closing round us as we rode past the Eleanor Cross at Charing. Joseph Anderson stopped his horse and turned to me. 'But if you are on the Bead-roll as a traitor, Henry Morane,' he said, 'you will never get past the guards outside the Palace. They will have orders to arrest you, and the sight of you is too well known . . .'

'Are you not one of those same guards?' I asked him. He looked surprised, then agreed that he was, and I told him what to do.

The sentry outside West Minster hall saw him first. 'Hah, Captain Anderson,' he said, raising his halberd in salute. 'We thought you . . .' Then he frowned as he recognized me.

'Admit me and my prisoner,' Anderson said sternly. And after that it was only a matter of finding the Queen's court.

'Oh, Henry! Henry Morane!' Matilda cried, throwing her arms round me. 'For me you were dead when I heard of your name on the Bead-roll. I could not think what . . .'

'And now I am alive again,' I said, stopping her with a kiss, and smoothing the hair under her cap. 'And no traitor, either.'

'No traitor, Master Morane?' a voice said. 'Then what of your name at Paul's Yard?' It was the Lady Margaret Beaufort, and her face was hard.

We broke apart, and I bowed low. 'My lady,' I said, 'I seek audience with Master Christopher Urswick, and after, he willing, with the King's Grace itself. Pray restrain judgment until then.'

The grey eyes looked me up and down, but there was no expression in them. 'Mistress Morane,' she said without turning, 'do as your husband asks. Tell Master Urswick that it is my wish.' As Matilda turned to go, she added, 'And have more torches brought in here. The place reeks of damp and shadow, and I would examine Master Morane the better.'

But she did not. Instead she moved across to the glassed window, and stared thoughtfully out over the smooth flowing river. She was about to turn back when the arras was drawn aside. It was Thomas Howard, earl of Surrey. I looked at him with astonishment, for I had not expected him to be at West Minster.

When he saw me the pleasure on his face gave way to a frown. 'Why, Henry Morane,' he said, 'I had not thought to encounter you here. What Devil's work have you been up to now?'

By the window, the Lady Margaret cleared her throat loudly. Surrey swung round to her and bowed. 'My lady,' he said, 'I crave pardon.' He crossed himself quickly. 'I should have asked Morane why he has been called a traitor at Paul's Yard these last Sundays. There is . . .'

He in turn was interrupted by Christopher Urswick, with Matilda close behind. He wore a long, priestly gown, which increased his stature a little. Inclining his head to the Countess of Richmond and to Surrey, he turned dull eyes on me.

'So you have survived again, eh, Henry Morane?' he said, without any apparent satisfaction. 'We thought the Dowager Duchess had done for you in Burgundy.'

Matilda gave a long, shuddering sigh, which brought the Lady Margaret's arms out to her. At that she could restrain herself no longer and gave way to a flood of tears.

'Mercy me!' Urswick said, clicking his tongue. 'Your return seems to have caused some embarrassment. Perhaps we should leave the ladies to console each other.'

'There need have been no embarrassment had you told them the truth of the matter,' I said resentfully.

'Indeed?' He clicked his tongue again. 'The truth?' he inquired. 'When it was the King's express command that no one was to know it? Aye,' he added, inclining his head towards her, 'not even his own mother.'

'No one?' I countered. 'When the Duchess Margaret herself knew it to be false?'

That wiped the expression off his face. He pursed his lips. He was about to say 'Indeed' again, but thought better of it. 'Then perhaps we must leave the others alone while you tell me of it. Yes, and Joseph Anderson, too.' He looked round. 'Where is he? Or did he not cheat the Burgundian executioner?'

'He did,' I said shortly. 'He waits outside, as my guard. How else do you think I should have gained admission to the palace?'

'Ah! I had not thought of that!' He smiled a little. 'It seems the Duchess Margaret did not take your resource from you, then.' He took my arm, bowing to the others in turn. 'You will understand,' he said to them, 'that nothing of this is to be spoken outside this room. Morane is not yet known to have returned to England. Or if he is,' he added, his eyes narrowing a little, 'it will be as a prisoner surrendering to the King's mercy. That is King Henry's express command.' With that he turned and led me out of the room.

I heard Surrey say, 'Well, thank the Good Lord for that! I should have known that Henry Morane could be no traitor.' And with that Matilda gave way to a further flood of tears.

*　　　*　　　*

'And so,' Christopher Urswick said when I had finished, 'you think this Sir Robert Clifford carried a letter from the Duchess of Burgundy to Sir William Stanley?' He eyed us both in turn. 'Then why did you not seize him and take if off him?'

'Because,' I said patiently, 'such a letter would not bear any inscription. The risk would be too great. You could not prove it was for Stanley until the act of delivery. That is why we outpaced Clifford from Dover so that you can arrest him as he hands it to Sir William Stanley right here in West Minster.'

Christopher Urswick gave a long sigh. 'But Sir William is not here!' he told us. 'He has begged leave of the King to attend his estates and hear the audit of his stewards' management of them.'

'At Chester?' I said, taken aback.

'Yes. At his seat. Holt castle. So it seems that Sir Robert Clifford will have to journey there. And ...'

202

his voice fell as he looked round the room '. . . it is of importance, because Charles of France has written privily in his own hand to King Henry, warning him that the Emperor Maximilian, with his new found wealth, has begun to furnish ships for this Perkin Warbeck in his designs upon this realm.'

'King Charles?' I said incredulously. 'Why would he do that?'

Urswick's smile was sardonic. 'Because he is now our friend. Trouble between England and the Archduke. . . the Emperor Maximilian would keep us both occupied while the French armies swarm over the Alps into Italy. But the information is correct, for we have it from another source also that Maximilian provides ships, and the Duchess Margaret the men for an attack upon this country soon, provided,' he added, 'that they are assured of support, military support from dissidents within the realm. Jesu!' he muttered, wiping his brow with his sleeve. 'Once Sir William Stanley pledges his power to Warbeck the invasion will commence.' He stopped suddenly and eyed us anxiously, as if he had said too much. I had never seen the little priest so distracted before.

'But King Henry must have had suspicion of this for some time,' I protested.

'Aye, suspicion, but no more. But suspicion is for dissembling where matters of state are concerned.' He fell silent, and we watched him.

'No,' he said at length. 'It would be pointless to arrest Stanley as the letter was handed to him. He would merely say that he was being importuned, and would denounce Clifford as the traitor. It is Sir William Stanley's reply to that letter which will be evidence. It will contain precise details of what he will do, and when.' He struck a palm with his fist. 'It is that reply which we must have, after it has been given to Sir Robert Clifford to take back to Flanders.'

'Then all we have to do is to seize Clifford on his way back,' Joseph Anderson suggested.

'That will not do,' was the reply. 'He might not return this way. He might take ship from Chester to Ireland, for instance, to try and persuade the Fitzgeralds to rebel for the second time. . .or from Bristol.' His eyes went back to me. 'Sir Robert Clifford has to be watched closely.'

I gave a loud groan. 'And we are to do it, you mean?'

'That is what I mean.'

'But Clifford knows us now.'

'So does Sir William Stanley, I believe,' he said with ponderous irony. 'You must leave for Chester forthwith, to be there ahead of Clifford.'

'God's Hooks!' Anderson muttered. 'And we only from Flanders today.'

'I am well aware of it,' Christopher Urswick replied. 'But it has to be you two. You know Clifford by sight.' He suddenly pointed a finger at us, each in turn.'And remember this. No one besides myself and the King is privy to this. No one,' he emphasised, 'but you two. And I have spoken at some length so that you will realise its importance. Sir William Stanley, as is his habit, will not raise the standard of revolt until he is certain of success. And that cannot be before the Garson's soldiers land in the realm. If the attempt fails, as, God willing, it will, he must never learn of our suspicion. Unless . . .' and the finger waved at us again '. . . unless you obtain proof of his complicity. If you fail to obtain it then your tongues must be stilled.'

'Is it implied that we cannot keep them still?' I said indignantly.

'All tongues must be stilled,' he emphasised, 'where the policy and welfare of the state are concerned, no matter in what esteem the King holds you, you understand?'

I began to understand, but Joseph Anderson did not. 'We can control our tongues,' he growled.

'There will be no need to if they are not there,' Christopher Urswick said, a sudden gleam coming into his eyes. With that he turned away, the tiny feet pattering the tiles as he went, while Joseph Anderson and I stood staring at each other.

204

CHAPTER 37

T H E cold November light came through the shutters and fingered away the reluctant darkness from the room. Matilda reached for me again. 'But now the King can require no more missions from you, Henry Morane,' she murmured. 'The war with France is over, and we can live in peace.'

'There is one more mission, my sweet apple,' I told her, 'and that will be the last.'

'One more?' Her eyes widened. 'Oh no! King Henry must allow you rest. I will speak to the Lady Margaret, who may persuade him . . .'

'You must speak to no one,' I warned her. 'Remember that the Lady Margaret did not know of my last adventure. This will be the last, I assure you, and it will be in England at least.' But I knew that, if I failed, I would kill Sir William Stanley myself, for the consequences would be the same.

'You have been much preoccupied since your return,' she said, running a hand through my hair. 'You have not even given much thought to dalliance with young Nicholas, and of you I speak to him constantly, so that he looks forward to your company. He will be downcast.' She eyed me curiously. 'Would it be your experience with the Dowager Duchess Margaret in Flanders? Did she try you, as she is reputed to try all Englishmen who visit her?' she added, and there was mischief in her smile. Then she added, and her eyes were very blue, 'But I have no thought of jealousy, Henry Morane, if you assure me there was no pleasure in it.'

'Pleasure?' I smiled back and held out my arms to her. 'Pleasure such as this? It was in the line of duty.'

'Duty?' she laughed, holding me close. 'Then may God make you rue the day when it comes to that with me!'

*　　　*　　　*

'Henry Morane,' Joseph Anderson said as we rode through the mud of the Strand, 'this is the last mission I undertake with you. You create too many alarms and excursions for my well-being. When this is finished I will beg the King a pension so that I can have some peace of mind at last.'

'But you cannot write,' I pointed out.

'Write? What has that to do with it?'

'How could you ask otherwise if you have no tongue?'

'Aaaah!' He cleared his throat and spat into the mud. 'All this talk of cutting out tongues! What is the little priest so agitated about? He knows that if we go into the Stanley domains we shall be recognized and hanged for sure. How can we follow Clifford there?'

I had been thinking of that, too. I had also been wondering why Christopher Urswick had expressed no curiosity about Sir Robert Clifford. I said, 'Clifford will first go to West Minster, seeking Stanley.'

'Then why are we riding along the Strand, away from it? And in the opposite direction from Chester.'

'You will see,' I told him, and he scratched his growing beard.

We pushed our way between the rolls of cloth in Mehmet's shop. The mouth under the great nest of hair moved into a smile when he saw me, but the Saracen eyes narrowed with suspicion at Anderson. I was about to explain, when Ali came running in from the street.

'Ah, Morane effendi!' he said, throwing his arms about me. 'And Captain Anderson too! This gives me much pleasure.'

Mehmet's eyes softened. He held out a hand to Anderson. The latter took it and muttered, 'So this is where the little fellow lives, eh? But, by reason of their faith, I suppose they will have no beer.'

'They have better, eh?' I said to Mehmet, and he smiled broadly.

'Indeed, good sirs!' he bowed effusively. 'There is a store in my horse stables at the back, but of course only . . .'

'Only for visitors,' I laughed. 'Not for yourself. And then I would speak with Ali alone, for it is better you do not know what I ask.'

206

'Ah!' Mehmet said. 'If you will put him in no danger then he is yours. For I have great affection for my nephew, and would have no harm come to his beautiful little head.'

Ali grinned. The golden tooth was still there. 'My wicked uncle speaks like one of the Christian angels,' he observed, ducking quickly away from him. I heard the latter muttering 'Scum!' as he went outside.

'And what was that we drank?' Joseph Anderson said as we rode somewhat unsteadily along London Bridge. He gave a loud belch, frightening two clerks as they scurried past. 'If the draw-bridge is down we can wash it away with good English ale at the taverns on the other side.' When he had ridden round an approaching ox-cart and joined me again, he said, 'And why do we need this spare horse and panniers you just bought from that bearded Saracen?' He belched again, this time bringing a protest from a balcony above the street. He waved a fist at it, and received a reply from the contents of a piss-pot. He would have stopped then and there and stormed the house, but none of the liquid had hit him and I led him on firmly. It was as well that the draw-bridge was down, for other citizens were growing angry at the interruption of their dinners.

'You think to find your way through these marshes?' he complained later. 'My horse will likely soon sink in the slime.'

The one-eared priest peered out through the matted door of his hut, then recognized me. 'Mother of God!' he exclaimed. 'Master Measles-man! And who is this?' he asked, eyeing Joseph Anderson, who stood rubbing his hands together in the cold.

'A captain of archers,' I told him. 'Once of the Earl of Surrey's division at Bosworth field, but now, like me, Captain Anderson is in the service of the Tudor king, although, as you well know, loyal to the memory of Dickon. We are as one in that.'

'Ah!' Wrinkles appeared on the brown and pink skin where once his hair had been. 'What brings you here, then?' Or . . .' he brightened '. . . do you bring news that Sir William Stanley has been accounted for?'

'Alas, no.' I shook my head. 'Although that accounting

might be closer. I come from West Minster to bring you news that Thomas Howard of Surrey who, like us, remains faithful to the memory of King Richard, remembers Martin Caillou as one of his chaplains, and would have you back in his service if you would consider it.'

'The earl of Surrey? You have seen him?'

'Aye. And he is no friend of Sir William Stanley either.'

A little tear came into the eyes above the grey bearded face. 'With service to the earl of Surrey again? But you said he was in the North?'

'He came to West Minster for the jousting and the festivities when the King's second son, Prince Henry, was created Duke of York.' It had been a fine show, I was told, with much ceremonial. The three-year-old prince was already a lusty boy, even riding his own horse in the procession, although he had to be carried to the ceremony itself in the arms of the earl of Shrewsbury, where Archibishop Morton had presided with no less than ten mitred bishops. But Martin Caillou was shaking his head.

'No,' he said finally. 'My respects to Thomas Howard, but I cannot do it.' He waved a hand at the thick belt of reeds and rushes around us. 'I am content here. No one disturbs me. My peace of mind is complete. To return to life . . .'

'Aye,' I said, 'to return to life. That is it! Here you survive, no more. You have to steal to live at all. And what peace of mind can that be? For one day the sheriff of Middlesex, who must already be alert, will catch you, and then you will hang, my friend, and quickly. Whereas as chaplain to the earl of Surrey in the north country, you will have a life of fullness. A life which you really hanker for, however much you delude yourself otherwise.'

Anderson was looking at me with astonishment. But the priest was wiping his hand across his face. 'Think on it,' I said to him.

'The north country?' His voice came from between his fingers. 'Where I come from. Beyond York . . .' he brought his hand down to grasp the other. 'But my appearance? The ear hewn off, the mark of a felon?'

'Did you not tell me it was hewn off at Bosworth Field? Could not that command respect, especially in the north where loyalty to Dickon remains as strong as ever?' I took his arm. 'Come, my friend, think on it. This life of yours is feckless. Responsibility and respect is what you need. Let me tell Surrey that you will serve him, and I know that it will give him much pleasure.'

'Then come inside, both of you,' the priest said. 'There is a brazier there, and good wine from Middlesex, as well as a pie of thrushes and starlings, feathered and clawed and ready to bake. We will talk of it, and . . .' he looked round at the rushes '. . . I could always come back here if it did not succeed.'

'I would not serve under any but the earl of Surrey,' the priest said. 'You understand that?'

'Of course. But the opportunity was there, and I spoke of you. Thomas Howard remembered you.' That was nearly true, although his memory had needed prompting. 'But now,' I added, 'he will have returned to his duties at York, and to travel there you will need a letter from me.'

'A letter from you.' Martin Caillou waved his hands in the air. 'That is nothing to what else I should need! Clothes . . .' he indicated the rags he wore '. . . some money, and a horse.' Anderson cleared his throat, and I knew he was thinking of what we had outside.

'We have a horse to lend you,' I told him, 'and spare clothes in its saddle-bags, which would fit you enough. As to money, why, I know I should be repaid for what I lend you.'

'And the letter?' He waved at the hut. 'There is nothing to write with here, my friends. You will need to bring . . .'

'It is already written,' I said, taking a paper from my pocket.

The priest eyed me sharply, and then began to laugh. He was in such a state of exhilaration that my heart warmed to him. After a moment he tilted his stool back and began to laugh the louder, so that we joined in.

'Your Henry Morane is a wily fellow,' he said to Anderson. 'But I will forgive him, for he has convinced me, my son.' He got to his feet and stood upright. 'There!

209

You see I already speak as a priest again. I will leave at dawn with the ferryman, and the Middlesex men can go to the Devil in Hell.' He crossed himself quickly, remembering his new office. It was as if a man with wasted legs had risen and walked again.

'There is one favour I would ask you first,' I said to him. That brought him down to earth again and his eyes became wary. A chuckle from Anderson died stillborn when I glared at him. 'It will be to the discomfort of Sir William Stanley,' I went on. 'For on the way north you could pass through his domains.' I told him why we could not do that easily, whereas he would not be known, and could watch the activities of Sir Robert Clifford.

'Sir Robert Clifford?' he said. 'I know of him, if it is the same fellow. Chamberlain of Berwick after Dickon took it from the Scots.'

'It will be the same,' Anderson said, 'he spoke as if from the north.'

'Ah! He was known then for a subtle and wily . . .' he stopped and smiled at me '. . . knight. Yes, I recall! He changed his coat to Buckingham when he rebelled against Dickon. Not a nice fellow.' The priest held his hands out to us. 'I will do what you ask, Master Henry Morane,' he said, 'and may God help you in your design to unhinge Sir William Stanley.'

CHAPTER 38

JOSEPH Anderson sat by the trestle at the Wandsworth tavern and stared into his ale-mug. After a while
he looked up at me. 'You used that priest for your own
purposes,' he said accusingly. 'And while I hold little
brief for Holy-men, that one seemed to be more honest
than most. He is also poor,' he went on, 'which sets him
apart from other priests. He is also skilled in the matter
of survival on his own without wailing to God to look
after him and other such hypocrisies that they never
cease to mouth. You have used him for your own purposes,' he said again.

'No,' I said, 'that is only partly true. I owed him my
life, and in return have given him the opportunity of ful-
filling his, which he has taken. To do so, he must go to
York, and there is no danger to him in visiting Chester
on the way. Besides,' I added, 'it will give him as much
joy to see the discomfiture of Sir William Stanley as it
will do to us.'

'Aaah! You do not convince me, Henry Morane. And
I think you are trying to convince yourself.' He put a
hand down to stroke a black cat that was stepping dain-
tily over the sawdust on the floor. 'You had in mind to
use him before we set out. And that is the point.'

'I did,' I admitted. 'But you saw the pleasure it gave
him.'

'And how did you persuade Thomas Howard? Or is
that a lie? For when did you speak with him about it?'

'See here,' I said with asperity, 'I do not employ
people by using lies. I sought audience with Surrey before we set out.'

'But you had a purpose,' he objected.

'Of course I had a purpose! I had two purposes; the
greater being to help the priest, the other being to help
ourselves. Is that immoral?'

He shook his head slowly. 'Maybe not. But you were
always subtle.' He smiled. 'And wily. So fetch more ale
and tell me what we do next.'

211

As I began to reply, I saw a man come through the doorway, his breath still making steam from the cold. I gave him no more than a glance, for a longer look incites curiosity in the recipient. 'The man who entered,' I said to Anderson, 'if he has a dagger scar on the forearm, will be one of those who waylaid me here when I had the fever.'

Joseph Anderson, as versed as I in not provoking attention, kept his eyes on me. 'The arm will be covered with a coat this weather,' he said. 'Will you ask his permission to remove it while you search for scars? And if he has one, will you pursue private vengeance when there are other matters to attend to?' He held up his mug to me. 'If he recognizes you then I will help, but otherwise it is an alarm I would forego. As I told you, I seek only the completion of this mission before I retire.'

'You are growing old,' I said to him.

'Old? Older, maybe, but still not too old to fight a proper battle with my companions around me, and not these lone excursions that you promote.'

I took his mug and sighed. 'The fellow has gone out again. Only searching for a companion, it seems.' I signalled for more ale.

'Good! Then what do we do next in the matter of Sir William Stanley?'

'Atherstone?' he said, when I had finished. 'You mean to wait there?'

'That is what I told the priest. It is a convenient place, on Watling Street, half way between Chester and London, small enough for him to find us there, and close to High Cross where the Fosse Way will lead him to Lincoln and thence to York after he has finished his business with us. It is also along Watling Street that Stanley will return to London.'

'And the way Sir Robert Clifford will take to Chester.'

'Then perhaps he will ride back that way as well.'

Anderson pulled at the short hairs of his beard. 'But the Three Tuns? It is the inn where we had that trouble the night before Bosworth. And the landlord . . .'

'May recognize us? Not after nine years.' I shook my head. 'But what if he does? I carry the King's Writ. He will not dare trouble.'

212

'You have the King's Writ as well?' He laughed. 'You must have been busy at West Minster the few hours we were there. But why did you not tell the priest of it? He might have been persuaded the quicker.'

'It would have confused him. He has been a hermit so long that it might have been difficult to reconcile himself all at once to the Tudor rule. But as one of the chaplains to Thomas Howard it was easier.'

He eyed me, shaking his head. 'You think carefully, Henry Morane, eh?'

'I try to, Captain Anderson. It is a matter of survival.'

*　　　*　　　*

The Three Tuns at Atherstone was still the same. Its hall, built of wood in the Saxon manner, with its gallery high up along three sides, seemed as strong as ever. Only the three great tuns which gave it its name, and each big enough to hold four men, had the yellow tinge of age.

'At least they have changed the floor rushes,' Anderson grinned as we went in.

It was the same landlord; still huge, but now the red face was speckled like a song-thrush, the cart-wheel shoulders had sagged, and a vast belly preceded him wherever he went. He eyed us without recognition, and when we asked for beds he told us that, due to the time of year, he could put paliasses on the gallery, where the smoke from the fire below would turn the edge of the cold from us. When he had gone to fetch us meats and ale we turned to look at the village folk sitting on benches round the fire, which was in the middle of the floor in the Saxon way. Some of the customs of our forefathers seem to have advantages that we have forgotten, for the smoke rising to seep out through the roofing thatch prevents insects and other vermin from making their homes there, and I have even heard it said that in those days men never suffered from the sickness of the head which brings on sneezing, coughing and fluid running from the nose.

'Jesu!' Anderson said. 'This place brings back memories.'

'And none of them good.'

213

'Then why did you choose this tavern?'

'Because it is the only one in Atherstone, and has a name I remembered which I could tell the priest.'

When we moved over to the fire-place the conversation stopped. Strangers the world over are objects of suspicion. After a silence while several pairs of eyes inspected us, a young, short-cropped fellow asked us where we had come from. I gave him a friendly smile, then frowned and jerked my head towards the landlord. Lowering my voice I told him we came from London, and asked him with some concern if he was likely to report our presence to the Justices. That brought a few nods of understanding, and one old white-beard put a finger against his nose and winked.

'Not he,' he assured us. 'Not since that time when King Richard was killed over there at Bosworth Field, and we put him in one of his tuns, with water up to his neck.' He snickered, showing us two ancient, snaggled teeth. 'Stay here a few days,' he added, 'to see if there is any pursuit. If it comes there is my barn you can use. If not, then you can move on more leisurely. And if you cannot afford the charge made by that robber over there then you can use my barn this night.'

'Ah, no,' I said. 'But thanks.' I gave Anderson a knowing smile. 'We have a little money. But we will do what you say if it becomes necessary.' I called for ale and mead for them.

They nodded and resumed their discussion. The problem of the London men fleeing from justice was solved, and theirs was more pressing. They needed no aid from us in return, as we were city folk, and ignorant of country matters.

Two of the villagers were swineherds, and the welfare of their charges, out in the forest to find their own food until the winter, as is the habit, was in danger. A great boar, wild as the hills, had been seen. It was the wrong time of year for such a one. In the spring and summer there was food for all in the forest, and he would father new litters to improve the breed for the swineherds. But now, just before winter set in, he would kill off the villagers' boars, depriving them of their fresh meat during that season, and he would eat up what remained of the acorns and beech-mast in the forest, so that the herds might starve before they could be rounded up and brought in. Worse, as the winter grew harsher, he would invade the pens for pig-food, scraps such as cabbage stalks and the dead grain left over from ale-making, and there was no fence that would stop him. He would even smash down huts to get at the pens.

Something had to be done. To set about to kill it would break the law, for such a beast was the preserve of the Lord of the Manor, and he was away from his estates, no one knowing when he would return. They had been considering the question of killing the beast privily, not only to protect their herds, but also because the meat of a wild boar is the tastiest of all. And why should the Lord of the Manor have the privilege of this Boar's Head? But none in the village had the courage to face the fearsome creature. Besides, as White-beard pointed out, even the force of a longbow, fully drawn, would not stop the beast, as its forehead slopes at such an angle as to turn any arrow or spear. It would have to be shot from the side. But how to get to its flank? For a boar, once attacked and at bay, so places himself that only one man can get at him at a time. They needed trained dogs, and those were only kept by the Lord of the Manor. The close-cropped youth suggested it might be brought down from horseback, but he only drew cries of derision, for a boar can not only outrun a horse, it can kill one in momments if it is not properly placed, by ripping its belly apart with its deadly tusks. Besides, someone else put in, if the gentry considered it beneath them to go in for the kill on horseback, but to show their manliness by advancing against it on foot with the barred-spear, then why should they, even if they were only humble village folk, not do likewise? They had bills and some swords, he added proudly. But that suggestion, too, was rejected, which did not surprise me. Then the bell from the church summoned them for Vespers, and the meeting broke up.

When they had gone I said to Anderson, 'It seems they need one of these new-fangled hand guns, well primed with powder, to kill that boar.'

He sat up straight. 'If I had my bow I could do it for them.'

215

I raised my eyebrows. 'You could?' I inquired. 'But I thought you were too old for such lone excursions?'

'Aaah!' he growled, spitting into the fire.

The noise of horses outside told us that other travellers had arrived. The innkeeper yelled for the stable lad, then went out, waddling like an over-fed gander, and rubbing his hands together. Travellers at this time of year would pay well. But it seemed that the newcomers did not want their horses cared for, and they followed him back inside. Tall, well set-up, they eyed us incuriously as they crossed to the trestle by the serving hatch. Joseph Anderson nudged me. He, too, had seen that they wore the badge of the Hart's Head, the device of Sir William Stanley.

As they took their wine they told the innkeeper that they would require twenty beds the next night as a great magnate was passing through. He demurred, saying that two paliasses were already taken, and pointing in our direction. They turned round and surveyed us with cold eyes. 'Then have them put out,' the darker one said indifferently, going back to his wine cup.

Anderson started to get to his feet, but I restrained him. 'Wait,' I murmured. 'Listen to what they have to say.'

What they said was that provisions would be required. They did not want beef, as it would be salted because all the cattle would have been killed for the winter. They required poultry, and ten pigs.

That brought the reply that there were no pigs. They were still in the forest because a great boar had been seen, and the swineherds were afraid.

'Oho!' the second one said, slapping his thigh. 'A wild boar, eh?' He grinned at his companion. 'Sir William will be pleased to hear of it.' To the landlord, he said, 'Are there dogs for it? Boar hounds?'

'At the Manor, good sirs. The lord is away, but maybe the steward can be persuaded by me . . . at a price.'

'A price, you say?' He laughed. 'Well, Sir William will be pleased to pay it, if I know him.' He swung round to eye us again, then finished his wine and beckoned to his companion to follow him out. At the door, he turned back. 'See to our wants, fellow,' he told the innkeeper,

216

'and Sir William will pay you well enough too. There will be twenty of us, although carpenters will be carrying Sir William's own bed to put up by the fire over there. You have other mattresses?'

'Aye, sir, if those men over there . . .'

'Then get them out,' he said, without even a further glance at us.

Joseph Anderson started to get up again, but I held him back until they had gone out. 'Leave them,' I told him. 'Would you pursue private vengeance when there are other matters to attend to?'

He scowled at me, and spat into the fire again.

If Sir William Stanley was already returning to West Minster it could mean that the die for rebellion had been cast, but, whatever the case, Sir Robert Clifford had not preceded him, along the main highway through the village of Atherton at least. Perhaps he had taken ship from Chester or Bristol, or even from one of the smaller ports on the eastern coast which were nearer to Flanders. Whichever way he had gone he would have been in haste to take Stanley's letter back to the Duchess Margaret, and to have lost the track of him was a serious matter for us, but we could not move until we heard from the one-eared priest. We should have to efface ourselves until Sir William Stanley and his escort had gone by, and now there would be at least a day's delay while he hunted the boar. But, as in all affairs planned by mortal man, the Hand of God might dispose of them otherwise, although in what followed it seemed more to be the hand of the Evil One instead.

We were leading our horses towards White-beard's barn when there was a loud hallooing from among the trees. A score or so of huge dogs, some golden brown, others grey, but all with massive heads and upright ears, came bounding out, followed by the Hound-master and his assistants, each with his short hunting-horn. Close behind them came horsemen armed with spears, and a dozen or more men on foot with pointed staves. The spears had a small transverse bar below the head, for while the ordinary weapon will penetrate the boar's hide it will not stop his headlong charge. We moved aside quickly to let them pass, when one of the horsemen reined up and drew his sword. It was Sir William Stanley.

'Well, well, well!' he said, his angular face twisting into a sneer. 'What have we here? None other than our old friend, Master Henry Morane and ...' the colourless eyes took in Anderson '... his black-bearded familiar! Now what,' he inquired loudly, turning to his companions, 'can two Yorkist spies be doing in these parts, I wonder?'

It was a question that did not call for an answer, for, at his signal, we were promptly seized and bludgeoned to the ground by staves. Sir William Stanley looked down at us disdainfully as we lay bleeding on the road. 'It is high time you were hanged,' he observed. 'Both of you.' He waved at the trees. 'Over there,' he told his men, while the villagers watched with open mouths. 'And...' Then he was interrupted by the sound of a horn.

'The quarry is scented, sir,' one of the horsemen said.

'So I hear,' Sir William Stanley replied, moving his horse round. 'See that you hang them well,' he instructed. 'And I will inspect your work later. . .no! wait!' he added suddenly. 'Hang that one ...' he pointed at Joseph Anderson. 'As to Morane ...' he began to smile '... I think we shall have better sport with him and the boar. Bring him with you.'

The point of a stave went into my back and I was forced to my feet. I was prodded into a run down the slope to where the track crossed a wide but shallow stream. It was there that I was able to look back. Two of Stanley's men were standing under a tree, laughing to each other, as they swung the kicking body of Joseph Anderson from side to side like the pedulum on a huge clock. My stomach began to fill with ice. It was the end of my world. I ran on, the stave at my back, with tears coursing down my face.

218

CHAPTER 39

W H E N we reached the stepping stones in the stream I saw that it flowed between rocks and boulders along the bottom of a valley, which terminated at a thickly forested ridge across its head about a mile away to my right. On each side of the stream the slopes were quite steep, and held many large rocks, but with flatter spaces between them where trees and undergrowth sprouted, so that it was not a difficult climb for either man or horse. From some distance up the valley came the baying of hounds, shouts, and the noise of horns which told me that the quarry had been found. But there was no means of bringing it out of its thicket until the men escorting me came up, for six of them carried bows.

Sir William Stanley and his horsemen were among the trees on each side, while the hounds and their attendants waited in the shallow water among the rocks. The huge dogs had been unleashed and were baying impatiently, but would not attack until the beast was driven from its cover. Two men stayed to guard me, while the others moved up, feathering their arrows. Then, at the short blast of a horn, the dogs became quiet, the shouting died away, and the archers drew their bows. All at once I could see something big and dark among the brambles and dead bracken. The bowmen saw it too, and, almost as one, six strings made the musical note of battle that a soldier knows so well. If they found their mark I did not see, for there followed the loudest grunt I had ever heard, the bushes parted, and a gigantic boar came out.

He stood higher than a man's waist, as black as seacoal, with stripes of grey running along his body and a great broom of bristles erect all the way down his spine. Little eyes glared out above foot-long tusks, curved like a Saracen's dagger, that drooled and dripped with spit; tusks yellowed with age, barber-sharp and which I had heard were always poisoned to bring death later if they did not do the business first. Even the Hound-master whistled at his size before he sounded the attack.

The leading dog gave a loud bay, and the rest of them went along the stream after him. But this was no ordinary wild boar. He was not going to run. With another loud grunt he put his head down and charged straight at them, the tusks swinging from side to side, slashing at everything in their path. The dogs were at a disadvantage in that narrow space. Two of them died instantly, their bellies ripped wide. Another fell with its head nearly severed, and two more limped back with their legs trailing after them. The stream became bright red as it gurgled round the stones towards me. The boar stopped as suddenly as it had started, and swung round at the dogs that had got behind it. They were brave enough, but no match for that ferocious monster. Three more lay dying before the rest drew back along the ravine, yelping and whining at their wounds.

By this time the bowmen were poised for another shot. More arrows sang towards the beast, but he had turned again, and those that found their target bounced ineffectually from the massive head. Then the horsemen came riding down the slope with their spears at the ready. But the old boar seemed to know what they carried, for he ran backwards as quickly as he had charged out, crashed into an unexpected rock, fell over with his legs waving in the air, but recovered himself at once, and was away up the ravine before anyone could get to him.

The pursuit continued, but the way became too difficult for the horses, one of them seeming to break its leg in the uncertain bed of the stream. Sir William Stanley ordered a halt. It was time to dismount and hunt the animal on foot. No knight worthy of the name will keep his saddle in such circumstances. But on this occasion there had been no opportunity of wounding the animal with spears first, for the old boar, wise to the ways of the hunt, had not charged the mounted men after disposing of the dogs.

Horns sounded again, and the men with staves began splashing their way along the stream and round the boulders. They moved cautiously, with points well forward in case the animal charged out again from a hidden

220

cavity. Behind them came Sir William Stanley and his company with drawn swords.

The great boar had travelled a long way. The stream dwindled, and more trees began to thrust upwards between the rocks and thickets that lay on either side of the defile. Then there was a shout in front, and I saw a man pointing upwards with his stave. On a shelf below an overhanging rock two reddish eyes were glaring down at us. A great yell of triumph went up. The quarry had been brought to bay, for there was no way out of there. It only remained for a man with a sword to climb up there and kill it.

Sir William Stanley stopped and looked round until he saw me. 'There you are, Master Yorkist spy,' he called. 'Now you can provide us with the first sport.'

They untied me and pushed me staggering along the stream. I would have gone straight for him with my bare hands, but he had stepped back among his men. 'Up there, Morane,' he said, waving his sword. 'And I shall not be far behind you, for once the boar has disposed of you it will be my honour to have it for the kill.'

The Hound-master was standing with his hands on his hips. 'Even if he is a spy, he should have a weapon, sir,' he called.

Those about me drew in their breaths. But the Hound-master was no obsequious servant. He was the Lord of the Manor's retainer. He had no qualms about incurring the displeasure of Sir William Stanley.

'Ah!' the latter said, pulling at his beard. 'It might be better sport, at that.' He drew a short dagger from his belt. 'Here you are, then, Morane.' He threw it up the slope, where it fell soundlessly on to a blanket of dead leaves. 'Pick it up as you go. And if you think to turn and use it on me then think also of this longer sword. And . . .' he waved it at the bowmen '. . . there are six arrows aimed at you if you try to escape.'

But there was no escape. The way was narrow, and here devoid of trees. Yet I would try, somehow, if only to have the chance of avenging Joseph Anderson. Matilda would at least have young Nicholas to console her grief, but I put the thought of her aside, for it did no good to me. Instead, I began to curse. I cursed Christopher

Urswick, I cursed King Henry and all the Tudor brood, but above all I cursed that sneering face behind me. As I stopped to pick up the dagger I saw that he had two spearmen with him. Aye, I thought, he would have the honour of killing the boar, but only after the spears had pinned it down. I moved on slowly towards the cleft where the monster lay, slavering on its tusks and watching me with tiny, fiercely glowing eyes.

The path led up beside a steep rock, with the stream winding between other rocks and thick brambles some twenty feet below. None of the others had come that far. There was no need, as the boar had only one way out, but there were two dogs nosing the stones, thin streaks of blood coming from their damaged muzzles. They must have been left to roam, and had scented other prey. But it was useless to essay a leap down there, for the hounds would have seized me if the rocks did not cripple me first. With six arrows to prevent my escape up the hillside there was nothing left to do but face the wild boar.

He got up slowly at my approach, the bristles on his back scraping the top of the cavern above him. He grunted twice, watching me, but made no further move. I stood, stomach taut as a drum, while the stench of pig ordure rolled out towards me.

'Give him a stave,' the Hound-master shouted, 'and let him prod the beast out. Or the sun will have set before it is killed.'

'He needs no stave,' Sir William Stanley laughed. 'Go in, Morane, and prod him with the dagger.' More sycophantic laughter followed.

The dagger was a woman's weapon, no wider than a thumb and but six inches long. I held it out before me as I went down on my knees, my feet seeking a stone to press against. The great beast lowered its head a little, its hot eyes uncertain. I carried no spear or stave, and could not be much danger. Yet what was an unarmed man doing there?

Then, with all the force I could muster from my feet against the stone, I projected myself forward on to my stomach beside him, at the same time planting the dagger straight into the eye above that slavering yellow

222

tusk. As the blade found its mark I rolled aside quickly, but the brute swung round with the speed of an arrow. There was a sudden searing pain in my leg, I was shoved aside, and the next moment I was falling through the air on to the rocks below. I heard the valley filled with shouts and yells before I hit the bed of the stream and then a blow on the head drove my senses from me.

CHAPTER 40

IT was dark, or I was blind. I did not know which. I must have made some sound, for gentle hands raised my head. In the dimness there was a face above me. On one side of it there was no ear.

'Praise be to God!' he said. 'And you live! He must have placed that dog there for you to fall upon.' Hands came under my shoulders. 'Can you rise?' he asked anxiously, dragging the brambles off my body. 'For we must put tar on that wound soon, or you will die of the boar's poisoned tusk.'

'Jesu!' I muttered. 'A moment more yet. Then I will try.' He set me back slowly, and I lay panting for a while. Then I put my hands under me and felt a cushion of fur and hide. It was the body of the dog. More hands came to my shoulders, stronger ones this time, and I stumbled to my feet. I stood up straight in spite of the pain in my leg, and grunted with satisfaction. 'I can walk,' I announced, swaying like a sapling in the breeze.

'God's Hooks!' another voice said. 'The fellow is indestructible.' The speech was thick and sore, but there was no mistaking the baldness of the head and the black beard below it, even in that gloom. 'How. . .?' I began wonderingly, and then pitched forward unconscious again.

*   *   *

'The priest cut me down before I could strangle,' Joseph Anderson said. 'He walked straight up to the first guard and, before the man knew his intent, stove in his chest with a club.'

Martin Caillou steepled his hands together. 'A priest may not draw blood,' he said sententiously. 'But a club. . .'

'It was a mighty blow for an old man,' Anderson grinned. 'And when the next guard tried to interfere the villagers joined in with pitchforks and spades. They had

224

heard us called Yorkists, and it seems there is still some sympathy for Dickon hereabouts. They cut me down, but . . .' he put a hand to his throat '. . . I cannot eat or swallow ale, although they tell me that it will pass. But now we must see to you. They have gone to fetch tar, before the wound festers up and kills you.'

'They?' I said. 'Who are they?'

'Why, Master White-beard and his friends,' Anderson replied. His voice was very thick. I sat up and looked round. We were in a barn, and the smell from the cloth round my leg showed that it had been bound in wine.

'You have lost much blood,' the priest said. Then his face set hard. 'But I pray that Sir William Stanley has lost more.'

'More?' I asked, and they told me what had happened. The village folk knew where I had been taken, and where the boar would hide. They had shown the priest and Anderson the way across the ridge from the other side, and it had been as they were descending the slope that the two dogs had scented them and come to investigate. At that moment they had seen me leap into the cleft at the boar, and be tossed out, bloody and sprawling on top of one of the hounds. Anderson had killed the other dog, while the priest had clambered over the boulders to me. They saw the boar, half blinded by my attack, come charging out of its cavern. The two men with spears had been watching me, and were caught off guard. The first died quickly after his side was ripped away, the other, on the blind side of the animal, having time to plant his spear in its neck before he, too, fell against its deadly tusks. All this happened so quickly that Sir William Stanley could only leap for safety behind another boulder, but not before those same tusks had gouged a sizeable piece of meat from his scrawny buttocks. Then the boar, its brains coming from its empty eye, had charged down the slope finally to be despatched by staves, arrows and a score of spears. And even in that last fracas two more men had been wounded and were lying up at the Three Tuns along with Sir William Stanley.

At that I tried to rise to my feet, swearing that we must go up there at once and kill him, when White-beard

225

and two others came back with a cauldron of pitch, and it took all of them to hold me down while they poured it over me in clouds of steam and the stink of burning flesh, so that once again my senses left me.

*   *   *

Two days later, when I could hobble about with a stick, they told me that the men at the Three Tuns had been taken away in carts, Sir William Stanley among them, for, although mostly recovered from his flesh wound, he still could not sit a horse. They had gone towards London, as expected, and I asked the priest what news he had of Sir Robert Clifford.

'Now that, my son, is the mystery,' he said. 'For no man from London called upon Sir William Stanley.'

'You are sure?'

'I am sure. I entered Holt castle each day with the folk who brought in food and other provisions, and no other person was there, much less a knight such as Sir Robert Clifford, or there would have been gossip of it. There are none so curious about the doings of their lord as country folk.'

'Curious . . . country folk . . .' I repeated. 'Of course! I had not thought of that . . .!'

'Something you had not thought of, Morane?' Anderson inquired drily. 'Is that possible?'

I ignored him. 'But Sir William Stanley would have been aware of it,' I went on. He would have told Clifford to wait for him in London, where it is easier to meet privily.'

'You mean that Clifford has been in London all this time?' Anderson said with disgust. 'And all this has been to no purpose? Me, hanged, and you gouged by a wild boar?'

'But no!' the priest exlaimed. 'There *has* been a purpose! It was God's design.' He pointed a finger at me. 'If you, Henry Morane, had not thought that Clifford was journeying to Chester, and used me for what you thought were your own ends to spy on him, I should still be living as a hermit, forgotten in the marshes of Putney. Whereas now I am chaplain

226

to the Earl of Surrey,' he concluded cheerfully.

I stared at him, and he began to laugh quietly. 'It was God's design, Henry Morane. He knew you for a wily man, and used your deviousness for my benefit.' He turned. 'And now I will go up to the church and give Thanks. And you,' he added to us, 'could well do the same for your deliverance. God does not forget,' he said as he went out.

Joseph Anderson eyed me, and began to chuckle. But it did not last long, his bruised windpipe changing the noise into that of a choking frog. I glared at him without sympathy.

'Well now,' I said to Martin Caillou as we came out of the church. 'As God has given you so much benefit from my deviousness, perhaps in return you would do one more service for me, this time straightforward.' He smiled at that, and I went on. 'Take horse to London, for even with two days' start your old bones can still outstrip Sir William Stanley on his litter, and give a message to my wife.'

'Your wife?' He looked startled. 'A man of your turbulent nature with a wife?' His expression changed to one of mock concern. 'Poor woman! Her life must be one of constant anxiety. I will go at once. She will be in sore need of God's comfort.'

Anderson began to laugh, then thought better of it. 'She is as turbulent as he is,' he told the priest, 'save now she has a child to consider.'

The priest threw his hands into the air. 'A child! God save us! Then I will pray that it will grow up without its father's guile.'

'And what do we do now?' Anderson asked me as we watched him ride away, his gown flapping behind him like a tattered flag.

'We follow as quickly as we are able. We cannot reach London before Stanley, because I do not ride so well yet. But now I think I know where Clifford will be.'

*　　　*　　　*

'Thanks be to God!' Matilda said, putting her arms round me. 'That one-eared priest you sent made so much

227

praying to Him for my comfort that I thought it meant you were dead. And for the second time within a month!' She held me away, and her deep blue eyes were wet. 'This goes too far, Henry Morane . . .'

'It does indeed, madam,' Joseph Anderson said from behind me. 'If you have any power over him, Mistress Matilda, it were time to exercise it. For my sake at least,' he added with feeling.

She smiled at him. 'Maybe I will, at that, Captain Anderson. A woman can always refuse her favours,' she said, her eyes alight again.

'I would I were in a position to refuse mine,' he muttered.

Matilda laughed, and turned back to me. 'So I went to see this Saracen. I had forgotten he was Ali's uncle, or I should not have been so afeared at walking down that narrow street. You have used him too?'

'He uses them all,' Anderson said. 'Saracens, priests, dwarfs, and soldiers without eyes.'

'Not to mention the pimply whores . . . and the duchesses,' Matilda added mischievously.

'So you went to see Mehmet?' I said with some impatience.

'Yes,' Matilda said, looking back at me. 'And you were right . . .'

Anderson gave a loud groan.

'. . . Sir Robert Clifford was lodging at one of Stanley's more privy houses. The one not far from ours, at the top of Wall Brook Lane.'

'It seemed to be a good place,' I nodded. 'Where he keeps his whores,'

'Only one at a time,' Matilda smiled. 'But you recall there is a back way from ours, along the passages between the houses?'

I did. Only too well.

'So I went along there, and peered in. He was in residence, with one of Stanley's fatter whores.' She made an expression of disgust. 'Then, soon after, Sir William himself came back to court. He made apologies for his delay, limping somewhat from what he said was a dog-bite in the knee.' She saw my face. 'So that was you, then, Henry Morane?'

228

'Me? Am I supposed to be a dog now?' I complained, and Anderson laughed.

Her eyes narrowed. 'It seems there is more to this, which I shall expect to be told of. But meantime . . . I waited until he left the court and went to observe his house again. I saw him in conversation with Clifford, but could not hear what was said. It seemed that Stanley was sending him off on some errand, for he clapped him on the shoulder as he left. But Clifford dallied until yesterday . . .' she made a face again '. . . it seems he also has a liking for over-fat whores.'

'Yesterday? Then we must be off too.'

'No, no!' Matilda cried. 'Not again! Not so soon!'

'There will be no trouble this time,' I assured her grimly. 'I go to arrest Sir Robert Clifford, and he will make none. Have you told Master Urswick of this?'

'The priest said, before he left for York, that you wished it secret.'

'Good! I want Clifford for myself.' I took her in my arms. 'There will be no more trouble now, my sweet apple. I promise you that. Ali will have left word with his uncle as to which road he has taken, probably to Dover now, and once I have Sir Robert Clifford the business is finished.'

CHAPTER 41

B E F O R E we reached Dover, the snow came. At first
it was no more than flakes in the wind, then there
were thick horizontal streaks of it that plastered one
side of the trees and houses inches deep, leaving the
other bare, as if the Hand of God had thrown a giant
bucket of freezing plaster straight across the countryside.

We found Ali at the docks, below the castle, his slight
figure encased in dark sheepskins, looking more like a
bear from Muscovy than a Saracen from warmer climes.
'Morane, effendi,' he said, a hiss of steam seeming to
come from his golden tooth, 'Sir Clifford lodges at the
King's Head, awaiting a ship for Boulogne.' Beyond him,
I could see the vessels at the quay, their ropes and poles
gleaming in the frost.

'At least it will be warm in there,' Anderson said. 'But
he will know us!'

'It makes no difference now,' I said.

At first the place seemed full of sailors in their coloured garb, then I saw others, more soberly dressed;
citizens come in from the weather, and weary-eyed
travellers, waiting for their ships. They moved aside to
let us warm ourselves by the fire, and then Sir Robert
Clifford saw me. He touched his companion on the
shoulder and they began to get up.

I wasted no time. Going straight up to him, I said,
'Sir Robert, I carry the King's Writ, and I arrest you for
treason to his royal person. Put up your sword,' I added,
for his hand had crept towards it.

'A moment, sirs!' the landlord said, thrusting himself
forward. 'I want no trouble here. I will see your warrant, if you please.'

Brushing the snow off my cloak, I drew out the paper. Clifford and his man had moved towards the door,
but Anderson was in the way. The innkeeper inspected
the Writ and gave it back to me. 'I will not meddle with
the King's justice,' he said, looking round at the curious

faces that were watching us. 'And neither will anyone else,' he added warningly. That brought some smiles, nods and shrugs, and the mariners turned back to their wine. 'You will take them to the sheriff?' he asked me.

'Aye, sir. But bring some ropes to bind them first.'

While we were waiting, Sir Robert Clifford pointed at one of the ship-masters. 'You,' he said, 'give me back my passage money, so that I can return to London and answer this false charge.'

The mariner laughed, looked him up and down, then raised his eyebrows at me inquiringly. I shrugged. It was not my concern.

Clifford began to draw his sword. 'Draw it full, Sir Robert,' Anderson said from behind me, 'and then let it drop on the floor. Like the landlord, we want no trouble here.'

'The rope has gone!' the landlord put in, looking puzzled. 'Someone must have . . .'

Then he saw that Ali had slipped in through a doorway with a length of it in his hands. The landlord started towards him, but I held him back. 'It seems he found it before you did,' I said, and in the laughter that followed he gave a shamefaced smile.

'To the sheriff's jail?' Anderson inquired, once we were outside.

I nodded. 'And you for London, forthwith.'

'What?' He looked round. 'It will be dark soon.'

'Forthwith,' I repeated. 'Where you will find Christopher Urswick and give him the message I will dictate to you.'

'God's Hooks, Morane! This is no night for travellers.' He spat into the snow. It made a tiny hiss, and then there was a hole as if a finger had been poked into it. 'And will you bring those two on your own?'

'I will,' I told him. 'With Ali. We will start at dawn. I have matters to discuss with Sir Robert Clifford. He will make no trouble after that, I think.'

'You think?' he muttered. 'You and the Saracen boy.' He climbed stiffly into the saddle. 'What is the message, then?'

*   *   *

231

The sheriff of Dover, a fat, balding man with drooping moustaches, was not too pleased at my intrusion. He read the King's Writ, raised his wide shoulders with resignation, and gave me the key to the wooden cell behind the building. I pushed his servant in there, then led Sir Robert aside.

'Now, Master Morane,' he said, eyeing me with disdain. 'I will hear more of this.'

'You will, sir,' I assured him. 'For there is evidence that you have been in communication with Sir William Stanley.'

'What of it? Is that supposed to be treason?'

'It is,' I told him. 'Because Sir William is known to be plotting it.' That wiped the sneer off his face. 'You carried a letter from Flanders to him,' I went on, 'and it is his reply that I will have.' I held out my hand in a gesture, even though his arms were still tied.

'His reply?' A gleam of something crossed his face, and I knew at once that there was no reply in writing. Sir William Stanley had been too careful. I changed my hand into a finger that pointed at him. 'His reply,' I repeated, 'the one that he dictated to you to take back to Flanders.'

'Reply? I carry no message,' he said haughtily. 'You had better return to your master and tell him you have made a mistake. And if it is alleged that I have been in 'communication' with Sir William Stanley, whether he plots treason or no, then you can tell him that, also . . .'

'Yet you have admitted that you met him.'

'Why not? He is no more than an acquaintance, and the meeting was fortuitous.'

'Fortuitous?' It was my turn to sneer at him. 'So much so that you journeyed to London to meet him, and no one else? That you hid privily in his house by the Wall Brook until he came there to see you, and were deep in conversation for several hours?'

Sir Robert Clifford looked at me, his eyes a little wider. Then I added brazenly, 'And that conversation was overheard.'

His little mouth popped open like the bung-hole in a beer barrel. 'Jesu!' was all he could say.

'Aye, overheard,' I repeated. 'So that the treason is

232

known. You will therefore come back to London and testify to that conversation.'

'Testify?' he said after a long time. 'Give evidence as to my own treason?'

'I did not say that,' I pointed out. 'It will be as to Sir William's treason, not yours.'

'What?' He looked uncertain. 'To Stanley's and not mine? How . . .?'

'Because . . .' I spoke slowly, emphasising each word '. . . because it will be asserted that your part took place in Flanders. In Flanders,' I repeated, 'which is outside the realm. And treason against the King's person, as you may already know, can only occur within the realm.'

'But Wall Brook is within the realm.'

'Agreed. But that will not be adduced against you, for it will be asserted that you were being suborned.' I waved a finger at him again. 'Provided that you testify against Sir William Stanley.'

'*You* assure me of that? I must take your word?'

I indicated Ali, leaning against the cell door. 'Would you have his as well? For I do not see anyone else to give it. But I will be frank with you, sir. There may be a lesser charge to put a face on the matter. That of misprision of treason, in not reporting to the proper authority the attempt by Stanley to subvert you. But that charge will be lifted once Stanley is found guilty, I can assure you.'

'You assure much . . .'

'Aye, Sir Robert, and there is one thing else . . .' I smiled suddenly at him '. . . I can also promise you that you will be well rewarded. The King does not part readily with money, as is well known, but in this case, while you yourself are of little account, your testimony is worth more.' I hoped I hadn't gone too far, but I had at least asked Joseph Anderson to put in such a request.

Sir Robert Clifford shrugged. 'Even if I did not believe you, Master Morane, it seems I have little option. I will therefore come to London peaceably with you. But what of my servant? It was his brother who was killed that day at sea, and he holds you responsible for it. You should not trust him to give evidence, which in any

233

case can provide no details, as he overheard nothing of what passed between myself and Sir William Stanley.'

'I will leave him here, then,' I said with some relief. I did not look forward to having two prisoners on the road to London in that weather. 'If he is required,' I added, 'we can always send for him from Dover.'

CHAPTER 42

THE journey back to London took three days, for winter had closed on the countryside with a fierce hand. The roads were already deep in snow, and we could not have travelled far without the wrapping on our horses' hooves. Along each side, the forest trees stood stiff with cold, and the thickets and brambles that were able to keep above the white blanket held the bodies of many little birds, frozen where they perched, the ice on their feathers glittering like tiny jewels in the winter light. That weather, in fact, had gripped all Europe, almost as cruelly in the south as in England, for I heard later that frost had destroyed thousands of olive trees along the Mediterranean, and even the port of Genoa was closed by ice, an event unheard of before.

Ice, too, scraped the pier at the village of Bermondsey, and I had to use threats as well as gold to persuade a waterman to take us across the river. The Tower stood over there against the darkening sky, its walls and battlements shrouded in snow like a magic castle in a children's tale, unreal in that December gloom.

Joseph Anderson, thick in sheepskins and furs, stamped up and down on the narrow wharf below the Cradle tower. 'Hah!' he grumbled when he saw us, 'I have been waiting all day, never thinking you would be so long, and without even a cup of wine to warm me.'

'Wine, sir?' Ali said, climbing out of the boat with a flagon. 'I have some.' He held it up to inspect it, then announced that it was not yet frozen.

'Where did you get that?' I asked him.

'At the inn, while you were swearing at the boatman.'

'What? And left our prisoner unguarded?'

He gave me an innocent stare. 'But, sir,' he said, 'you had bound his hands to the pommel as we approached London, and while we waited for the boat I made more sure, and tied the legs of his horse to a post on the quayside. Was that not enough?'

'It seems to have been,' Anderson laughed as he took the flagon. 'You are to take Clifford over there . . .' he pointed a gloved hand '. . . to the Lanthorn tower, and wait while I report your arrival at the Wakefield tower. Urswick will be impatient for news.'

'Has Urswick been waiting?' I said with some surprise.

'Oh aye, but they are in the Royal Apartments, where it is warm, and there is plenty of wine you may be sure. Come with me,' he said to Ali.

As I led Sir Robert Clifford across the narrow bridge over the moat I fell to wondering why it was so important to question him so soon after our arrival, but my mind came back to its business when I slipped on the ice-covered steps that led up to the small, squat Lanthorn tower, one of the lesser bastions in the wall that faced the river. A heavy arras had been drawn across the entrance to the upper chamber. The sentry brought the butt of his halberd to the stones with a bang, glad of some movement to induce warmth in his aching body. 'Aaaah!' he spat. 'Any more of this and even Christ's gonads'll be frozen off.'

I gave him a grin as I pushed the arras aside. The room was bare, except for a brazier that sparkled a welcome. We warmed ourselves while Clifford and I inspected each other.

He shivered a little. 'Now we shall find out what your promises are worth, Morane.'

I had some apprehension too, but I eyed him sternly. 'Even if they are worthless,' I said, 'there is little you can do about it now.' Then I heard the weapon outside bang on the stonework again, and turned round. The heavy cloth was drawn aside to admit a thin figure in a plain brown cap and a fur-lined coat. Bottle-green eyes took in Clifford, and then turned to inspect me, and a smile came slowly on to the long face.

'How now, Master Morane? It seems you have carried out our commands with diligence.'

Recovering my astonishment, I went down quickly on to one knee. It was the King, and he was alone.

*   *   *

236

'Now leave us, Master Morane,' King Henry said, waving me outside.

'But Sire,' I protested, 'have you no escort?'

'Do as I say.' The voice was patient. 'We would converse with this man on our own.'

I got up slowly, eyeing Sir Robert Clifford, but his head was sunk down on his narrow shoulders. 'Untie his hands,' the King said, 'else how can he warm them when they are behind his back?'

Shaking my head with disbelief, I did as I was told, then left the room reluctantly. I glanced at King Henry Tudor as I went, but the green eyes were on the prisoner. Outside, I waited by the arras, which was too thick to allow me to hear any conversation, but a sudden cry for help might penetrate it. I could not think what madness had overcome the King.

The sentry was puzzled, too. 'He's in there alone?' he asked me.

'Did you see an escort of armoured cavalry ride in with him?' I snapped, and immediately regretted it. But the sentry was not one to take offence.

'You are as nervous as I am,' he smiled, fingering his dagger.

A little while later there were careful footsteps on the stairs, and Christopher Urswick appeared. He was cased like a woolly caterpillar that wriggles in the summer grass. The dull eyes took in the dagger I was holding ready. He clicked his tongue at it. 'There is no need to wait further, Henry Morane,' he said. 'The Queen's court is at West Minster, and there is a boat ready to take you to your wife.'

'But sir,' I said, 'the King risks his person in there. Sir Robert Clifford is a self-confessed traitor.'

'As to that we shall see,' he replied complacently. 'You have done well, Henry Morane. Little else may be required of you . . .' he gave his thin smile '. . . for the present, at least.'

What passed between King Henry Tudor and Sir Robert Clifford on that December night in the Lanthorn tower will never be known for sure, but within a week high judicial commisions were set up in no less than twenty-six counties to investigate suspects in a conspiracy that seemed to have ramifications everywhere.

The number of arrests grew as each day went by. William Worsley, dean of Saint Paul's, was the most prominent, but there were others well enough known: Lord Fitzwalter, Sir William Mountford, Sir Thomas Thwaites, William Daubeney, John and Robert Ratcliffe, Thomas Cressenor, Thomas Astwood, and a leader of Dominican friars with his assistant, as well as two other priests. Even old Thomas Rotherham, archbishop of York, was brought before a tribunal, and only released on the personal surety of John Morton himself. All were convicted, and while Worsley and the other churchmen were spared by reason of their office, the rest were seen to by the executioner's dripping hands. All, that is, except Cressenor and Astwood, who were reprieved at the last moment on the scaffold at Tyburn. This act of mercy immensely pleased the crowd, already sated with butchery, for they were both little more than boys. But it was before the executions took place that King Henry, still in residence at the Tower, summoned his Great Council.

*   *   *

'What does it all mean?' Matilda said, taking my hand as we looked out over the snow on the palace yard. 'How did this come about? Even here at West Minster, everyone is sombre. Queen Elizabeth has not laughed, nor even smiled, this past week, and as for the Lady Margaret, her expression is like one who suffers a plague of the stomach.'

'It was Sir Robert Clifford . . .' I began.

'Aye, that is obvious enough. But it seems the conspiracy was deep rooted, and spread throughout the realm.'

'All pots boil their contents to the top in the end,' I said sententiously, 'and it was high time this one did, with Perkin Warbeck ready to sail from Flanders with his invasion fleet. Sir Robert Clifford has betrayed them all. All,' I added, 'except the highest one, and that I do not understand. He must have spoken to the King of Sir William Stanley, yet the fellow still goes free as air, still Lord Chamberlain, and in close attendance upon the King.'

'Yes,' Matilda sighed, 'it seems you may be right. Perhaps the King has some aberration of the mind . . .'

'That,' a voice said curtly, 'is a remark near to treason. Too near for safety these present days.'

We swung round. It was the Lady Margaret Beaufort, and her face was hard under the tight-drawn wimple.

'Madam!' I bowed. 'My respect and affection for you precludes an answer such as I might have given to anyone else. I am confident that my wife's loyalty will stand any questioning of it.'

I heard Matilda gasp. But if tempers were to be strained I did not see why others should have the monopoly, no matter who they were.

The grey eyes, beyond a first widening with astonishment, regarded me steadily. 'You may be so, Master Morane,' Lady Margaret said. 'But I, too, have an affection for your wife that would suffer if it were put to the test. I have not yet heard you called a fool, and would suggest that you cherish the respect I have for your single-mindedness towards her. Come, Mistress Matilda,' she added, holding out her hand, 'the Queen requires your attendance. Her court moves to the Tower this afternoon.'

'Jesu!' I muttered under my breath. But she heard me.

'Neither will I tolerate blasphemy, Master Morane. You will go to the chapel forthwith and ask forgiveness, paying whatever penitence is asked. And,' she added, as she turned to go, 'while you are there it will do you no harm to pray to the Holy Virgin to curb both your tongues.'

CHAPTER 43

THE Great Council assembled in the Presence Chamber of the royal apartments at the Tower. Its members said little, eyeing each other carefully while they waited for the King. All the churchmen were there, save Thomas Rotherham of York. Christopher Urswick stood close to the dais with Richard Foxe, bishop of Durham, who was clutching his secretarial equipment. There were the bishops of Exeter, Winchester and Ely and of course John Morton, resplendent in his new Cardinal's Hat, with his young acolyte Thomas More, fresh-faced and precocious. Jasper Tudor leaned on a stick, still somewhat crippled by a fall from his horse. I saw John de Vere, booted and spurred as if ready for a campaign, and the earls of Devon, Arundel, and Ormonde with many knights, those best known to me being Sir John Dynham, the Treasurer and once the Lieutenant of Calais under Dickon, Sir Richard Guildford and Sir Thomas Lovell. But it was the portly figure of Lord Thomas Stanley, Earl of Derby and his brother which held my attention. They regarded each other coldly as if they had just finished a quarrel.

King Henry Tudor did not keep them waiting. He came in with short steps, gave a general smile of welcome, and then stood with his arms folded while the bows of obeisance were being made. Before he could say anything Sir William Stanley stepped forward.

'Sire,' he said, 'if we have been summoned to decide upon measures to meet the threat from oversea, then I would have it known that I and my brother . . .' he waved an airy hand at him, and got a frown in response '. . . can equip as many men between us as the rest of your lords and barons here assembled.'

'We all know that well enough,' Archbishop Morton said, 'but it would be as well to hear what His Highness has to say first.'

The royal eyes watched them both without expression, then turned to take in the others. 'My lords,' he said, 'before we discuss the threat from outside the realm, we will first consider that which exists inside it.'

'Does any still exist, Sire,' John Morton said, 'since all the trials and convictions which have recently taken place?'

'It does, my lord bishop,' Christopher Urswick said, looking up at him. 'And too close to the throne for royal comfort.' There was a startled silence while he turned to the King and, receiving a nod of agreement, gave orders for the prisoner to be brought in.

All eyes turned towards the entrance, and nearly all of them showed disappointment when they did not recognize who it was. But Sir William Stanley did, his face showing a flush which he could not conceal.

As Clifford went down on his knees before him, King Henry looked round at his Council. 'My lords,' he said, 'this man, Sir Robert Clifford, has confessed his treachery and seeks our pardon. He has confessed freely and without persuasion . . .' John Morton coughed '. . . telling us many names, most of whom have been arrested. But,' he went on, his green eyes turning to Urswick, 'we are informed that this plot approaches our royal dignity.'

He paused, and turned to the prisoner. 'Sir Robert Clifford,' he said, 'you have been brought here so that our Council can witness the pardon we shall bestow upon you.' He beckoned to Morton. 'My lord Chancellor,' he went on, 'you will formally bestow that pardon, so that this knight can go free and without molestation for his offence.'

While the Archbishop's sonorous tones droned above Clifford's head Anderson nudged me. 'Look at Stanley. He is like a hawk that has swallowed an angry bee.'

'Quiet!' I whispered fiercely. 'Do not show yourself. Our turn will come.'

When it was done, Clifford rose to meet King Henry's hand on his shoulder. 'There is one further duty required of you, sir. You have asserted, I am informed, that the treasonous plot approaches our throne. Therefore, you will look round this assembled company and tell us if any here are concerned. Speak freely, sir, for you have our protection now.'

Sir Robert Clifford wasted no time. He looked round

241

quickly and then pointed at Sir William Stanley. 'Your Lord Chamberlain, Sire,' he said with a tremor in his voice. 'He is the instigator . . .'

'God in Heaven!' Lord Stanley exclaimed, and backed away from his brother in the long, horrified silence which followed.

Then Sir William Stanley recovered himself. 'Nonsense!' he shouted. 'Who is this man? He is not only a fool but a liar, and speaks for gain of some kind!'

King Henry put his hand to his brow. His shock and distress was so well feigned that even I was deceived a moment. 'Are you sure, sir?' he inquired of Clifford after a long interval.

'I am, my lord,' was the reply. 'And I have proof.' There was more confidence in his voice now.

'He had better have,' John Morton boomed.

Clifford turned to him. 'Aye, my lord bishop,' he said, 'for it was Sir William Stanley himself who sent me in the first place to seek out this Perkin Warbeck and assure him of his sympathy.'

King Henry gasped, and the whole assembly seemed to follow suit. 'This is too much to bear, my lords,' he said. He looked at Stanley, who stood straight and taut as a drawn bow. 'My own Lord Chamberlain!' he murmured. He turned away slowly. 'We will depart forthwith, and leave you all to consider the matter.' Holding out his arm for Urswick to support, he added, 'Have my escort accompany me.'

It was our signal. Joseph Anderson and I stepped forward from the shadows. When Sir William Stanley saw us his jaw dropped with consternation and disbelief. I gave him no more than a glance as I took up my position behind the King.

*   *   *

The King's Council, led by his Chancellor, John Morton, interviewed Clifford and Stanley. They could not discredit the former, who stuck to his story, and Sir William Stanley's attitude was that he was above such a sordid allegation. His services to the King had been beyond question, he pointed out, and he reminded Morton

242

that it had been he who had placed Richard of Gloucester's crown on Henry Tudor's head after the battle at
Bosworth. But then Clifford further asserted that Stanley had told him that, if Perkin Warbeck's claim were
true, he had a more legitimate claim to the throne than
Henry Tudor. Moreover, Stanley was convinced that
the claim was true, as the Dowager Duchess of Burgundy
was giving Warbeck her full support. It was on the four-
teenth of March, 1493, and although now nearly two
years ago, Clifford was sure of the date, that Sir William
Stanley had sent him to France to offer Warbeck his full
support with men and money.

Sir William Stanley's past, and hitherto successful performance as a weathercock that could sniff a forthcoming change in the wind was well known. During the
civil wars he had abandoned the Lancastrians before
their slaughter at Towton; turning back to them in anticipation of the removal of King Edward of York; going
over to him again when he returned to settle the issue
on the fields of Barnet and Tewkesbury and, lastly, his
sudden change of allegiance during the battle of Bosworth. From all this the Council concluded that Sir
William Stanley was attempting to secure himself should
an invasion, even by a pretender, expel Henry Tudor
and reinstate the Yorkist dynasty. Archbishop Morton
therefore reported to the King that his Council was un-
animous in considering that Sir William Stanley should
be brought before a properly constituted tribunal and
stand trial for high treason.

*   *   *

Christopher Urswick warmed his hands at the brazier
and watched me. His eyes were pink in the glow from
the burning coals, like those of a basilisk examining its
prey. He seemed to be about to say something when
Jasper Tudor hobbled up on his stick.

'A sorry business, eh, Master Urswick,' he said. 'But
at least the treachery at home is stamped out. Although
I confess to some anxiety as to whether the judges will
accept Clifford's testimony, a traitor saving his own skin
...' he lowered his voice '... especially if it is known

243

that he was rewarded as well.'

'Aye.' Urswick turned back to me. 'I was about to tell you, Morane, that the King honoured your promise to Clifford.'

'How much?' Jasper Tudor asked him.

'How much, my lord? Why . . . er . . . five hundred pounds . . .'

'Five hund . . .!' I began, but Jasper Tudor's whistle drowned the rest.

'Enough to ransom an earl,' he said. 'Then that increases my anxiety as to his testimony, if the judges hear of it.'

'They will accept it, my lord,' Urswick said slowly, turning to watch me carefully. 'Because all the time Sir Robert Clifford was our man.'

'What!' I almost shouted. 'Clifford was your man all the time? Are you telling me that all my services, all I have been through, were to no purpose? That he would have come to the King with his denunciations without my efforts? This is too much, Master Urswick.' I turned to go. 'You can have . . .'

'A moment, a moment, Henry Morane!' He took my arm. 'Compose yourself, and listen.'

'Aye,' Jasper Tudor said, 'I would hear more, too.'

I turned back, glaring at Urswick. Then he began to speak.

'It is true that Sir Robert Clifford was in the King's service,' he admitted, 'but that was at the beginning of the business, two years ago. It was then that he met Sir William Stanley for the first time, and was sent by him to Flanders . . . with our full knowledge,' he added with a bleak smile. 'But he tarried there over long, and we had reports that he was becoming too familiar with the other dissidents there, and especially with the Garson, so that we became concerned. Aye, especially . . .' and now his expression changed '. . . as the Garson Warbeck is a pretty creature, and we have it that Sir Robert Clifford has little liking for women . . .'

'Huh?' I said, astonished, and Urswick stopped to eye me curiously.

'Not like Morane, look you,' Jasper Tudor said, waving his stick at the brazier. 'But continue, Master Urswick.'

'Aye, sir,' he said, still watching me. 'In any event, when Clifford returned to England to see Stanley for the second time, he did so privily and without advice to us, and very soon after left for the Duchess Margaret's court. It was then that you were employed, Henry Morane, as it seemed he might be swerving from his duty. But . . .' he brought his hands together as if to emphasise the point '. . . no one else knew of his wavering allegiance, and so, as far as the Council and the judges are concerned, he has been our man all the time. So, Morane, you see that, but for you, Sir Robert Clifford might have encouraged a rebellion by the King's most powerful subjects, and brought about the civil wars all over again.'

'Ah!' Jasper Tudor laughed. 'Set a Mole to catch a mole, eh?'

But I was not amused.

CHAPTER 44

S I R William Stanley was tried before the court of the King's Bench in West Minster Hall on the thirtieth of January, 1495. The great hall was cleared of the other courts, and suddenly the place grew very cold in spite of the multitude of braziers that had been set up. London was suffering a dreadful winter. The river had by now frozen hard along the edges, and several urchins were drowned when they ventured too far out on the ice. Horses stumbled and broke their legs on the hoof-hardened snow of the streets, and a thick white pall covered the piles of refuse so that their familiar sight and smell were obscured from the dogs and other scavengers, and they took to eating each other. But all that was nothing compared to the ice in my stomach as I watched Sir William Stanley.

He stood up, arrogantly denying all charges of treason, yet agreed that he had said that if it were proved that Perkin Warbeck was of Yorkist descent he would not fight against him. His overweening pride would not let him see that this alone was an admission of disloyalty to the throne, if not more. The rest of the business was mostly a repetition of what had been said at the King's Council and, while it took two days, it ended in his conviction and sentence to a traitor's death. And, more significantly, with that sentence went the forfeiture of all his estates to the crown. King Henry had been very careful. His hands in the matter were unsoiled. The disclosure of his Lord Chamberlain's treachery had appeared to have been a complete surprise to him and, shocked, he had left the proving of it to others.

*   *   *

Early in February writs were sent to the more important soldiers of the realm summoning them to attend the King in Council at the end of the month. The long interval of notice was due to the inclemency of the weather, but in spite of it Thomas Howard of Surrey made the journey from York in little over a week, in time to witness the execution of Sir William Stanley, which was to take place on February the 16th.

Falling snow did not keep the crowds away. The execution of one who had been so high in the King's counsels was an event not to be missed by the London mob, especially as by now the legend of his wealth had reached fantastic proportions. It was even said that he was to be despatched by a sword inlaid with gold, which he had paid for himself, and which would be the headsman's reward for a quick performance.

By then both the King's and the Queen's courts had returned to West Minster. None made the journey from there to the Tower save for Christopher Urswick and I, for which purpose one of the royal barges was placed at our disposal. The oarsmen, though, demanded double wages due to having to break the ice at the river's edge, yet the King accepted it without demur.

'There can be no reprieve now,' I said to Matilda as I made to go.

'You think not? The King has already commuted the sentence from that of the full treatment for a traitor to a simple beheading. And are you sure that Urswick does not carry a Royal Pardon under his cloak? Else why does the King send him? He needs no witness of the execution, for the great boom of artillery from the Tower can be heard well enough from here.'

I shook my head to ease the doubt she had placed in my mind. 'You would be a better witness,' I told her, 'after all the mischief Sir William Stanley has done us.'

'No, no!' she cried. 'I could not bear it! I only wish to see an end to this matter, so that you can live in peace henceforth.' She reached up and kissed me. 'Can you not understand that, Henry Morane.'

Christopher Urswick said no word all the way to the Tower. Even the excitement of shooting under London Bridge left him unmoved, his face impassive, his eyes on the way ahead. The snow that covered Tower Hill was trampled hard by the crowd, so that we slipped often, and found Sir William Stanley already on the scaffold.

He stood, stripped to the waist, and shivering, but whether it was from the cold or from fear no one could tell. I saw that the chaplain was giving him unction, while the executioner and his assistant warmed their hands at the steaming cauldron of tar. Then Stanley saw our movement as we pushed through the crowd. He shoved the chaplain aside and called to Urswick.

'Ah, Master Urswick,' he said, 'you bring the King's pardon. It is his nature to delay it to the last moment.'

Those near us were suddenly silent, and glared at Urswick. Was the show going to be cancelled after they had come out in this weather?

Christopher Urswick funnelled his mouth with his hands. 'Not so, Sir William. I come as a witness, that is all.'

I let my breath out in a long sigh, but it was drowned by those about us. Sir William Stanley's eyes widened in disbelief, but before he could say more the headsman's assistant seized him, bound his hands quickly behind his back, and thrust him forward to his knees with his head across the block. The crowd grew quiet again, as in the pause before the thunder strikes. And thunder it did, as the drummers began their dreadful, monotonous roll.

The executioner, naked behind his leather apron — the easier for washing himself after his work — shivered as he picked up the sword. If there were murmurs of disappointment that it was only of steel after all I did not hear them. Someone waved at me, and I saw that it was Thomas Howard of Surrey. I returned the salutation, then watched the scaffold above me. The drums had stopped, and the silence was such that I could almost hear the snowflakes as they floated down. Then the headsman raised his weapon, but perhaps because his hands were not properly warmed to take their grip, bungled his work. The blow took Stanley on the head, which must have killed him, but did not sever it from his body. A howl of rage went up from the spectators. Infuriated, the headsman raised his bloody weapon and made a threatening gesture with it. The howl grew fiercer, so that he swung round and made another stroke, this time too quickly. It seemed as if the crowd might storm the scaffold. But then, at the third attempt, the business was done, the body stump tarred, and the head held up for all to see. Sir William Stanley's eyes, as is usual in such cases, were open wide, but they blinked suddenly as the head was lifted, and then went on staring, sightless at the crowd.

God's will be done! Dickon is avenged at last!' I said, and crossed myself.

'Aye, it is God's will,' a voice said, 'and the vengeance is His. Do not forget that, Henry Morane.' It was the one-eared priest beside me.

CHAPTER 45

I nodded at Joseph Anderson, standing stiff as his pike outside the Painted Chamber at West Minster.

'Now what are *you* doing here again, Morane,' he glowered. 'If the King is to send you on another mission I will not be part of it. But it cannot be so yet, at least, for they are all in their discussing military matters, and you are no soldier.'

'Nevertheless I am bidden to attend for a short while,' I told him, and brushed past before he could lower his weapon.

'Ah, Morane.' Christopher Urswick took my arm and led me forward. Those about the King stopped talking and looked round. Their expressions became irritated when they saw who it was, but King Henry beckoned me forward, and I knelt before him.

'Your pardon, my lords,' he said. 'I would interrupt you for a moment on a small matter of business.' He turned to Richard Foxe. 'I had meant to tell you, Master Foxe, to see to it that the body of Sir William Stanley be buried at Syon Priory — it will be at my expense.'

The horse-faced secretary looked surprised, then became busy writing.

'As for you, Master Morane,' King Henry Tudor said, 'we have considered your services in that and earlier matters, and have decreed that the bond you pledged us for five thousand crowns is fully redeemed, and we look forward to your continued loyalty.'

I looked at the greenish eyes, my head a-swim. I shook it violently, muttered some incoherent thanks, and began to back away. Matilda must be the first to know of our redemption.

'A moment, Master Morane,' the King said. 'Our gratitude is not yet done. We would grant you other favours, yet, apart from other money, which would not be fitting, we have no means of knowing what would suit you.'

They were all looking at me. I collected myself and stood up straight.

'Sire,' I said, 'there are but two, and each of little cost.'

'Two!' Morton exclaimed involuntarily.

King Henry glanced at him, then turned back to me. 'Then let us hear them,' he said.

'The first, my lord,' I went on, 'is that when one of the enemy ships is captured in the forthcoming invasion of the realm . . .' I waited, but he made no sign '. . . that one of them be given to my nephew, a mariner of Bristol, and ambitious for your service with his own ship.'

'That can be arranged, no doubt,' King Henry Tudor said with a smile. 'And the next?'

I drew in my breath. 'Sire,' I said, 'the greater of the two is that a tomb be erected for Richard of Gloucester, whose memory, as is well known, I still hold in much respect.'

There was a long, shocked silence. Then Archbishop Morton gave a loud exclamation. 'By God! That is a real impertinence! The fellow goes too far!'

'Does he?' Jasper Tudor inquired. 'Richard of Gloucester, usurper or no, was a good fighter, at least. And you would have some knowledge of that, my lord of Derby,' he added, turning to him. 'You fought with him to capture Berwick from the Scots, which fortress we still hold.'

But Lord Stanley was too frozen to answer, frozen, not with the cold, but with apprehension. He did not wish to become involved in any such matter, his brother not yet dead a week.

It was Thomas Howard of Surrey who spoke up then. 'Aye, my lord,' he said to the King. 'I have some knowledge of his military prowess. But then,' he laughed, 'I fought with him at other places.'

King Henry Tudor looked at him for a moment, then nodded. 'We have some recollection of that,' he said, a slight smile on his face. 'Very well, Master Morane,' he said to me. 'It will be seen to.'

*　　　*　　　*

And, six months later, an alabaster tomb was erected at Leicester for the memory of Richard, Duke of Gloucester, once known to all as King Richard the Third.